TAJ

Sandra Wilson

TAJ

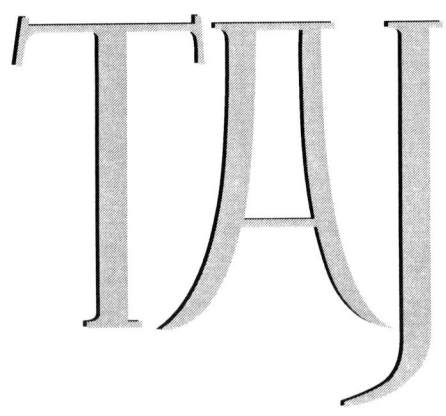

The Woman and the Wonder

Sandra Wilson

Amundson Davis Publishing

ISBN 0-9760575-4-9

Acknowledgments

There are people who have touched this manuscript in a significant way and should be mentioned for doing so. Their support fits into concentric circles that emanate from Taj.

The furthest geographical circle encompasses people in India: Sarlu and her enriching friendship, Salma for bringing the library of Jamna Hamdard within my reach, Dr. Nasim Akhtar at the National Museum who allowed documents from the Taj Mahal's construction to be photographed for the first time, and Anurag Gupta of Agra's Marble Arts Palace for the demonstration of the exacting inlay technique. Aman Nath, I thank you for Meerijan.

A closer circle encompasses my friends, family and particularly the readers who took the time to strengthen my manuscript. Your input was varied, thoughtful, and sincerely appreciated.

Taj has been artistically brought to life by Jane Jeszeck of Jigsaw Design through her cover design and graphics. This book owes its look to her. Laurie O'Keefe's illustrations explain more than thousands of words. Lowry McFerrin of ProForma Mactec Solutions helped beyond the definitions of his job description.

The very closest circle is around my husband Dave, who has lovingly supported my project even though we have decided to disagree on the total amount of time it has taken.

—Sandra Wilson

Text copyright ©2005 by Sandra Wilson
Illustrations copyright ©2005 by Laurie O'Keefe
All rights reserved. No portion of this book may be reproduced or utilized in any form, or by any electronic, mechanical, or other means without the prior written permission of the publisher.

Published by Amundsen Davis Publishing
Cover and interior design: Jane Jeszeck, Jigsaw (www.jigsawseattle.com)

Library of Congress Cataloging-in-Publication Data
#2004116493

ISBN# 0-9760575-4-9

Dedicated to A.I.S.

Characters

AKBAR ~ Third Mughal Emperor; Jahangir's father, Khurram's grandfather
ASAF KHAN ~ Mumtaz' father; Nur Jahan's brother; Minister of the Army
AURANGZEB ~ Third son of Mumtaz and Khurram
COBRA QUEEN ~ Nur Jahan
DARA SHIKOH ~ Eldest son of Mumtaz and Khurram
GHIYAS BEG ~ Nur Jahan's father; Mumtaz' grandfather, Chief Minister to Akbar and Jahangir
JAHANARA ~ Eldest daughter of Mumtaz and Khurram
JAHANGIR ~ Fourth Mughal Emperor, Nur Jahan's husband, Khurram's father
PRINCE KHURRAM ~ Mumtaz' husband, Son of Jahangir, Fifth Mughal Emperor
LADILI ~ Nur Jahan's daughter, Shariyar's wife
MEERIJAN ~ "My Life" (Taj's name for Prince Khurram)
MELHINRISSA ~ Nur Jahan
MUMTAZ MAHAL ~ Prince Khurram's wife
NUR JAHAN ~ Jahangir's wife, Mumtaz' aunt
SHAH JAHAN ~ Prince Khurram's regal name
SHARIYAR ~ Jahangir's son, Khurram's stepbrother
TAJ ~ Mumtaz Mahal

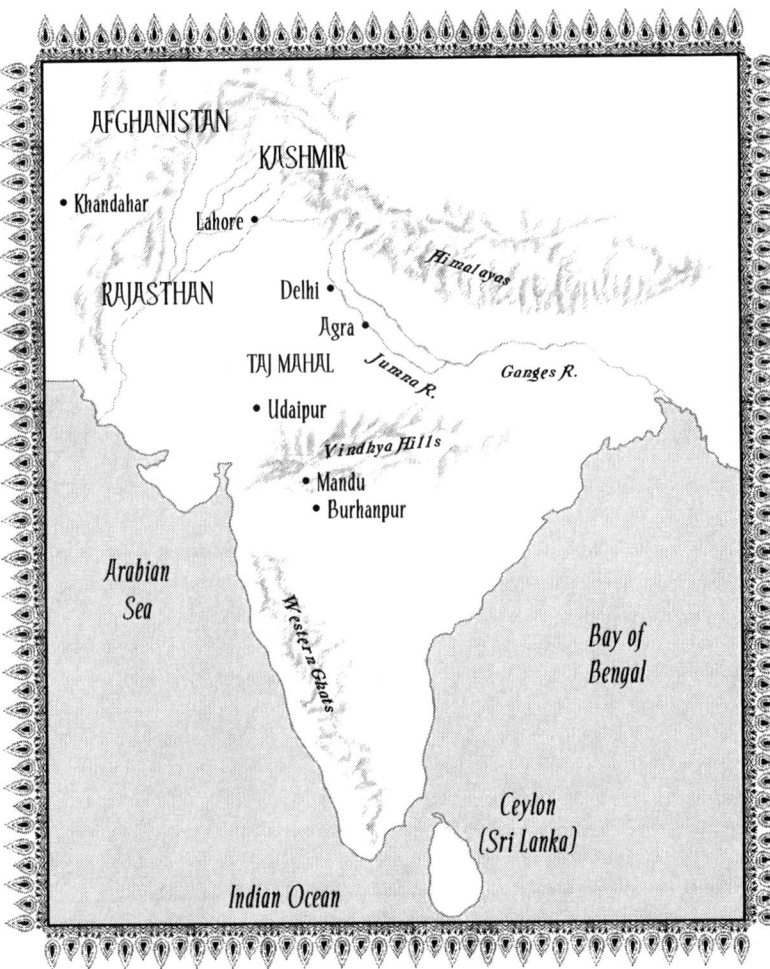

Taj Mahal

Prologue

Agra, India - 1666

Shah Jahan's shrunken body was covered with silken sheets and fine blankets as he lay without moving. Along the walls of his room, shrouded women were ready to wail their grief at the moment of his death. The former emperor had ordered his bed placed on the exquisite octagonal marble balcony, an extension of the large, airy rooms that had confined him for eight years. With effort, he looked past the nearby white pillars and low marble parapet inlaid with semiprecious stones. How many times he had walked onto this same open spot and gazed a mile down the river to admire the marble domes he had built as they reflected the color of the day—the golden orange of sunrise, the rose of sunset, the brilliant white of midday or, his favorite, the pearlescence of the moon's reflection. Though he intensely longed to visit them again, he knew he never would.

He smiled at the structure that meant more to him than any other. Even though his architectural genius was responsible for many changes in the skyline of his empire, Shah Jahan's dimming eyesight lingered on this favorite accomplishment of all: the Taj Mahal.

Knowing he had come to his final day on earth, his eyes sent a silent goodbye to his beloved daughter, Jahanara. She had chosen to stay with him during his humiliating years of house arrest when his son, her brother, had usurped him and begun his own rule as emperor. She stood close to her dying father as though she had the power to ward off the approach of the Angel of Death. Shah Jahan knew it would not be long before he would be free of his physical imprisonment. He no longer raged with the turbulent and agonizing anger that had pulsed through him years ago when he was suddenly transformed from Ruler of the World to prisoner. He had eventually found peace, assisted by the influence and memories of Mumtaz Mahal. He allowed Jahanara to gently feed him sharbet to relieve his thirst and help his soul resist Satan's tempting cup of sweets on the other side of life's curtain.

Surely, the angel who had been recording the good deeds of his seventy-five years would remember that he had been he emperor of a magnificent empire, had loved deeply and completely, fathered many children, and left a striking architectural legacy. This angel would be busier than the angel on his left shoulder who simultaneously recorded the bad he had done. The Islamic Tree of Life held a leaf with his name on it, and even now this leaf was fluttering to earth. Azreal, the Angel of Death, would read what the angels wrote before deciding if Shah Jahan was qualified to spend eternity with Allah.

As the Great Mughal he had created exceptional buildings, constructed an entire city of unprecedented lavishness and size, and sat upon a costly gem-studded throne. But it was not these accomplishments he remembered most vividly. His final memory was the deeply satisfying love he had shared with Mumtaz Mahal for the nineteen years they had been wed.

Thinking about his wife, the old man sighed and gazed again in the direction of the mausoleum he had built for her in his attempt to create a monument as lovely, as changeable, and as mesmerizing as she had been. It was his memory rather than his sight that filled his mind with pictures of the fine decorative inlay, the imposing yet delicate harmony of the entire complex, and the sound of the splashing fountains.

When the former emperor closed his eyes once more and squeezed his fist around a smooth yellow stone, he remembered a woman who exceeded even the beauty of the building which was already gaining fame throughout the world. She had made two promises to him the last time they met. One she had already kept. He would soon discover if her second promise, the most important, would be fulfilled.

He contentedly remembered the first time he had seen her. She was called Arjumand Banu Begum then. It had been their wedding day.

1

Agra - 1614

This is the worst part of the trip! I'm hot and we're so far from the Moonlight Mahal. The magic we had is leaving as quickly as this elephant is approaching the walls of the Agra Fort. I don't know which is worse, Mumtaz wondered crossly, *leaving our retreat or traveling in this heat. If only the curtains didn't have to remain down, I could at least feel the moving air and my howdah would be more bearable. If I were already in Agra, I'd be enjoying my garden or a cool bath where the thick walls keep heat out better than this silk ever does. I'd be in comfort now if I'd agreed with Khurram and left earlier. But then, I'd have lost our last lovely hours.* Dreamily she relived the moments shared with Khurram and knew they'd been worth their uncomfortable ride.

Mumtaz looked tenderly at her sleeping husband whose head was resting on her shoulder. *Instead of riding his horse in the breeze,* she reminded herself as she gently tucked a strand of his hair back where it belonged, *he chose to ride with me.*

The marriage of Mumtaz Mahal and Prince Khurram had changed not only the two of them, but also the rather cynical atmosphere of the royal court. There was a new contentment and a sense of optimism in the Mughals as a whole since Jahangir's son had taken a bride.

Though Mumtaz was always unseen in the zenana, she had already become the subject of storytellers and poets who lauded what they could only imagine. Her place in the heart of the empire's population was assured when she became pregnant shortly after the wedding. Khurram and Jahangir outwardly professed a desire for a male heir. Regardless, they rejoiced with Mumtaz when her baby was a healthy girl.

Together in the howdah, Mumtaz gazed at her husband. His smooth olive-colored skin glowed from the oil lightly applied earlier. The sun slivering through a crack in the curtain highlighted the crevices of his lean, angular face and his tightly trimmed black beard. Although tall, he hadn't inherited the large, muscular build of some of his ancestors, nor the added weight his father carried.

As Mumtaz caressed his cheek, Khurram awoke, took her hand and opened his eyes. Her fingertips on his face reminded them of recent touches, both gentle and urgent. Wordlessly, they re-lived their lovemaking and the hours they'd shared with one another in their private hideaway. Alone with Mumtaz, Khurram was her laughing husband, lover, friend, and confidante. But as they approached the walls of Agra Fort, Khurram's countenance became stern, cool, and public. Witnessing the transition, Mumtaz was saddened he felt the necessity of a protective appearance.

It had been this way between them since the beginning of what was supposed to have been a marriage of convenience. She had been fearful, angry and then resigned to her fate on their wedding day. He had been stern and aloof during the ceremony. When their eyes first met under her veils she had felt violated by his piercing look.

It wasn't until they were alone in the bridal chamber that night that she became aware of his goodness, his charm, and his laugh. How quickly she had changed from fearing this man to loving him. She smiled as she remembered the heavy, misshapen green bottle that her former ayah had given her before she left her father's house.

It was empty now and remained a favorite belonging of hers because with it they had first harmlessly plotted together. They had spread the contents upon the silk bedsheet and had it taken to the waiting guests as proof the marriage had been consummated. Then they sat together and began to learn of one another. It had

Howdah

been immediately obvious to her that she first realized Khurram's public demeanor was very different than his behavior when the two of them were alone.

She had so many memories from that first night. Even the earrings now brushing her shoulders came from that time. They had been given to her by the emperor himself and were so exquisitely worked that she was speechless by their beauty when she first saw them. The center of each was a stunning ruby encircled with two rows of small pearls. But what made these ear ornaments unique were the six strands of tiny pearls that hung to her shoulders from

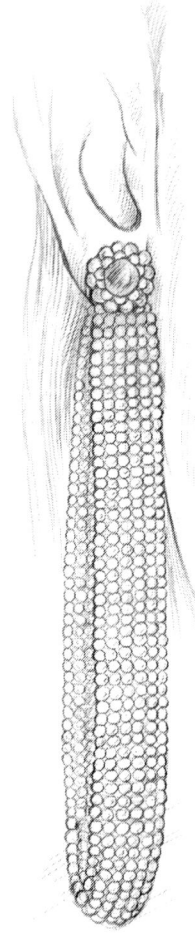

Wedding earring

the center and were long enough to loop up and attach again at her earlobe. She was rarely without them and frequently wore them when she and Khurram were together.

Nineteen years earlier - 1591

Khurram had no memory of the afternoon in his infancy when Fakir had visited him. Nor did he recall a man with flowing white hair, thin limbs, and strong walking stick who had traveled far to deliver a vision to the baby prince.

As Fakir had gazed upon the child within the royal cradle, Khurram had opened his eyes and stared back. There was no fear in the newborn eyes as they met the pair that returned his look from below bushy, black and white brows. Gently, so very gently, Fakir raised his hands and put one on either side of the small head. The baby relaxed into the support of the man's hands watching Fakir intently.

Fakir had carried the revelation he'd received from Allah in his mind since before he had begun his travels to the prince. Now, the vision flowed from his head, down his arms, through his fingers, to the young mind where it was meant to reside unnoticed for decades.

When the entire vision had been shared with Khurram, Fakir whispered, "That's all, Baba. I'll be back when you're older. Now sleep. You'll have no memory of me, but I'll leave you this small token." Still cupping the infant's head in his long, slim hands, Fakir gently applied pressure against the baby's temples, then slipped a smooth yellow stone into his hand, and left.

Khurram was comforted by the gentleness of the touch, the soft sounds encircling him, and finally by the points of tiny lights dancing in his head before they dispensed. He was sleepy. So very sleepy he could hardly keep his eyes open. There was a new picture in his head he wanted to see. He'd look at it more clearly after he closed his eyes for a short nap. He hoped, as he yawned and allowed sleep to overtake him, that the gentle man would be here when he awoke.

But he wasn't. When the prince opened his eyes, his adoring ayah picked him up and began cooing to him. Neither of them remembered seeing a thin man with zebra eyebrows.

It would be another thirty-eight years before Khurram saw him again.

❈ ❈ ❈

Now, Khurram remembered he had an important matter to discuss with Mumtaz. *No,* he corrected himself, *there is something I'm going to TELL her. There's no room for discussion on this topic as I've already made up my mind. Decision-making is something I've always done quite well,* Khurram reminded himself emphatically. *I was doing it before Taj came into my life and I can still do it—alone.*

He had known his wife as Mumtaz when they had married two years earlier. During that time, he had shortened the name to Taj. It was a name only he used. No other voice held the tender love that resonated when it was spoken by Khurram.

Before he and Taj were together, the prince would have been astounded by his feelings for her. He had been long aware of the necessity of wedding and heir-producing wife and had accepted such a marriage as one of his duties. Though he had never seen Mumtaz before the wedding ceremony, he could still remember the lurch in his stomach when he knelt to look in the mirror his stepmother held under the veils of bridal finery. Although he hid his physical reaction, when he met her eyes in the reflection he knew she was going to be important to him. He had even begun to wonder if he had been bewitched by the sight of her soul even as he waited for her to come to him after the ceremony. Pacing as he waited, he realized he wanted to see her again. Could he be so favored by Allah as to have a wife that would also be a woman he loved?

It had happened to his father whose wife, Nur Jahan, was beautiful, intelligent, and eager to rule the empire. Khurram had no doubt that she loved his father but she was surprisingly involved with the administration of the great lands ruled by the Mughals. Most women would have been content to live the life of luxury in the zenana where every material wish was granted. But not Nur Jahan. She soon grew bored and began to ease the burden of rule from her older and tiring husband, Jahangir. In a few short years she had become the power behind the throne.

That she had been at his wedding was one example of her daring. She had convinced Jahangir she should attend with the males though the other women guests were seated out of sight behind jali screens. Even more daring was her brazen arrival—unveiled. Nur Jahan and Mumtaz had seen the faces of one another many times as was common for aunts and nieces. Yes, the sister of his wife's father was none other than his own stepmother, Nur Jahan.

Why do I hesitate to tell Taj about my plans? To answer his own question, Khurram considered the chain of events that had gradually brought him to the present. At the beginning of their marriage, Taj listened when he talked about his duties. Appreciating her insight, he sometimes asked her for thoughts and opinions. What began as a courtesy became helpful and now he regularly consulted her.

Because they had agreed not to discuss their "outside" lives when they were at Moonlight Mahal, he had not told her yet. It could not be kept from her for much longer, because if she did not hear it from him soon she would hear about it in the zenana.

He wondered if Mumtaz was to him what Nur Jahan was to Bapu. His father had often said that all he needed was meat, wine, and Nur Jahan. Over the years of their marriage, he'd given much power to his wife. Lately, he had let her keep the Great Seal which stamped a document as unchangeable—even by the emperor.

He answered his own questions even as he asked them. *No, Nur Jahan is not the sort of woman I would want for my queen. Taj's intelligence, beauty, and charm are certainly equal to those of Nur Jahan, but she uses these talents to support rather than dominate me.*

Having concluded again that the woman in the howdah wouldn't try to usurp his power, he daydreamed about his upcoming adventure. *I'm going to lead the Imperial Army. Bapu has finally picked me to lead a battle for the glory of our dynasty. This has to be the last accomplishment expected of me before Bapu will definitely and irrevocably announce I'll inherit the royal throne and rule after him. This victory will bring me—and the empire—long-lasting glory.*

Then, amidst the thoughts he had about the thrilling experiences awaiting him, Khurram suddenly felt an ache of pain in his heart as he realized another consequence of the campaign. He would be apart from Taj.

The thoughts of what he would miss faded as he was once more lured by thoughts of the excitement awaiting him: marching to battle, victory in Rajasthan, and accolades heaped upon him when he triumphantly returned to Agra. His delight in desert travel, campfires, and conquest came honestly to him from his nomadic ancestors. The most recent of them had traded their tents for palaces, but the genes of Ghengis Khan, who had led the Golden Horde from Siberia to Europe, continued to flow in his veins. Ghengis Khan's life had been focused on conquest of land and treasure.

To a soaring hawk, the mighty Jumna River was no larger than a glistening ribbon curving crookedly through a hot and languid land. Sprawling on its shores was a city, Agra, from which the Mughals ruled their vast empire.

Agra wasn't a lovely city. Its elegance came from the river, lined with the palace/fort and the large, walled homes on both sides. The owners of these homes enjoyed the beauty of marble, crystal, and fountains. When the weather annually became too hot, they found refuge in their shady, fan-cooled verandahs. Here the punka wallas would push moistened reed screens back and forth cooling the space through evaporation and filling their air with the lovely, sweet aroma of khus khus. The Greatest population of the city, however, resided in smaller buildings, the poorest of them nothing more than one-roomed mud huts.

When he glanced through the howdah's curtain and saw Agra Fort's drawbridge, Khurram was dismayed at how close they were to the end of their journey. Soon, he would climb out of the howdah, mount the waiting horse, and enter the fort on horseback. Before he left Taj alone, he was determined to tell her of their upcoming separation.

2

Agra – 1614

The nervous garble he spoke to Taj concerned him. *How will I inspire my men when we're at battle if I can't even broach a topic of duty with my wife?*

Again he cleared his throat.

"Taj…" *Good. That sounded better. More definite.* She raised her eyebrows to signify he had her attention.

"Taj, our time at Moonlight Mahal was restful and exciting for me."

Understanding by the tone of his voice that he wasn't finished, Mumtaz waited wordlessly.

"And…well…I want you to know I'm looking forward to our return there when I come home."

Taj assumed a questioning expression, expecting to hear more.

Khurram felt relief spreading through his entire body. *There, it was said.*

Mumtaz remained still, and Khurram inwardly congratulated himself. *Yes, he thought, I've done this well. She needs time now to accept our first separation.*

The change Mumtaz had made in Khurram during the early years of their marriage was known to only to a few. All his life, men and women had bowed to him. Although used to issuing commands, he had learned quickly that words spoken from his heart were the ones his Taj heard.

The perfume only Mumtaz wore filled the air of the howdah reminding him of intimate moments. He was hoping she would understood what he had so plainly stated for he was not certain he could make the effort to tell her again.

She *had* heard. Her eyes took on a deeper intensity, though her countenance didn't change.

"Come home?" she asked softly.

Her question dissolved Khurram's reticence, and words came pouring out of him. In a rush, he told her about the Rajput kingdom to the south. How his father needed a military victory there and wanted the tribute it would bring. The emperor had previously been loath to send him away for so long but had finally agreed Khurram needed to experience war as a soldier.

Jahangir was not the robust and courageous commander his own father, Akbar, had been, so he had relied upon the military acumen of trusted generals. He was sending Khurram at the head of his army because while he trusted his son's skill in disciplines other than the military he understood the young man was eager to prove himself on the field.

Khurram barely paused for breath in his explosion of words. "It's the opportunity I've been waiting for, Taj! I spent my first fourteen years in the zenana; I've always been under the protection of my father and before him my grandfather. I've studied, trained, and designed buildings, but I've never done this—I've never led a military campaign."

Fingering the airy, spangled veil that lay beside her, Mumtaz knew by his passion for the topic that Khurram had already planned his campaign in great tactical and logistical detail.

"Father's showing the court he trusts and respects me," continued Khurram. "By leading his army in Rajasthan and living in the Red Tent, I'm certain to secure the succession. And," he reflected, "I'll be a better emperor for this experience."

The Rana of Mewar, a forceful and dynamic leader of many clans within Rajasthan, believed that he and his followers could—and should—resist paying taxes stipulated by the Mughals. To expand his own imperial authority, Jahangir needed to force the recalcitrant clan chieftains and their Rana to the path of obedience. It was time to put a halt to these desert men who had been out-maneuvering Mughal field artillery with their fast-moving skirmishes and small arms.

Mumtaz faced her husband in her usual posture of listening.

They both knew the decision to send Khurram to the south had not been made by Jahangir alone. There were more complex forces at work than simply an emperor's choice of field general. Through careful manipulating, Jahangir had been led by his capable wife, Nur Jahan, to choose Khurram. As Jahangir's helpmate, she subtly encouraged the emperor to believe her decisions were his own. Slowly and inexorably she was shaping the empire, and the men who ran it, as much as he was.

While she might be the smarter of the two, Nur Jahan knew that Jahangir, as the emperor, was able to deploy armies, give and retract wealth and promotions, and end lives. Not wanting to seem too authoritative, she kept her husband unaware of the full extent of her powers. Others knew the cold, even heartless, empress who ruled the country; but Jahangir knew only the gentleness and charm that flowed from her love for him. Though nobles and religious leaders understood the source of the true authority in the empire, their faces were innocent when speaking to Jahangir.

Jahangir's unpredictability unwittingly helped his wife. Nur Jahan wasn't accepted by those who whispered ominously about the bad luck of having a woman leader, but they were more reluctantly approving of her sensible control than if her husband had been a consistently competent authority to lead the empire.

As important to Jahangir as his authority were the frequent hours of eating, drinking, and entertainment he enjoyed with the court. The best singers, the most famed dancers, storytellers, poets with glowing reputations, and musicians unparalleled in the land, performed in the lantern glow of the Diwan-i-Khas. The partying frequently ended when Jahangir was carried to his bed after falling asleep from either the wine, the opium, or simply fatigue.

Jahangir could be a courteous and affable man—before he drank. With opium and wine, his mood would become dark and cruel. It was during these times that he had commanded heads to be severed, men to fight tigers, and soldiers to be whipped for obeying his own, now-forgotten order.

Listening attentively during the outpouring from her husband, Mumtaz wasn't surprised. She had known of his appointment through rumors that had been in the zenana for some time. It surprised her how innocent her husband was of the zenana's knowledge. He, like many others, assumed nothing, including news, entered the walls of the Royal Zenana without being heard first by the ruling male. The women knew differently.

When Khurram finished, another silence lived between them as the howdah continued swaying in time with the steps of the elephant's lumbering gait. The silence lengthened until Mumtaz asked, "When do we leave?"

Khurram looked at her in surprise. *Perhaps she hadn't heard what he said. Or, was this a deliberate misunderstanding?*

"What do you mean? I said nothing about you coming."

"There will be women on the trip," she stated.

"Yes," he replied slowly, "There will be soldier's wives, and, of course, the women who run the bazaars that feed us. Not many women, but some." He sat up taller. "This is, after all, a serious military expedition and not a place for the fragility of high-ranking women."

The firm tone of his words pleased him. Logical. Decisive. Yes, he had certainly delivered what this moment called for.

Mumtaz seemed totally engrossed in toying with her long, full skirt as he spoke. When he finished, she looked up as though she had considered all that he said, then made her own decision.

"I will be on the trip as well. There will be other women from your harem. I'll select them for you and inform them to prepare. I think thirty or thirty-five women, don't you?"

Her matter-of-fact tone hid Mumtaz' personal reasons for wanting to be part of the procession heading south under the command of her husband. She wanted to be with him. Her place in life was to be by his side. She was his wife and the mother of two of his children. She could not imagine spending weeks or months without touching this man who was central to her life. Knowing he felt the same about her gave her the confidence to assume she would be welcome with him.

Mumtaz leaned toward her husband, took his hands in both of hers and whispered to him, "Being with you is what I live for, Meerijan. Whether it's in Rajasthan or Agra, it doesn't matter. What does matter is that you and I are together." Her name for him, meaning My World, expressed her feelings.

Everything Mumtaz said was true, but it wasn't her entire truth. Having lived in zenanas her entire life, Mumtaz was aware that the women in them did more than provide pleasure and satisfaction to their master. She wouldn't allow her husband to travel without highborn women who were more fervently loyal to him than even his army or the courts.

She would see Khurram had the visibility the zenana willingly provided with their presence. The women would be there to brighten days of dimness, provide soothing and delightful entertainment and unchallenged support. They were bound by and committed to Khurram's honor and his integrity in return for his lavish provisions.

Khurram started to protest and then looked at the soft, loving eyes of this woman who had put into words his own feelings.

"Why," he asked after several heartbeats, "did it take so long for me to realize you must be with me?"

The howdah's sudden lurch propelled her into Khurram. After her initial startled reaction, Mumtaz smiled, lowered her eyelids seductively, and softly kissed Khurram's ear.

"We are from the same flame," she reminded him.

3

Zenana ~ Same day

Even as Mumtaz continued toward the zenana in her howdah, she was not the only woman pleased about the campaign to the south. Reclining in her lavish palace quarters, the Empress Nur Jahan was smug knowing her influence on Jahangir had been the deciding factor in the choice of Khurram as the army's commander.

Ghiyas Beg, Nur Jahan's gray-bearded father, was sitting nearby, dressed in a long tunic. The heavy silk cummerbund wrapped around his loose jama created a fashionable shape while providing a place to prominently display a short lethal knife and its heavily ornamented hilt. Shunning the inclination of other rich Mughals to bedeck themselves with many gems, Ghiyas wore only his trademark piece of jewelry; a large amethyst ring carved with his initials and set in rich gold. At this moment, Ghiyas Beg was nodding agreeably from a chaise and discussing Khurram's recent appointment with his daughter.

"Khurram, my stepson," she was saying, "is a talented man, and it's fitting he'll be leading our intimidating Imperial Army southward." Nur Jahan, already assuming the victory in Rajasthan was a fact, thought about the advantages of having Khurram on the throne. The young man was important for her to rule through him for another generation.

Ghiyas marveled at how far and how swiftly his daughter had

risen in the empire. He recalled her initial reluctance to take on more of Jahangir's responsibilities as the emperor became increasingly disinterested in the affairs of state. Once she started "helping" her husband, there had been nothing within her experience to defend her against the strong lure of sovereignty. Nissa, Nur Jahan's nickname from childhood, became addicted, not to drink or opium, but to the headiness of wielding supreme authority. She didn't lust for money: she craved power.

Ghiyas and Nur Jahan were both influential in what was informally named The Persian Junta. The third, and last, member was Ghiyas's son and Nur Jahan's brother, Asaf Khan. Being careful to keep their influence hidden from Jahangir, the three of them wielded much authority. Although the Junta's influence was felt throughout the empire, in no place did it cause more trembling and dread than in the court of Agra.

The Junta preferred to allow the Great Mughal to believe their plans were indeed his original ideas. Jahangir wouldn't admit, even to himself, that his wife, his Chief Minister, and his Chief of Armies would join together to diminish his power.

An important decision of the Junta had been their choice of successor to Jahangir. They bargained their support for their candidate in return for a favorable attitude during his reign. They had long ago chosen Khurram, because of the love between him and his father as well as the prince's leadership abilities.

Primogeniture, the passing of rule to the oldest son, had never been more to the Mughals than a preferred option and remained informally accepted but not automatic. This, and Jahangir's proclivity toward the unexpected, created the uncertainty of Jahangir selecting his heir from outside the family.

Nur Jahan was comfortable speaking openly with her father, so many years her confidante and mentor. "Khurram is so focused on his own future, he's barely thought about mine or why you and I want him on the throne."

"Nissa, why *do* you want Khurram on the throne so strongly?"

Shaking her head at his naïve question, Nur Jahan became

excited as she answered. "Father, you know the limitless power the Great Mughal wields. He has control of the brimming treasury...immediate respect...irrevocable orders... All of this I have with Jahangir, but I want more. I'll have it with Khurram."

Ghiyas loved his daughter but wasn't certain she was the one to make life and death decisions, be the final recourse to justice, or mold the laws of the land. Khurram was born to royalty and was comfortable with the pageantry of the court as well as possessing the ability to become a capable leader.

Nur Jahan continued freely expressing the feelings she had kept to herself. "The biggest difference between me and Khurram is our gender. Unlike him, I must control the throne behind screens rather than in front of them. Since I must, by tradition, remain a shadow, I need someone to do my bidding." They both knew she was planning for the years after Jahangir's death.

"Does our prince know how you manipulated Jahangir to choose him?"

The look that flashed across Nur Jahan's face was one her father seldom saw. Nor did he want to see it again.

"If he's ignorant enough *not* to recognize the obvious, he'll be even easier for me to manage," she hissed.

Because he'd been trusted by both Jahangir and before that by Akbar, serving them both with great skill, Ghiyas had much to teach his daughter. Sadly, Nur Jahan was consumed by a power lust that Ghiyas had not embraced. He sometimes feared his haughty daughter might use her brilliance to attempt being the first woman to openly rule this mighty empire. She'd not overstep *that* tradition and sit publicly on the throne, would she?

"Khurram will comply with my wishes because he knows the power I have over his father and the Persian Junta." She paused and thought for a moment. "And I have my niece, Mumtaz, to supply the proper nudge to her husband." The younger woman's value to the empress would soon be tested. A slight frown creased her forehead when she realized how long Khurram and Mumtaz had remained close. Her scheme would be brought to life quickly after there was dissatisfaction between the two of them. Khurram had no second wife yet, she remembered as she yawned, but there would surely be one soon, now that Mumtaz had delivered two babies.

Watching his daughter's satisfied stretch; Ghiyas remarked reflectively, "Our family has done well."

Indeed they had. In one generation—only one generation—his Persian family had risen from penniless refugees to highly influential members of the Mughal Court. He and two of his children had direct access to Jahangir. Of them all, it was Nur Jahan who had reached the greatest height. Jahangir had even ordered drums to be beaten to announce her arrival...*after* they had played his music, of course.

Ghiyas knew that his Persian background was a factor in his acceptance in the court of Akbar. Though the Mughals had been powerful and influential when he arrived, there existed a strong respect for the ancient Persian culture. The Mughals, eager to camouflage their rawness, wore Persian fashions, collected Persian paintings, followed Persian garden design, and spoke the Persian language. Only in the area of borders were the Persians defied. Otherwise, the Mughals strived to emulate their well-established and valued culture.

He had watched his daughter grow into a strikingly beautiful, self-confident woman, radiating health and energy. Her dark hair was cleverly twisted and braided in trendsetting patterns when she was in public. But whether her hair was loose or tight, there was no disguising the intelligence of the dark eyes above her high cheekbones. Small, elegant, and wise to the ways of the world, Nur Jahan disguised her intensity with attractiveness. While she grasped tightly to all that was hers, she was continually scheming for more.

This was part of her appeal to Jahangir, who, as a young man, had been given all but one thing he petulantly continued to wait for—his father's throne. In frustration, he threw himself into a life filled with personal debauchery shocking even to the permissive

Mughals. He consumed vast amounts of wine and opium, surviving until he wore the royal turban in great part because of the robust constitution he'd inherited.

Jahangir adored Nur Jahan's brazen attitude, physical beauty, and quick mind. As his favorite—and most politically powerful— wife, she soon became a force recognized by the court. She handled the petty jealousies and possible usurpation of her power in the zenana through diplomatically marrying rivals into advantageous —and distant—positions.

Depending increasingly on Nur Jahan for the administration of the empire, her loving attentions, and her nursing talents, Jahangir nonchalantly transferred to her the power to disperse imperial grants of land to women.

Admiration shone from Ghiyas' eyes as he gazed upon the woman before him. *She's where she wants to be,* he smiled to himself, *and doing what she wants to do. I can think of nothing that would get in her way.*

4

The zenana

The women's zenana was an extravagant city of waterfalls, fountains, plants, and buildings. Although it took up a large portion of the main palace area, it was accessible only to females of the palace, the emperor, eunuchs, and a few chosen men.

High-ranking women were surrounded by rooms and gardens brilliant with paint, inlay, and mirror work as they lounged on ornamented cushions and rugs. Queens, servants, sisters of the emperor, and concubines shared the zenana with royal relatives, female slaves, female guards, female entertainers, and female soothsayers. Children, including young boys, filled the city with their sounds and energy. Eunuchs served and guarded the emperor's women. These emasculated men moved between the zenana and the rooms of men, linking both worlds, belonging fully to neither.

Fierce large females, easily distinguished from the predominantly petite women they were hired to protect, arranged themselves inside the zenana. They carried the bows and short daggers they had been trained to use. Eunuchs also defended both the inside and the outside of the women's living quarters. In addition, armed soldiers patrolled the outer walls to insure safety. At sunset, the zenana doors were closed and torches were lit for further protection. Mughal honor required that women were kept secluded no matter the cost.

❁ ❁ ❁

THE MORNING AFTER HER RETURN from Moonlight Mahal, Mumtaz was awakened by a young servant gently rubbing her feet. After she stretched and stood, a group of serving women moved silently toward her. One slipped her into sandals as delicate as her soft feet. Another carefully pinned back her loosened hair. After she had been robed, they all accompanied her to the Bath. Her skin was brightened with a fragrant paste of turmeric, gram flour, and rose water. She was soaped and rinsed, then rubbed with scented oil. When dry, she was dressed and cosmetics were applied. Flowers were added to her hair, and she was given breath-freshening cloves to chew. Before she left for this morning's visit with Nur Jahan, she glanced in the nearby mirror and smiled.

Had this been a "special occasion" Mumtaz would have required a more thorough preparation: bathing would have included sandalwood fumes to infuse her drying hair with its sweet smell; a black paste would have been applied carefully on her eyebrows and around her eyes, a red paste would have adorned her lips; henna would have been painted in complex designs on her hands and feet; and she'd have worn many jewels. She knew some of her zenana sisters regularly took a half day for their personal beauty routine but she chose brevity when she could.

This morning's visit to her father's sister, her Auntie, the empress, was considered more of a family time than a special occasion, and Mumtaz was eagerly looking forward to it. Her relationship with Nur Jahan had become more important since she had moved into the Agra Fort as Khurram's wife. Nur Jahan knew the expectations of the palace, was familiar with the zenana, and had known Mumtaz when she was still called Arjumand. The older woman's irreplaceable mentoring had enabled Mumtaz to adapt quickly to the opulence she now enjoyed.

Mumtaz chose to walk alone between the two apartments, enjoying the variety of sounds she heard. Jahangir, following the precedent set by his father, had brought women of all faiths into his zenana so while some women chanted from the Koran, others sent prayers to their Hindu gods, and a few rang bells. A small group of concubines sat on carpets beside a pool, playing the stringed sitars and tapping the drums they were encouraged to master. Others practiced dances. She listened to the cooing doves, the splashing of fountains, and the chatter of scampering monkeys. The nearer she came to Nur Jahan's apartment, the more lavish were the silk carpets and the seasonally changed brocades hanging with heavy gold and silk tassels.

Nur Jahan had already been reviewing her business interests that morning. She had become wealthy since marrying Jahangir. Through trusted eunuchs, she had purchased cargoes of goods for her ships and chosen the ports to trade the items for the greatest profit from the grants of land she had received from Jahangir She reviewed the income from taxes and tolls collected from travelers and merchants, and the success of her many-roomed inns, or caravansaries. In addition, Nur Jahan received valuable gifts from the emperor as well as from foreigners and supplicants who understood her sway with the emperor.

The two women strolled on carpets laid for them under the embroidered awning that extended from one of Nur Jahan's rooms. They talked, leaning on large silk pillows as they plucked at mangoes, grapes, and pomegranates while servants poured fresh juices from golden pitchers. They shared reminiscences of family days before either of them lived in the Agra Fort. They discussed the years Nur Jahan had lived far to the east in Bengal with her husband and the arrival of their baby girl. The empress spoke of how she had returned after her first husband died to eventually marry Jahangir and become the highest-ranking woman in his zenana. She told her niece again the story of how she had successfully insisted upon becoming the emperor's queen rather than his concubine. All of this was known to Mumtaz who nevertheless enjoyed hearing it again in this quiet and personal time with her auntie.

"Are you enjoying your life here?" Nur Jahan asked as she

helped herself to more sharbat. With this question and others following it, the empress began steering the conversation in a different direction.

"Is Khurram a good husband to you?"

"Is there anything I can do to make you more comfortable here?"

"Isn't it true that when women work together we have great influence over our men?"

"Even your husband, as intelligent as he is, will interpret the events surrounding him according to how he is involved with an issue. Don't fret if you are puzzled, Mumtaz, for I can translate what you hear from him. Feel free to talk to me when you feel confused."

Though she was aware her auntie was talking, Mumtaz was barely listening. She was watching Nur Jahan bite her lip. Her auntie only reverted to this unconscious and lifelong habit when she was thinking secret thoughts. Mumtaz had been taught her entire life to respect her father's sister, but now she realized conflicting currents existed under the smooth words and easy manner of the woman before her. The seemingly casual questions were not innocent at all, but were an attempt to tunnel into her private hours with Khurram. Mumtaz maintained a guileless face to suggest to Nur Jahan the seed of her idea had been planted.

"Thank you, Auntie," she spoke as she rose to leave. "It pleases me to know I can confide in you."

Strolling back to her own apartment after the visit, Mumtaz was thoughtful. Nur Jahan was both a member of her family and the Padshah Begum, the highest ranking woman in the zenana. From now on when the two of them were together, she was going to be certain which one of these two "relatives" was speaking.

The sounds of women ahead caused her to put aside the troubling conversation. Her pace quickened with pleasure when she remembered there were displays set up this day for the women of the zenana. Because the emperor's women were not allowed to travel to the markets, merchants sent women to sell cloth and ornaments to the wealthy customers living in the Agra Fort.

Lakiti, Mumtaz' favorite among these merchant women, spotted her and smiled broadly as she approached with her arms filled with expensive cloth. She had been waiting to reveal the preselected lengths of glimmering, diaphanous fabric she had for the wife of the emperor's son. Mumtaz smiled and sat on the carpet to make her selection. Almost immediately her smile vanished and her body froze when she heard, from the group of chattering women next to her, the seldom-spoken phrase, "Cobra Queen."

Mumtaz turned her head to catch more of the conversation. "Cobra Queen" was a title carefully used to describe her Nur Jahan. Before this morning, Mumtaz would have ignored the comment or even defended her auntie. After hearing her auntie's curious questions earlier, she listened.

Unaware that they were being overheard, Asha and Saleen, were telling Dari, a newcomer, how Nur Jahan's father and pregnant mother had traveled from Persia to India across the great desert. They were poor and their caravan had just been robbed leaving them even more destitute. When their child was born a female, it was the last straw, a sign of continued bad luck.

Dari, her eyes following the descending silk that floated to the ground in front of her from the hand of the merchant's daughter who had deftly thrown it above her head, continued the conversation still gazing at the colorful sight. "They couldn't very well just leave her there, could they?"

"That's exactly what they did!" Asha leaned toward her listener and lowered her voice. "Her mother protested, but her father insisted the newborn wouldn't survive either the intense heat of the day nor the equally intense cold of the night, so they left her and continued on their way to India. They didn't get far before the mother collapsed unable to go on without her daughter."

Nodding affirmatively to conclude her selection of silk, Saleen continued the story. "Her father, Ghiyas Beg, yes, the man who is now Chief Minister, was not a bad man. He'd made the decision because he sincerely believed it was best for both the infant and his wife. He was easily persuaded by his distraught wife to return to look for their daughter."

Adding drama to her next words, she continued. "When they retraced their steps and saw their baby, they found her alive but in mortal danger."

"Yes, mortal danger," echoed Asha. "Nur Jahan received her nickname because her parents witnessed a huge black cobra was raised over her. Its hood with its spectacle mark was spread wide. He was soundlessly oscillating so its shadow shielded the little one from the burning sun of the desert. The baby wasn't even crying. She was motionless and seemed to be staring at the steady, small red eyes of the snake above her as though the two of them were communicating."

Fascinated, Dari turned away from the patient seller of silks. "What did they do?"

Putting her head closer to Dari, Saleen whispered, "Without thinking, Ghiyas Beg stood up and began running toward the two of them. Of course, the snake could have bitten the baby, or him for that matter. Instead, it simply lowered itself and slithered away."

"So that's why she's called the Cobra Queen?"

"Yes, but you must never use the title when she can hear it. She doesn't believe anyone knows about this experience she had as an infant."

Dari's puzzled face revealed she did not comprehend what the Cobra had to do with Nur Jahan's current position.

"Think about it, Dari. When her parents arrived in Agra, her father was a penniless man hoping to find a new life. He very quickly was brought into the court of Akbar and eventually raised to an exalted position. And look at Nur Jahan now. She is an empress. This is a woman who had been left to die in the desert."

Asha and Saleen exchanged glances and nodded slightly as if deciding they had said enough.

Dari saw the look and asked. "Are you going to tell me the rest?"

Hesitantly, the two women agreed. They went on to speak of the rumor that questioned the source of Nur Jahan's decisions. Perhaps she received counsel from a source not available to everyone...

"Like the Cobra?"

Neither Asha nor Saleen answered.

❊ ❊ ❊

MUMTAZ HAD FIRST HEARD this Cobra story when she was still in her father's house. Hearing it again reminded her of the dark side of her auntie. "I don't want to be her enemy. It would be both foolish and against my heart. But I simply won't let her into the private time I spend with Khurram by opening it to her." She shook her head in disbelief. "Did she really ask me to be her spy?"

Not wanting to believe the worst about her auntie, Mumtaz concluded that the woman she'd just spent hours with had more important things to occupy her thoughts than information about her husband.

Indeed, Nur Jahan did have much to concern herself with and the lavish zenana was only part of it. She made the decisions concerning not only its physical aspects but also the women within who were, for the most part, content to live in their gilded cage, and enhance their physical beauty. Many were sophisticated, self-assured, and happy with their lives. Many, but not all.

A minority resisted contentment and instead focused upon what they were forbidden to have: men. These were the women who had flaunted their sexual association with the emperor and the costly gifts they had received from him. Usually surprised when replaced, they would rage with jealousy, exchange angry words, plot against others, and even use spells and potions to thwart another's good fortune.

Jahangir thought nothing of using his privilege as an emperor to sexually enjoy the beautiful women in his own zenana. Because he assumed none of his previous partners minded, and because he expected his women to show only happiness when he was near, he was unaware of the harsh fate that could be dealt to a new favorite in the hands of a jealous "sister."

Jahangir's patterns changed after he married Nur Jahan. No longer was there tension generated by his fickle choice of one woman to the exclusion of another for Nur Jahan satisfied him in bed every night he stayed awake. Because the emperor was no longer a source of intermittent sexual satisfaction, unhappy women schemed even more diligently than before to sneak men into their rooms and discover which eunuchs might still have the ability to satisfy them. Many learned how to gratify one another.

The greatest threat to those who called the zenana home was a pregnant woman. Each woman wanted to give birth to the emperor's first son, hoping she might attain the enviable position of seeing her child on the throne. Even a concubine, who enjoyed the pleasure of the emperor without marriage, was delighted to carry his child knowing that through her baby she would be well provided for even if her son had little chance of wearing the royal turban.

Old and conflicting political allegiances as well as routine jealousies were additional causes of quarrels between women who had been brought to Agra from all around the empire These were partially balanced by many adult male friendships that had beginnings in shared childhoods in the zenana, in spite of the fact that they had inherited the prejudices and feuds of their mothers.

One detail in the construction of the zenana silently but inarguably reminded women that they, and their belongings, were the property of the Great Mughal. Although they could enter and exit their apartments at will, all their doors led into other areas of the zenana. The lock on the door leading to the world of men was on the outside. The zenana existed for the pleasure of the emperor who assumed anything a woman would want was already within the walls.

5

Agra ~ 1615

"We should have already marched, Taj!" Khurram, rhythmically clenching and unclenching his jaw was alone with his wife. "Why don't they simply allow me to lead the troops the way I want and stop nattering amongst themselves? The old men have been eating and drinking with Father, going over and over the battle plans and ideas. It's time for action in Rajasthan!"

Mumtaz was alert to the impatience she had not heard from her husband for months. It had frequently been close to the surface when he had began conferring with the experienced generals Jahangir had summoned to Agra. His early feelings of superiority changed to respect for the experienced men who shared their wisdom with a prince who had never before led an army.

Khurram's wife saw her husband learn as he absorbed the ideas spoken in the exclusive Shah Burj with its painted ceilings, thick carpets, tapestries, and bolsters of velvet and silk. Khurram was taught the necessity of making the water supply a high priority in the desert and the difficulty he would face rolling cannons through the sandy grit the Rajasthanis called soil. He tucked away in his mind the suggestion from a popular general that celebrations and entertainment assist men far from home forget their hardships. He understood how a fierce reputation was by itself a powerful weapon for both a soldier and an army. He listened intently when the conversation turned to tactics for battling small, fast-hitting bands of men.

Though he valued and respected their input, he couldn't push them toward an earlier departure. Surrounded by comfort, the older men reminded the impatient prince that Rajasthan had existed since time began and would surely be there when the army arrived.

"Have another glass of wine."

"Have another mango."

"Take yourself to the coolness of the underground rooms."

"Enjoy this leisurely afternoon."

"Departure is just now coming."

The eyes of the fighting men, who had all spent years far from the appealing bustle and luxury of the palace, devoured the sight of the fountains, shade trees, dancing girls, cool drinks, and marble floors they would soon leave behind. Each wondered if Allah would permit them to see any of them again.

The full army of thousands of soldiers was not in Agra, but maintained within various territories of the court. Soldiers had to travel from the provinces of the nobles who lived throughout the empire and had been paying them until they were called to serve the emperor. Each noble sent soldiers according to his rank. The higher his rank, the higher his standing in court, his income, and the number of soldiers he was obligated to maintain. By an unwritten rule, the number of soldiers actually expected by the emperor was seventy-five percent of the total number of the rank. A nobleman with a rank of 5,000 was expected to send 3,750 mounted, equipped, and trained men. High rank significantly increased a noble's income from the Royal Treasury, only some of which was spent maintaining his expected portion of the Mughal army. Through this system, the emperor was relieved of the responsibility of maintaining a large standing army.

Because the wealth of the nobles reverted to the Crown upon their deaths, there was no incentive to save. Their lavish lifestyles emulated the emperor's, and increased their competition amongst themselves for higher rank which would afford them even greater ostentation.

As if overseeing the activities of the army, men, weapons, animals, food, and armaments was not enough preparation and commotion to keep Khurram busy, Mumtaz made him aware of the flurry in the zenana. She insisted on particular tents and food for the women and separate tents for their servants, slaves, jewelry, perfumes, and clothes.

"Why are you doing this, Taj?"

"Doing what, Meerijan?" Her term of endearment for him and her innocent tone did not distract the determined Khurram.

"You are complicating my military strike into Rajasthan with such things as perfume, chiffon, and jewelry. I'm organizing a military campaign, not an outing for women."

Mumtaz sighed and smiled at her husband's lack of zenana sophistication. "Your women are important, Meerijan," she said, flashing him a look he had come to know as decisive. "We need your help so we can do our best for you. You will see to enough tents for us, won't you?"

Taj knew her husband was learning his military role but it was up to her to help him learn how to use the zenana. The talents of women living in the zenana went far beyond their attractiveness. Many were intelligent and could write poetry, sew, design, organize, paint, and play games. While it was true the indulged women spent many hours everyday deciding which jewels they would wear, there was more to them than self-pampering. They were useful as emissaries, protection, or symbols of power to their master.

But Khurram was not able to see or even care about the value of his zenana—he was impatient to begin his campaign. Mumtaz stood quietly waiting for her agitated husband to stop pacing back and forth.

"Why is it all taking so long?" Khurram asked again. Throwing his hands in the air he groaned, "Why can't we just get on our animals, tie the cannons to the elephants, and leave?"

Mumtaz knew he had the answer to his own question. Pageantry was an essential part of Mughal movement. The population of the empire, court regulars, and peasants all expected a show. It wouldn't do for an army representing the Great Mughal to simply march away without a fuss. Extravagant rituals would consume the day of departure with a string of balcony appearances. blessings, and the giving of gifts.

Court astrologers had declared the auspicious departure date was two weeks hence and Mumtaz wondered how Khurram would survive until then. Already, he was losing his usual tact and diplomacy. He had yelled at his Keeper of the Bath about the water temperature. He had kicked a saddle left on the ground. He had turned away from a soldier while the man was still speaking to him. She knew his temper would only escalate until he was irritating everybody. Khurram needed to distance himself from the clamor, the hustle, and the dust of a preparing army, and she had an idea. She touched his arm, and looked into his troubled eyes.

"Have you noticed the beauty of the moon in the last few days, Meerijan?" She mentioned how she had been watching it from her apartment. Even though her unsuspicious husband heard her words, he was distracted by his thoughts of Rajasthan.

Aware that his thinking was distant, Mumtaz continued with a deliberate vagueness in her voice. "As it becomes more and more rounded, I've been thinking we should be some place as beautiful as the moon itself." She stood and deftly adjusted the lengths of her gossamer skirt. Continuing innocently and casually, as though the thought had just come to her that moment, "It's a pity we won't see Moonlight Mahal for so long—the full moon is always so lovely there..."

She left the room, certain Khurram would put the two thoughts together.

6

Moonlight Mahal - 1615

 As the small sandalwood door inlaid with ivory opened for them, Khurram was glad to be spending several days at the Moonlight Mahal. It was exactly what was needed as the troops sent by nobles arrived in Agra and continued to prepare and pack for their departure south. Lists for equipment were filled. Tents and weapons were examined for usability. Food was amassed. *Yes, this is a good time to be away. These days in Agra will be filled with clattering, clanging, and people dashing about with short tempers. Moonlight Mahal will rest me for when I am needed in the future.*

Could it only have been three months ago that the two of them had first spent time in this hideaway of Takarrub Khan's? The tall Muslim nobleman was known for his height and thunderous voice and was a longtime friend of Jahangir's. He had mentioned this small pleasure garden to Khurram and Mumtaz, and pressed them to stay as his guests.

Later, Takarrub questioned his own generosity. He thought it strange that never before had he allowed, much less encouraged, another couple to spend time at Moonlight Mahal. Perhaps the two young people reminded him of the way Zebinissa and he had been when they were together so many years ago. Happy as most of his memories were, even this brief thought of Zebinissa momentarily saddened him.

Reminders of the consuming love and sensuality they had shared had painted his world with sunshine. Khurram's unhidden passion for his wife brought Zebinissa's forever-young face to the tall Muslim's mind where she still laughed with delight as she had done every day of her life.

Years ago he and Zebinissa had designed the beautiful walled garden and abundantly filled it with lush trees, bushes, flowers, butterflies, and birds. They had drifted under the moonlight in a specially designed float upon the bordering lake. A white silk tent with fabric arches, multiple rooms, wooden floors, and large openings drew garden views inside.

His hideaway held too many achingly personal memories for Takarrub to return. He couldn't bear to be there with another woman nor could he return alone. He was pleased when his twelve-year-old daughter visited the favorite garden of her parents bringing the two most tangible results created by the love he had shared with his wife were together. Because of his daughter, born the moment before his wife died, Takarrub had ordered the garden to be continuously maintained. Now after meeting Khurram and Mumtaz, he was moved to allow another man and woman to open the nearly hidden gate of his own Abode of Love, his Moonlight Mahal.

❋ ❋ ❋

As Mumtaz followed Khurram through the gate wall she remembered so fondly, she prepared herself to see the garden again. *Surely, Moonlight Mahal bewitched me when I was here before,* she thought. *Nothing can measure up to my memories. Perhaps it isn't a good idea to return. Please, Allah,* she implored silently, *make it lovely still.*

When she looked beyond the gate, she relaxed. Allah had been listening. Moonlight Mahal was even more appealing than before. Mumtaz understood clearly now that she had returned, that she was in the home of her heart. Her quarters at the Agra palace were without question refined and elegant. Though she had been surrounded with beauty her entire life, the sight before her held a uniquely personal quality.

Here her soul and her spirit soared and joined in harmony with the imagined music swirling around her. It was here she most strongly felt surrounded by Allah. She closed her eyes and allowed the garden to caress her while she listened, filling her heart with the sweetness of the lakeside paradise. A silver ribbon of water in a narrow stone channel bisected the garden. A fine white silk tent seemed to glow at the edge of the lake. She smiled, remembering what they had shared there only three months earlier. Several fountains created rainbows by spraying misty plumes of iridescent droplets into the air. Entranced by both spray and sunshine, Mumtaz lingered along the path toward the lake.

Khurram paused when he realized his wife was no longer walking with him. Looking back, he raised a questioning eyebrow. She said nothing, just smiled. Khurram waited.

Mumtaz suddenly whirled in a full circle with her arms wide, a physical exuberance erupting from her happiness. Then she did something she never did in court; she clasped her husband's hand in a demonstration of possessiveness, intimacy, and joy.

Sun reflected from the silver poles holding their shimmering silk tent and filling their Moonlight Mahal home with a radiance of filtered sunshine enhanced by pink and gold embroidery. Carpets with floral patterns brought the encircling garden within.

While the sun still brightened the day, Mumtaz and Khurram teased the peacocks with sweets and answered the agile, vociferous monkeys with their own version of the animals' chatter. They pushed lotus-petal "boats" across the waterways and shouted if the competition was meaningful.

Under the full moon, they enjoyed the unique pleasure of drifting in the garden's own round, disk-like float, upturned at the edges, padded, and covered in white fabric shot with silver. Reclining on pillows of a similar fabric, they viewed the sky and the moonlight-iced lake.

Although they were on the water for hours, they were never further from shore than the length of silver chain that connected them to the lake's edge from below the float. They had entered their craft from a small bridge which was then smoothly retracted. As the bridge disappeared from view, so did the servant who had withdrawn it. When it was time to disembark, Khurram had only to strike the small drum at his side for a servant to return, draw in the chain, and pull them in.

Mumtaz and Khurram drifted among the watery moonbeams, nibbling at the fruits set on low tables, and sipping sweetened drinks. In the warm, scented night, they claimed the luminous moon for themselves, as many lovers before them had done.

Hidden musicians added faraway music to the delights of perfumed flowers, peaceful murmurs of the water, and the gentle swaying of the trees' shadows upon the surface of the lake. Cradled in a moonlight embrace, Khurram and Mumtaz were gently rocked as they listened to the sounds of lapping waves, faint music, crickets, and the tinkling of distant bells. They recited words of poetry to one another. It was only here Khurram sang love songs.

As she watched a white jasmine bob away from her fingertips, Mumtaz thought of Takarrub Khan and Zebinissa who had created Moonlight Mahal with their love and laughter. She was momentarily saddened to think that those who brought this place of bliss into existence would never be there again.

7

Agra – 1615

 Departure day finally arrived. Men were equipped and mounted; luggage was packed; bazaar keepers were supplied; animals were loaded with cases and tents; Mumtaz and the women were prepared to leave.

Khurram, his impatience surfacing once again, clasped and unclasped his hands behind his back as he paced, barely keeping his eagerness in check as he waited for his father to begin the first ritual of this important day. Dressed before dawn, Khurram had summoned Ahktar, his manservant, from outside the door to make certain he looked as grand as the day deserved.

He was resplendent in pale green. His matching turban was adorned with emeralds and diamonds. The egret feathers added height to his headgear. Ropes of pearls and large tumbled rubies and sapphires covered his chest. The gleaming silk of his jama needed no other adornment, so Ahktar added only three heavy rings and green embroidered slippers for Khurram's feet. The prince's waist was sashed with a length of crimson satin; completed by the ever-present dagger.

The cost of subduing the Rana of Mewar would be high in the number of soldiers that would be lost, the drain on the treasury, and the time and effort expended. Still, Khurram was eager to expand the Mughal Empire and—equally important to him personally—to ensure himself the crown. His confidence and belief in his destiny to rule were unshakable.

"I'm ready," he said to Ahktar. Both knew he had been ready for months.

※ ※ ※

JAHANGIR THOUGHT ABOUT the coming day with a mixture of happiness and sadness. Although he anticipated being the center of the pageantry, the imminent departure of his son was source of unhappiness. The emperor had disappointments in his royal life, but Khurram was not one of them.

It was too early in the morning to soften his melancholy with wine because he had promised Nur Jahan he would not drink until after noon. A rotund man with a dark moustache that grew down both sides of his mouth and a stomach that drooped over his lowered cummerbund, Jahangir had been born into the kingdom his father, grandfather, and great-grandfather had created. His great-grandfather, Babur, was athletic enough to swim across every river he came to between his northern home in Afghanistan and Agra, but Jahangir didn't swim at all. He was carried almost everywhere, even to his bath. Since birth, all of his desires had been met.

Mementos of his careless and hedonistic life of with wine, opium, and a prodigious number of women showed on his body as extra weight, pudgy bags under his eyes, and the asthma that shortened his breath. Regardless, Jahangir still dressed his role as the emperor, ignored most counsel except his wife's, and was the Great Mughal.

A ring he wore had been a gift from one of the many women in his zenana. He had not worn it for many months and now it reminded him that he had not been to his city of women since shortly before he married Nur Jahan. Surely, his absence was a source of sadness to his women there. Gone were the days when he took upon himself the royal duty of visiting each of the zenana women at least once a year. As he drifted into a momentary reverie he recalled Zelna with her seemingly boneless body covered only with paint, the intoxicating musk aroma and flashing eyes of

Salara, and how Jorlin had moved beneath him.

There had been years when he had slept with uncounted women in each night. They came to him after they were bathed and rubbed with sweet-smelling ointments and special salves had been applied to their erotic areas to bring increasing sensitivity and responsiveness.

He in turn had been prepared for these nights with pastes and ointments that enabled him to remain firm and be aroused multiple times. It was his pleasant regal duty to have them in his bed and plant his seed in their willing and fertile bodies. He smiled in memory of the ritual that had been so good for the women, the empire, and for him. These thoughts tired him now even as he recalled the tantalizing aromas and exquisite bodies of those nights. He wondered just how active he would be even if he did not have Nur Jahan to satisfy his diminishing sexual needs.

Complex and contradictory, Jahangir sought the company of holy men even as he fed his addictions. He had both loved and hated his father. At his command a head could be severed, yet he was the idealistic emperor who ordered a long chain of golden bells to be hung from his jharoka balcony offering direct access to his justice when they were rung. Jahangir could be childishly naïve yet cruel enough to order, and gleefully watch, a battle between a tiger and a man.

Although he could be merciless, Jahangir was thought by many to be kind, noble, and gentle. He warmed water for his elephants so they would not be chilled when they sprayed themselves, he built a lavish feeding spot for a favorite deer, and he cried heartfelt tears when a grandchild was injured.

Coveting the throne, he had twice rebelled against and was defeated by his ruling father. Eventually Akbar allowed Jahangir back into his good graces and reluctantly bequeathed his thriving kingdom to his hedonistic son.

Jahangir had been thirty-six years old before his vigorous father had died, and forty years old when he married his heart's true love. Fortunately for both the emperor and the empire, Nur Jahan, his twenty-second wife, was capable and intelligent. Jahangir was becoming comfortable with her ability to direct additional affairs of the empire and wearing more frequently the mantle of sovereignty that had previously draped his own shoulders.

There was no doubt Jahangir loved being the ruler of a large and powerful empire, but his primary source of pleasure was neither his dazzling lifestyle nor the size of the land he ruled. He thrived on pomp and rituals. Fortunately, his reign had been a peaceful one, and he was minimally involved in the state affairs he considered tedious. Most of his energy was spent sitting at public and private durbars, making judgments, and watching processions.

His lifestyle hid the keen mind behind Jahangir's small, puffy eyes. This Great Mughal, sharply aware of detail, traveled with an artist who was directed to capture the likeness of any new animal or flower the emperor came across. Jahangir scrutinized miniature paintings frequently presented to him from the heavily patronized Royal School of Art and could tell which artist had painted a particular face and sometimes which man might have painted the eyebrows on a face.

Jahangir was becoming even more unpredictable as he aged. During his increasingly formalized schedule of durbars, meetings, and presentations, his routine had evolved into more and more ritualized actions, words, and ceremonies. The announcement of his arrival, presentations of his food, preparation of his bath—all were events that had become loaded with repetitious, and sometimes meaningless, movements. He became less and less involved with the details of the empire his father had found so fascinating.

To shock the clergy and declare his superiority, he flaunted his wine drinking and pork eating in front of the leaders of Islam. Confident his position as emperor and, therefore, head of the Islamic religion was more powerful than the ulama, Jahangir declared that if the Koran decreed he was not to eat pork and drink wine, he'd no longer support Islam. The frowning and concerned religious leaders left to confer. When they returned, they had agreed upon an interpretation of their holy book that justified Jahangir's actions while continuing to safeguard their position as caretakers of the empire's religion.

"The Koran, Your Majesty, states a man must not eat pork or drink wine." The small group of somber men looked at one another and nodded their heads in agreement. "It does not say what a King can eat or drink." They were relieved that Islam remained the empire's religion, they continued to hold power, and Jahangir could eat and drink whatever he liked.

In a land where there was nothing to counter or balance the emperor's decision, no body of men to pass restricting rules, no judges with authority, Jahangir's word was law. People gathered at the Justice Durbars held their breaths, not knowing if his decision would be spoken gently or harshly with a nod toward the nearby hooded men who held long knives to administer his decision immediately.

When he finally stepped onto the jharoka balcony on this day of his son's departure, he gazed benignly at the people gathered below. He had timed his appearance to coincide with the rising of the sun to link the power of the two. It was a conscious decision that the gold clothes he wore represented light and power.

The crowd of subjects below had become used to their symbiotic part of the morning ritual. They gathered before breakfast for proof that the sun would rise and imbue the Great Mughal with the right to rule them for another day. They were in place to confirm that the empire was well and the dynasty remained strong.

This day's gathering was larger than usual, for news of the significance of this morning had spread throughout the bazaars. This was the day the Imperial Army would leave. Prince Khurram, the commander, would be on the balcony with his father. Jahangir had arranged for his beloved son to join him there only after he'd inhaled the initial joyous greeting and basked in the first rays of the morning sun.

Khurram had learned long ago the jharoka appearance was important to Jahangir and contented himself to wait in the shadows behind the curtains of the room until his father motioned him to step forward. It did not occur to him as he watched without being seen that he was momentarily observing the world as Mumtaz always did.

Gems other than the ones worn by both men were part of the ceremony as Jahangir lifted high a golden tray of many-colored jewels and tipped it slightly over Khurram's head. The sparkling baubles showered the prince, signifying exalted honor and respect from the emperor.

8

Agra ~ 1615

"Try to relax, Khurram. There is more to do before we leave." Mumtaz spoke to her pacing husband as he tapped his fingers against his dagger.

Startled to hear the very words he had been thinking, Khurram stopped. He was ready to leave this very moment but knew he still had to summon enough patience to participate in the Ceremony of Luck and The Ceremony of Gift Giving.

Khurram's eagerness to begin his adventure was at odds with Jahangir's love of ceremony. This was to be a memorable day for an emperor who adored the trappings of his position. The prince asked Allah for patience during the hours his father would be center stage before he could depart.

After his sunrise ceremony on the balcony that protruded from the palace wall, a sleepy Jahangir had returned to bed. When he had been carefully redressed, he leisurely, as though nobody was waiting upon him, strolled down the wide staircase to the beat of thunderous, deep-throated kettledrums. He appeared in a room filled with waiting noblemen and accepted the teslim they performed in unison. The men placed the back of their right hands on the floor, raised them until they stood erect, then put the back of their hands upon the crowns of their heads, thus saluting Jahangir and signifying their total obedience to him. After receiving these salutations of honor and respect with the calm acceptance of what was due, the emperor motioned for the ceremony to begin.

As soon as he had seated himself on his throne, a servant brought him a large animal's head on a jade platter. Another uniformed servant held a matching bowl filled with a deep brown glutinous mass of starchy root. Jahangir raised his index finger, paused to be certain all eyes were upon him, then slid his finger into the contents of the bowl. Everyone in the room focused upon the swirling royal finger as though it might find something specific. Satisfied, Jahangir removed his finger and applied the residue that came with it upon the head of the plattered lamb.

Male Mughal dress

This age-old ceremony for good fortune, whose origins Jahangir no longer knew, was performed to bring Khurram safety and victory. The nobles watched silently until it was their time to shout their praises of both Jahangir and Khurram.

Weighed by his jewels, Jahangir was somewhat awkward as he stood. A chosen noble appeared holding in his outstretched hands a magnificent and bejeweled bow with diamonds and rubies inset along the curved strip of wood.

No longer the lightweight and effective weapon it had once been when used by Babur, the bow now represented the founding Mughal Emperor's valor. This same bow had been used when Babur successfully fought his initial battle on Indian soil and established the dynasty now ruled by Jahangir.

A second noble came from behind the first, bearing a quiver clearly belonging with the bow Jahangir was now solemnly holding. Covered in deep green velvet and jewels, the case, filled with its thirty cutting arrows, was slipped over the emperor's shoulder.

Holding the symbolic bow and quiver, Jahangir was a magnificent sight. On either side of his silk turban hung a pair of walnut-sized tumbled stones—a diamond and a ruby. A larger green emerald was nestled above his forehead, nestled into the folds of the silk that had been wrapped around his head. Ropes of pearls, rubies, and diamonds were wrapped around his waist belt which already sparkled with interwoven gold and silver threads. Pearls hung over his chest, he wore diamond armlets and bangles,· and rings adorned most fingers. His long sleeveless coat of fine satin and his matching embroidered footwear completed his undisputedly regal appearance. Jahangir epitomized the strength and the ostentation of the Mughals. This was the image he wanted prominent in Khurram's mind during the campaign, so he would remember he was fighting for an empire and an emperor of great wealth and power.

Khurram now moved from the side of the throne to face his father. "My son, you are the light of my eye and the hope of my heart. When you go forward you represent your father and the Mughal Empire. It is fitting that you possess the prestigious and wealthy principality of Hissar Feroza." Khurram's heart soared, for he knew this particular piece of land was traditionally the property of the heir apparent. Jahangir continued to increase Khurram's rank and give him a royal standard to be carried into battle.

The emperor then nodded his head quickly to call forward a waiting attendant who carried a tray piled with fine cloth. The prince held it up and everyone in the room was able to admire the exquisite golden robe adorned with fine embroidery of small pearls. This Robe of Honor, so called because it had been passed across the shoulders of Jahangir himself, was carefully draped upon Prince Khurram. Now he was attired not only in his own finery, but also with this gift from his father.

"You will shine as gloriously as the sun," beamed Jahangir.

Other gifts included precious stones from the royal treasury, weapons, and a million solid gold coins for his personal use. There were also ten million rupees for the military chest to cover expenses of the campaign.

Jahangir leaned on Khurram for support and together they walked to the adjoining courtyard, the assemblage respectfully behind them. There, head held high and stamping his hooves in what Khurram recognized as impatience as strong as his own, was a dark brown stallion with a jeweled saddle on his back. The brocaded silk saddlecloth was woven with golden threads, padded, lined, and tasseled. Hanging from the saddlehorn was a gem-encrusted sword.

"You must ride in splendor, my son, for the House of Timurid. Take these small tokens of my best wishes with you," smiled Jahangir, knowing full well the extravagance of the tokens.

Although accustomed to fine gifts, Khurram found himself speechless at the generosity of the animal, saddle, and sword. Even as he stroked the steed, another animal was led into the courtyard. Jahangir cleared his throat meaningfully, and Khurram, responding to his father's implied command, turned to see a tall, muscular elephant lumbering toward him. For transportation of both goods and people, elephants were invaluable in warfare and no man could have too many. As a gift, an elephant increased the prestige of both giver and recipient.

"I know you already own many elephants," spoke Jahangir with false modesty, "but I hope you will find room for one more."

"This admirable animal, the finest I've seen, shall have a suitable home." Khurram spoke the truth in his respectful reply. The unblemished animal before him was magnificent in every way, including his long curving tusks banded in gold.

"Perhaps when you are riding this elephant, Rumchun," said Jahangir in a voice heard only by Khurram, "you will feel your father is riding with you in spirit."

As a prince, Khurram was not allowed to show his feelings in public. But when the young Commander of Imperial Armies smoothly swung his leg over his new stallion and sat straight, he stopped and turned to look into the crowd of men before leaving. He caught his father's eye and flashed him their private hand signal.

When very small, Khurram had proudly practiced the teslim he had seen others perform for his grandfather. His first concentrated effort to perform it was perfect, except for one detail. He had put the back of his pudgy little hand over his eyes rather than on the crown of his head. Since that time, Akbar, Jahangir, and Khurram had raised one hand over one eye, palm outward, toward each other. With this private signal, Khurram wordlessly conveyed how much the gifts had meant to him.

Jahangir watched until his son was merely a spot in the distance. He would miss Khurram, but he realized the gifts and his sorrow were the price he had to pay to remain in the comfort of his palace while others assumed responsibility of military leadership. After watching another moment, he turned and retired to his private quarters for his first cup of wine of the day.

9

Rajasthan ~ 1615

The army Khurram led in 1615 differed greatly from the first Mughal forces that rode into the western portion of the Indian continent. In 1526, Babur, Khurram's great-great-grandfather, invaded the mystical land of jewels, cobras, and spices to claim what his ancestor had seen. This ancestor, Timur the Lame, Tamerlane, had darted into India only then returned north to his Afghani home in Samarkland with captured treasure and skilled workmen. Tamerlane had legitimized his invasions by stressing his blood relationship to Ghengis Khan. Babur had heard stories about the riches of Hindustan even before he had become homeless. The year he rode into India had been the year he either had to leave Afghanistan, the beloved land of his birth, or live there as a bandit finding refuge in his country's cold mountains.

Claiming the right to return to a land his ancestor had once invaded, Babur, bigger than life, outgoing, gregarious, and daring, defeated India's defenders. He found success with a combination of superb tactics, strong leadership, and the first use of gunpowder his foes had ever encountered. Thus the Mughal Dynasty began.

Babur built watered gardens in the land he had conquered, and began to establish comfortable living circumstances. His son, Humayan, succeeded him and rather quickly lost the land won by his father to outside forces and to his own ungrateful brothers and was forced to flee. With the aid of the Persian army, he reclaimed what had been given to him. Shortly after his return to India, he tripped coming down the stone steps of his library after prayers, hit his head, and died. His son, Akbar, then thirteen, became emperor.

It was during Akbar's reign that the empire began to amass size and wealth. Akbar's generosity, intelligence and farsightedness transformed his family's rule in Hindustan from a handful of quarreling, loosely organized Islamic overlords into a mighty empire. He amalgamated the fragile country and expanded Mughal land until it covered the area between the Arabian Sea and the Indian Ocean. From Kashmir in the Himalayan Mountains southward for a thousand miles, the subcontinent belonged to the Mughals. To increase even further the size of the empire, Akbar used ruthless daring, common sense, and a determination to become a leader of all religions. As a result of Akbar's reign, the Mughals were no longer strangers in India but residents who called the land 'home.'

Even though he was Muslim, Akbar accepted—even wooed— valiant Hindu soldiers to his army and Hindu statesmen to his court. He offered them positions, rank, and an increase in salaries. Even though orthodox Islamic leaders would despise this dilution of their religion, Akbar held fast to his beliefs. Ignoring the ulama's animosity, he made changes that developed the Mughals into rulers accepted by those they dominated rather than resented as invaders.

Religious harmony in the empire was a continuous issue. Akbar attempted to weave Islam and Hinduism into a new and dynamic culture with results considered brilliant by some, sacrilegious by others. He, a Muslim, married Hindu princesses and allowed them to continue to perform the rituals of their beliefs, abolished the jizya tax which had been levied on all non-Muslims, and seriously studied the teachings of Hindu religious leaders.

His success met resistance, but his power was great enough to surmount the opposition. By the early 1600's, before the Pilgrims sailed for the New World, the Great Mughal ruled over much of the subcontinent of India, lived in ornate palaces and had developed a complex court and administrative system. Music, painting, and poetry were supported by royal patronage. Taxation was an important pillar of the empire. And, as Khurram was now experiencing, uniformed and well-equipped armies of both Muslims and Hindus marched forth under the same banner—one showing a lion crouching in front of a blazing sun.

❋ ❋ ❋

THE SERVING GIRL MOVED NOISELESSLY as she scanned the tent for anything out of order before Mumtaz arrived. Jinka could already hear distant elephant bells as the animals approached the Royal Camp, a tent city that hadn't existed a day earlier. She had never imagined mere tents could be as splendid as these. The traveling furniture was arranged as prescribed, and incense perfumed the tent. Mumtaz' trunks of clothing and jewelry were nearby. The bathing and screened courtyard tents had been erected close to those of the prince.

Jinka relaxed knowing the canvas-walled room was ready. Low tables were spread with bowls of cashews for Mumtaz' empty stomach and cold lassi to soothe her parched throat. Rugs added images of birds, animals, flowers, and vines to the space.

She shook her head at the sight of the heavy green bottle. With everything else in the room of such quality, she simply couldn't imagine why that poorly made container traveled with her mistress. What Jinka did know was that Mumtaz would change her clothes and partake of the light prepared for her as soon as she arrived.

Because of her Muslim upbringing, Jinka was shocked to learn of a man taking dinner with his wife. She'd been in Mumtaz' room enough to know Khurram frequently ate with her instead of before her and separately as was more traditional. She had noticed other differences as well. The prince spent time with Mumtaz to the exclusion of other women; they touched frequently, and they laughed and talked, truly seeming to enjoy being with one another. *It must have something to do with being royal and having no worries.*

A refreshed Mumtaz emerged after her bath and massage. She would not have felt travel stiffness and aches from the day's journey, except that she was again expecting a baby. This was her third pregnancy in three years. Even though carrying a child and giving birth seemed less demanding on her than on other women, she would have preferred more time to be without child since the birth of Dara who was still only a few months old. She was to be with child for nine months as a result of being unwilling to stay away from her husband. She was pleased her babies would have fine attention and care after they were born. They all added joy to her life and she loved to hold them, play with them, and watch them grow. Knowing wouldn't ever become the ruler of an empire, make far-reaching military decisions, or design fine buildings, she accepted what she could do: bear children.

At that moment, Khurram strode into her tent, seated himself, and grabbed a tall glass of lassi that Jinka had ready for his visits. He lounged on a divan drinking Jinka's secret combination of diluted yogurt, peppers, and herbs while he waited for his wife to arrive.

Mumtaz quietly approached him from behind, admiring his turban, the fringe of hair protruding darkly below it, and the richness of his clothes. The thrill of seeing him in her room still caused her to catch her breath.

Tenderly, she touched the small portion of his exposed neck, as she had done so many times. Her touch and the scent of her exclusive jasmine and gardenia perfume filled Khurram with happiness. He was with Taj again.

Sighing with contentment as her fingers moved from his neck to his shoulders, he raised his hands and covered hers in their established way of greeting.

"The fresh air seems to agree with you," observed Khurram as he guided his wife around to face him.

Mumtaz recalled how the sun relentlessly sucked the air from her hot, stuffy howdah as she was transported to this city of tents.

She also knew the discomfort somehow increased the adventure of her chosen travel which would eventually be much further than her trips to the Moonlight Mahal.

"It does," she replied, choosing not to mention how difficult it had been to find a satisfactory position. "Most enjoyable. Suraiya was in the howdah with me, and we laughed, told stories, and played games...when we weren't peeking out the curtains so we wouldn't miss anything."

She related how her elephant had lumbered under the inner archway and through the royal enclosure then past still another barricade before reaching the elaborate traveling Diwan-i-Khas. The embroidered canvas and waxcloth walls were nearly close enough to touch from her howdah.

Her elephant had stopped near Khurram's Red Tent—the physical center of the Royal Tents as well as its military hub. She had passed the well-guarded painted wood and canvas fort, within which there were tents of the zenana. Encircling the tents of the women was a high, sturdy barrier. It was made of heavy poles lashed together then covered with yards and yards of thick cotton cloth that could be dismantled and reconstructed frequently as they journeyed.

Soldiers protected this enclosure that was within the more extensively guarded perimeter. As in Agra, Tartar women and eunuchs protected the traveling women; only one man, the prince, was allowed access. Comfortable in her spacious tent and surrounded by familiar people and familiar sights, Mumtaz was only vaguely aware of the enormity of the mobile city.

Khurram, assuming Mumtaz would never see the rest of the camp, described it to her, so the mosques, hospitals, bazaars, and the mobile stables for war elephants and cavalry horses became real through his words. This was his first experience with the traveling city, and he respected its masterful organization, immense size, and mobility. He knew that a second and identical tent-city was already being set up farther along the route, waiting for their arrival the next day.

Because they descended from tent dwellers, it was natural for the Mughals to use portable homes when they traveled. This tradition had been greatly modified in style; the Royal Camp had become, as had other accoutrements of the Mughal Court, complex, magnificent, and expansive. 'Mahal," the Mughal word for palace, originally meant "exalted camp," an apt description for their new cities. Spread out over a twenty-mile circle, it accommodated two to three thousand people in a variety of tents organized in a strict and unvarying plan. The prince's center was surrounded by striped and patterned tents topped with flapping banners belonging to the military commanders. Behind these tents were the smaller canvas living quarters of the soldiers and behind them the tents for families, animals, and equipment.

The largest circle consisted of the vendors and their stalls. When the camp moved, these stalls were quickly packed, loaded on animals, and moved ahead of the ponderously slow-traveling camp to be erected before the next evening. Humble and essential, these merchants provided the Mughal army its supply line of food. The royal family brought with them their own kitchen tents, cooks, and food.

Eunuchs, servants, and attendants had separate tents, as did the elephants, horses, camels, hunting dogs, falcons, and cheetahs. There were temporary structures used as storerooms for weapons, harnesses, and other animal gear: saddles, cannons, ammunition, palanquins, howdahs, litters, and medical supplies. Tents for Ganges water, condiments and spices, fruits and vegetables, and other foodstuffs such as rice and ghee surrounded the elaborate food-preparation tents. Brocades, chiffons, and jewelry were separately stored near the zenana.

❋ ❋ ❋

KHURRAM'S THOUGHTS WERE NEVER FAR from the challenge of his command. Even his grandfather, Akbar, who had encouraged many Rajputs to join his army, had been unable to subdue the powerful and long-established Rana of Mewar. The rana's confidence against the mighty leaders of much of India came from the historical claim that his family was descended from the sun. His Rajputs, fierce Hindu warriors, were aggressively loyal to him. He had never accepted Mughal domination, had never sent tribute to the royal court, and had offered none of the princesses of his house to the Mughals. Khurram knew his opponent would fight to maintain those points of pride.

Assuming the lack of reprisals from the Mughals as an admission of his superiority, the emboldened rana had been ordering quick, devastating attacks. Before the large Imperial Army could respond, the attackers melted into their barren, hilly, desert homes, regrouping to assault again.

The task Khurram had undertaken was complicated by the potentially divided loyalties of the Rajputs who served in both armies. The prince took very seriously the impressive foe he would be facing but knew his personal need for victory was equally strong. After weeks of traveling, he shared his thoughts with his wife.

"I see so clearly what needs to be done, Taj. My troops must not believe my plan is too harsh."

Khurram and Mumtaz had retired, and he absently stroked her back as she stretched out on her side next to him. Khurram's attention, usually with her at these times, was elsewhere.

"You will know just what to say and how to say it," she reassured him, feeling his distance. Mumtaz caught his stroking hand and brought it between her breasts. She pressed it firmly and gently until she felt him relax and knew he would soon share more of his thoughts. Tonight, he now knew, she was his confidante rather than his lover.

He was still for a moment, and then moved closer to her. She released his hand, which again began to absently stroke the length of her side.

"This is a vital mission I've been assigned, Taj; the honor and prestige of the Mughal army rests on our success."

Mumtaz waited for him to continue.

"We'll be fighting brave and sometimes reckless Rajputs who are proud and strong warriors. He laughed without humor. "It won't be simple, but the defeat must be so total and undeniable their rana will be forced to sue for peace. We must win by any means. We must be victorious."

Khurram stopped talking and thought about the destruction and the brutality his plan included. It was with wrenching mental anguish he admitted what he had never disclosed before when he whispered, "I will be asking my men and my officers to do great harm. We must be willing not only to destroy the people but the land they live on, Taj. I've asked myself if I can do this."

There was a silence between them in the dark before Mumtaz spoke in a low voice. "The approach used by your grandfather didn't work for him, Meerijan. Is there any reason that it would work now?" She could feel him shake his head in answer.

"Perhaps," she continued softly, "you must change tactics. Perhaps you have no choice. Your father has ordered you to subdue this rana. You know you must not limit yourself to what has been previously done."

He knew she was right. The knot inside his chest began to loosen, and he felt more at ease with his plans than he had since leaving Agra. His mind was at last comfortable, his course set, and his pre-battle doubts gone. He was now eager to pay more attention to the sensuous woman lying beside him.

10

Rajasthan ~ 1615

While dawn was spreading over the sky like a bouquet of roses and jasmine, Mumtaz took her hidden place behind a traveling screen and watched a cross-legged Khurram on his cushioned throne. Neither his posture nor his facial expression suggested he had ever questioned what he was going to ask of his men.

Each soldier came into the presence of the prince and clasped his hands in front at waist height to indicate allegiance and obedience. They all knew the full teslim was reserved for the emperor.

When the troops stood before him, Khurram greeted them with solemnity and gravity. In his first speech as their commander, he spoke to them in a resonant voice that reached to every ear. He asked them to respect their uniforms as they represented the honor and prestige of the Mughals.

"We are born to command by force of arms." Khurram was getting to the portion of his speech that would spell out the plans he was prepared to carry out. "We have to match the recklessness and inventiveness of the ferocious Rajputs we'll be facing. These warriors have a disdain for life that we'll have to emulate to conquer them. Remember that Allah is our friend and our guide. He'll be with us as we battle these Infidels!"

Aware he was pitting his Rajputs against others with a shared background, Khurram recalled part of the previous night's conversation with Mumtaz.

"If you choose to fight with me, some of you will be sacrificing more than others because you share traditions and perhaps even family ties with our enemies."

"Rajputs are born to fight. They live mainly to be warriors. When they aren't at war with a common enemy, they'll fight other Rajputs from the next village to stay trained. When we are in their land, their focus will be our defeat."

"We shall not be content with anything less than total victory!" shouted Khurram to his army. He stood. His listeners rose with him and copied his raised fist and his challenging cry for success.

❋ ❋ ❋

THE DRY DESERT'S STEEP CRUMBLING CLIFFS reflected incessant heat upon the determined soldiers. Only intermittent, dark gorges and strips of mountaintops resembling giant reptilian vertebrae broke the sere earth. Flowing rivers that cut earth and sand into deep jagged canyons were defined by the swath of green life growing along their shores. In other places, flat, seemingly featureless, land dropped sharply into dry ravines, carved by ancient rivers and further eroded by centuries of wind and driven sand. Only rain could add touches of green to these otherwise dry gullies. Brown hills of dirt, rocks, and distant cliffs were tinged with gold. Only when the sun sent a low, strong light did the single color become tinged with gold. At those times, ridges were most clearly shown and protuberances larger than hills, yet smaller than mountains were noticed. The Mughals marched, fought, and burned leaving nothing but some of the animals of Rajasthan unattacked.

The men Khurram commanded acted with the same determination they had heard in his voice, inspired to focus on nothing less than the goal of total victory. They sweltered in the cruel sun. Loath to remove their protective garments, they fought most conflicts wearing long sleeves, steel helmets hung on mail neck guards, and high collars studded with gilt-headed nails. Each carried a hard round shield of hide, a dagger, and a sword hanging from his belt. In addition, some carried a three-foot matchlock gun.

Khurram's skill and strategy were unstoppable. In addition to directing his ruthless and well-equipped army, Khurram ordered the Mughal cannons—previously deemed useless in the heavy, wheel-burying sands of the Rajasthan desert—to be pushed further into the desert than ever before.

He was ready for the rana's lightning strikes and retaliated with small squads of horsemen trained to relentlessly track these men from one spot to another.

Khurram ordered outer walls of fortresses to be destroyed. To accomplish this, he directed his men to tunnel from a safe distance, working under protective roofs when they were close enough to be within range of the city's guns. After the fortress' wall was breached in one spot, the Imperial troops rushed forward, even as the defenders of the fortress used cannons, guns, mortars, and rockets to repel them. Additional mines were detonated until the defenders surrendered, usually only after vicious hand-to-hand fighting.

The prince set up a series of military checkpoints in the hilly areas thought invulnerable by previous commanders, sent columns of cavalry to harass the rana and his soldiers, and made hostages of families of the most prominent Rajputs.

The prince's attacks were felt by more than the Rajasthani soldiers. Men, women, and children alike lived in fear as ruin and death became the fate of citizens. Wheat planted to feed families was burned to short, charred stalks. Pavilions proclaiming the location of treasured water were surrounded by bodies announcing the presence of poison in the wells. Nearby were dead camels still wearing their neck ornaments and padded saddles. Lifeless cattle, eternally yoked to their carts, rotten in the blazing sun.

Cities were blockaded. New craters from large detonations pocked the landscape. Bridges were destroyed. Roads became unusable. Soldiers witnessed at least one burned cluster that was once a former village. Silent, blackened, and empty, they were grim reminders of the pitiless battle.

When Anjit, a Mughal soldier, saw the toy horse near one of the huts, he picked it up for his young son, knowing Ajun would enjoy it. He had proceeded only a few paces when he realized it was likely the toy's owner had been burned out of his home, perhaps burned to death. He stopped, opened his hand quickly as though he, rather than the village, had been torched. After the wooden animal fell back into the dust, Anjit's heart softened, and he shed the tears of a father mourning the child that had loved the toy horse. He stood without moving until he heard the sound of a bugle calling him to resume his duty. Raising his head and wiping his face dry with the back of his sleeve, he again became a soldier fighting for victory.

❈ ❈ ❈

UNABLE TO DISCOURAGE the grimly determined Mughal prince any longer, the Rana of Mewar capitulated and sued for peace.

11

Rajasthan

 Harsh as they were, Khurram's ruthlessly devastating tactics had accomplished the goals he had demanded of himself and his men. Though Khurram had focused on defeating his enemy, it was only when the Rana of Mewar surrendered that he permitted himself to relax and accept the victory.

Lying in the dark, his mind was far away from his regal surroundings. He had shared his success earlier with Taj and now was alone with his thoughts. The next day, the Rana of Mewar was going to surrender formally to him. It was to be the first time he would meet the proud, strong man who would endure the humiliation of submission. This was a ruler who'd sent a petition asking to pay homage to the Mughals only because of the terrible damage being done to his people and his lands. He had given up all hope of escape and had stoically accepted that he would lose his life, family, and honor. Even so, he chose surrender as his last desperate chance to escape total devastation of his rule and his land.

Khurram rolled over and drifted into a satisfied sleep.

In the morning, turbaned Mughal soldiers followed the defeated rana as he approached the awning-covered platform where Khurram waited. His loss of status was made clear when his own men were not allowed to accompany him into the open tent. His ceremonial dagger had been removed from his cummerbund, leaving him weaponless. Khurram was waiting in solitary splendor under his canopy as he watched the rana, dressed in white with a gold-stitched belt, approach. Wearing swords and turbans and carrying their circular shields, the Mughal soldiers continued to be a silently threatening force, standing in proximity to the commander who had led them to victory.

The courage I can feel coming from this rana tells me his personal bravery is not lacking. This man before me would have fought to a Rajput death if his own life were his only concern. It was the slaughter of his people and the devastation of his land that compelled him to teslim to a Mughal Prince where all can see.

The following moments would reveal to the rana how the Mughals, who had already proven themselves to be ruthless, would treat him. He could be put in chains, imprisoned, watch his personal wealth plundered, or any combination of these alternatives. All he knew for certain was the Mughals were not known to murder a foe that had capitulated, even reluctantly, as he had. If the defeated ruler had been more focused upon Khurram, he would have seen the glimpse of deep satisfaction that his low bow had given not only to the handsome man before him, but through him to Jahangir and Akbar. The rana waited in silence, his head lowered. Even in this humble position, he could not change his belief that he and his family had received their right to rule from their ancestor, the sun

When Khurram spoke of the terms of surrender, the Mughals close enough to hear couldn't believe what was being said. Jahangir's initial intention to allow Khurram to crush the rana had changed only when the rana asked for forgiveness. Realizing the value of not destroying old families, Jahangir accepted obeisance instead. Following the wishes of his father, Khurram's demands seemed to be lenient, much too lenient to the men who had fought the battles and lost friends in doing so. Soldiers muttered among themselves. Had the fierce battles been worth the price in time, expense, and lives? they asked. Formerly expressionless faces reflected disbelief and even anger as they heard the easy terms the Mughals were extracting. Only a few valued their wisdom.

After his son's victory, Jahangir demanded, and received, a pledge of peace and friendship between the rana's kingdom and the Mughals. It was clearly understood by the rana that the Mughal army could—and would—bring more devastation to Rajasthan if there were ever a cause to do so.

The rana wasn't asked to present himself to Jahangir in Agra. He wasn't required to raise troops for the Mughals or pay future tribute in either cash or services. It was understood by all that the great portion of the rana's current wealth was to become property of the Mughals. However, his independence was to be respected, his women would be safe, and he wasn't ordered to become a military ally of the Mughals. As long as there were no physical or verbal attacks on the Mughals, the previously powerful rana could live and rule in his desert kingdom. These terms had been clear in a royal firman Khurram had received imprinted with a symbol of authority no less powerful than the palm of Jahangir's right hand.

The battle was over for the victorious Mughals and their leader. The train of people, baggage, animals, and tents began their lengthy northeastern trip home to Agra. Anxiety the army previously carried upon their shoulders as they moved toward battle had been replaced by the contentment of conquest, lingering resentment over the lenient terms of surrender and grief for the men lost

"You have been totally successful in your first military campaign, Meerijan. Why are you not as happy as could be?"

Khurram stopped rubbing the smooth yellow stone he kept with him and looked at his wife before he spoke. "There is part of me that wanted to slash the rana as I have slashed his land. Even though my head tells me that the terms my father ordered me to convey were reasonable, I didn't want to be reasonable. I represented all the men in the field, knowing that what I was going to say was in conflict with everything I had exhorted them with earlier. We had defeated the rana by being more vicious than he had been, and then at the very moment when I should have shown the greatest strength, I had to step aside from my own anger and serve my father."

"Was your father wrong?"

Khurram sat without speaking, his only noticeable movement the automatic working of his fingers and thumb of his right hand as he rubbed the stone. It was one of the surest indications to the observant Mumtaz that her husband was deeply in thought.

"No," Khurram's equivocal word was not deeply felt. "While I would have been immediately satisfied to demand much harsher terms, I can see why my father did what he did. The empire will be better off in the future if we leave the prestige and revenue to illuminate our glory. I will have to be content knowing that I brought the rana to his knees."

And the Rajasthan "cow" would also be content. The word reminded him of the philosophy of his skillful, brave, and far-seeing grandfather. In his time, Akbar had shamelessly used flattery and money to swell his army's size and strength by enlisting the very warriors he'd defeated. He offered much more income than they'd been receiving, didn't suggest they change their religion to match his, and allowed them to continue their fervent fighting under his banner.

"A contented cow will always give more milk," Akbar had said in reference to the care he gave his new soldiers. "But first," Akbar sternly added, his voice at odds with the twinkle in his eye, "you have to catch the cow." Khurram smiled to himself. He knew he had caught the cow in Rajasthan. The terms may have been lenient, but the "cow" of Rajasthan would remain contented and continue to supply a sweet stream of support, friendship, and, through taxes, money to the court of the Mughal emperor.

Khurram admired and emulated Akbar's open mind. His grandfather's inclusive vision, however, was the exception of the times rather than the rule. The imams believed those not of their faith were doomed as Unbelievers. With equal fervency, highborn Hindus believed if one was not of their religion they were below the lowest caste, they were Casteless. To be Casteless was to not exist in the eyes of their religious triumvirate. Thus men in the Mughal army fought with soldiers they respected in battle but had been taught would be deprived of life after death.

12

Agra - 1616

Protocol for the return to Agra Fort required Khurram to ride on the lead elephant and enter the royal gates at the head of the military retinue. Surrounded by cheers and welcoming music, he enjoyed the honor even as he maintained his unemotional public face. As the victorious commander of an army, he nodded to thousands of onlookers lining the route of his parade, remembering to glance upward toward the hidden women.

In the palace, Khurram was bathed and massaged, his beard was trimmed, his mouth was freshened, and his hair was combed. During his grooming, his mind reviewed the battles, the valuables he brought for the Mughal treasury, and the details of the next day's Victory Durbar.

The durbar would demonstrate how Khurram's status had changed. No longer an untried prince, he was returning his army with a victory over the Rana of Mewar. He would be honored during the durbar, he'd show the captured wealth, parade the animals, and present special items to Jahangir. The engraved ruby he'd already sent to his father was the finest but not the only present for his gift-loving parent.

❋ ❋ ❋

IN HER OWN APARTMENT, Mumtaz was being treated to the zenana's luxuries. Nimble and experienced fingers soothed her skin with scented oils, then massaged and bathed her body, her hair was washed with fragrant shampoo; she was covered with suds, then rinsed. Again scented oils were worked into her skin helping it remain supple, unlined, and soft. While bathing their mistress, the Washing Maids were careful of the rounded protrusion suggesting another royal birth was in the future.

❈ ❈ ❈

JAHANGIR HAD JUST STEPPED INSIDE from being adored at the jharoka window. Seeing his wife waiting for him was his second pleasure of the still-early morning. The previous night, he'd been petulant about not spending time with the newly returned Khurram. Jahangir knew his son needed to rest, bathe, and sleep, but he still felt ignored. Knowing Khurram was in the palace and had not come to him was an irritation. He pouted even though he had been the very one to declare he and Khurram should not meet until the morning. Nur Jahan had not condoned her husband's sulking behavior. Noting he was on his eighth cup of wine and predicting he would simply slide further and further into a foul mood, she did what no one else would have dared to do—she left the emperor without his permission.

Jahangir had roared and threw a nearby wine vessel at the wall. The metal object made a satisfying thunk as it hit.

"That's for Khurram not coming to visit me tonight!"

Then he put his hands on a priceless jade vase and threw it to the floor. The crash and sound of shards flying satisfied his frustration. "That's for Nur Jahan!"

He had then collapsed in a nearby chair and submitted to self pity. The two people he loved the most in the world were treating him as though he were a mere peasant. He could have them jailed. Or he could order them to be tied to a stake so he could watch an elephant trample them. Or maybe he would have them buried up to their necks with only their heads showing in the deadly sun

The ugly thoughts and his anger diminished as swiftly as they had arrived. *All I want is Nur Jahan's smile and touch.. and another cup of wine.* Wheezing from the exertion and stress, Jahangir remembered a tactic that had worked for him in the past. Giving the appropriate commands to servants within the sound of his voice, he trundled off to bed.

Now it was morning, and he had recovered his agreeable outlook. Excited about the upcoming day and anticipating the gratifying ritual at dawn, he had had himself readied for his time to be observed from below. Even before stepping onto the balcony, he called for Nur Jahan's maid.

"Waken the queen and have her come to my room before I return."

The empress obeyed the summons from her husband, wearing a long robe of fine cotton adorned with green and blue designs. The cotton was of such fineness that her figure was outlined by the sunlight coming through the window behind her. Her face and hair were as lovely as ever, and Jahangir, when he returned and found her in his room, was again pleased she was his queen. As emperor, he could cause people to quaver when he spoke, yet he was drawn to this woman who treated him as an ordinary man.

That Jahangir was still alive he owed to Nur Jahan. He had only a partial awareness of her exact knowledge of how much wine and opium he consumed, listening to the doctor's comments seriously, and making Jahangir adjust his habits. She listened to the doctor's other suggestions and was the only person who could cajole Jahangir into adopting changes.

How did I ever run the empire before she came into my life? All I really want now are food, drink, celebrations, and adoration. I'll happily leave the business of my duties to my trusted wife who will attend to the empire as I would want it done.

The beating of the drums announcing the upcoming the Victory Durbar could be felt and heard even though the jharoka window was far from the drummers high in the music room above the entrance arch to the courtyard.

"We have hours before we are due at the Diwan-i-Am, My Light. Let me apologize with this little bauble for my behavior last night."

He held out his hand with the fingers tucked underneath his palm. As she had done on other occasions, Nur Jahan put both of her hennaed hands with the perfectly tended nails under his much larger hand. Slowly he opened his fingers and into her waiting hands plopped a ring made from a single ruby. The ruby was the same shape as the prized one Jahangir wore daily. This one, although smaller, was noticeably different because of the tiny pearls encircling it.

Slipping it on, Nur Jahan studied her exquisite treasure. "Jahangir," she sighed, "it's beautiful. I love you."

"I know you do," he said softly as he removed his turban. He slowly reached out to remove her single garment. "We have time for you to show me how much before the durbar."

❋ ❋ ❋

EVEN THOUGH HE KNEW there was nothing more to do, Khurram went over his plans for the durbar one more time. Every detail seemed to be in place. He was comfortable with the balance between displaying the treasure and the pomp and grandeur of the marching animals his father enjoyed.

The ceremony, the fuss, and the tribute are all for my father, realized Khurram as he walked among the dozens of baskets of valuables waiting to be shown to the emperor, *but the glorious victory will always remain mine. My grandfather failed when he clashed with the Rana of Mewar and it pleases my father to claim this particular accomplishment for his own reign. Today's durbar will enhance not only the treasury, but be a balm for Father's heart. Bapu struggled with inferiority because of the wild success of his father's long reign. The victory will glorify his rule.*

Khurram wondered again if Jahangir would publicly declare him heir. "We shall see," he sighed. "We shall soon see."

❋ ❋ ❋

Alone again before the Victory Durbar, Jahangir indulged in daydreaming about the gifts from Rajasthan. If the rumors about the Rajasthani wealth were even half-true, there'd be much to see. If their wealth matched their ability to defend against the Mughals in the past, then it was certainly worthy of his respect.

Jahangir's smile revealed the satisfaction he felt at the outcome of the campaign. He wanted his states to retain most of their assets—after his own tribute was removed, of course. Adding his new ruby armband, a gift from Rajasthan through Khurram, to today's jewelry, he smiled again in anticipation of other gifts he'd soon inspect. "We shall see; we shall soon see."

❋ ❋ ❋

Returning to her room with her new ruby ring, Nur Jahan was in a much better humor than she had been the night before. As she studied her face in her enameled-back mirror she caught the reflection of the new gift. Looking at the ring, she remembered yet another reason to embrace this day that had already started so well. Khurram, the man who would rule for her, would most likely be declared the heir. She happily basked in her wealth, her power, and her beauty. This moment was perfect.

Or was it?

Something flickered in the back of her mind. Something was telling her all was *not* well. Even as she was prepared, dressed, coifed, jeweled, and enhanced with cosmetics, she continued to worry about the subtle but definite warning noise within her head.

She'd been in tune with this mental signal many times since childhood. When her first husband had been killed, she had been guided to return to Agra. When Jahangir became fond of another in the zenana, she'd arranged a suitable marriage and the woman was moved away. When the emperor was obviously imbibing more than his health could stand, she was shown how to assist him. Supporting Khurram in his desire to follow Jahangir to the throne had been guided by other internal messages. Every time she'd felt this sign and acted upon it, she was rewarded. She did not know what was needed this time, but she'd learned to trust her guidance. Whatever was suggested, she'd do.

"We shall see," she murmured just before she left to attend the Victory Durbar. "We shall see."

❈ ❈ ❈

TODAY MY HUSBAND WILL BE, *next to his father of course, the most important person at the durbar.* Mumtaz smiled thinking how handsome, assured, and capable Khurram was. *Jahangir will no doubt see that he is everything he had hoped for in an heir.* Her thoughts floated happily as she was made ready to observe this important durbar. *Khurram's dream may come true today,* she thought as her maids drifted around her. *I wonder if Jahangir will actually announce his choice or simply make it obvious Khurram is to follow him on the throne. My guess is the emperor will revel in today's happenings and leave the announcement for yet another gathering.*

Mumtaz knew the flutters in her midsection were not from this pregnancy, but from the excitement of the celebration. There was no particular hurry for her to get ready and rush to her place behind the side screen of the throne balcony. Her status as the daughter-in-law of the emperor, the wife of Prince Khurram, and niece of Nur Jahan, assured Mumtaz her spot would always be waiting for her when she arrived. She could hear the general music played to announce the Durbar and knew she still had time to wander in her zenana garden to find a rose.

When the attending women were finished with their preparations, she went outside and stood looking up, inhaling the fragrance of a newly-picked flower and noticing the cloudless blue sky. It was symbolic of how she felt about the future. Then a small cloud, seemingly from nowhere, darkened the light of the sun. Glancing upward, she was startled that the shape of the cloud reminded her of Nur Jahan.

"How silly of me," she spoke to the empty garden. "Auntie has been so helpful and thoughtful. I've been cautious with her but I've never thought of her as evil." But her admonition to herself didn't dispel her feeling of foreboding. .Mumtaz silently recalled Auntie's nickname, "Cobra Queen." The thought sent a slight shiver through her body. She wondered if the story behind the name was true. *If it was, what exactly did pass between her and the snake?*

Mumtaz scolded herself for the gloomy thoughts. Still, she couldn't rid herself of the feeling something was amiss. Somehow today's grand events no longer resonated with powerful optimism. Hoping to be wrong, Mumtaz promised herself she'd be particularly observant of Nur Jahan during the durbar to prove her strange feelings were unfounded.

"We shall see," she spoke to the flower in her hand as she inhaled the aroma deeply. "We shall see."

13

Agra ~ 1616

Khurram rode to his prominent position in the courtyard, dismounted and handed the reins of his mount to a waiting servant. He stepped confidently to the center of the front row surrounded by high-ranking soldiers, noblemen, and courtiers. The assembled men nodded respectfully to him, not guessing how he felt now that this durbar he'd been planning during the trip back to Agra was finally happening. He had to remind himself frequently to relax and enjoy this day; everything was ready. All that remained was to greet his father, tell his story, and present the riches he'd brought home.

Burning incense filled the air with ambergris and aloe as tendrils of aromatic smoke escaped from the gold and silver censers hanging from the canopy poles. Servants swung wands over their heads releasing the scent of roses into the air.

Khurram thought of his wife and deliberately ran his index finger slowly down the length of his nose; their secret signal to tell her he knew she was watching from her hidden spot. Remembering Nur Jahan's invisible nearness as well prompted Khurram to think of his feelings toward his stepmother.

I know I should be grateful for all of her help to put me where I am, but I'M the one who marched from Agra at the head of the army. I'M the one who planned a victorious strategy, and I brought Jahangir great treasure. Even so, I feel uneasy about being obliged to her.

A loud drum roll from two large brass kettledrums behind the throne interrupted Khurram's thinking as it proclaimed the arrival of the emperor and time for the group teslim.

Khurram smiled to himself at his father's habit of heavily adorning himself with jewels and fine fabrics. Jahangir had chosen to honor the Victory Durbar by looking every bit the emperor he was. His light green turban was decorated with long feathers and a large emerald, his gold brocade sash held a diamond-studded dagger, jeweled rings had been slipped on his hands and strings of pearls hung atop his green silk jama In a prominent position was the ruby armband Khurram had sent.

Jahangir looked for his son, found him, and smiled broadly. His pride and love were evident to all as the emperor basked in the knowledge that it was his own male child who'd brought this day's fame and honor to the Mughals.

Slowly moving his eyes from his son's face, Jahangir retained his smile as he spoke to the men gathered before him.

"Today is a glorious day for your emperor and for the Mughal Empire. This Victory Durbar celebrates the triumph of our invincible Imperial Army over the Infidels to the south. With the blessing of Allah, we sent our own son as the army's leader to demonstrate our empire's strength. Our desires were granted, and the Rana of Mewar has been defeated.

"I've asked the commander of my army to come before you so we can praise him for his enlightened leadership and his exalted efforts in bringing to us not only a proud victory but vast riches."

Khurram stepped up onto the small platform usually occupied by the Chief Minister. In this position, he looked up at his father with his back to the spectators. Speaking loudly so all could hear, Khurram summarized his version of the strategy, the execution of the war. He shared the credit of victory with his generals and soldiers. Then his voice changed to signal the next part of the durbar was about to begin.

"Your Highness, I'm pleased to bring to you great riches from the newest expansion of our borders to the south." Khur-

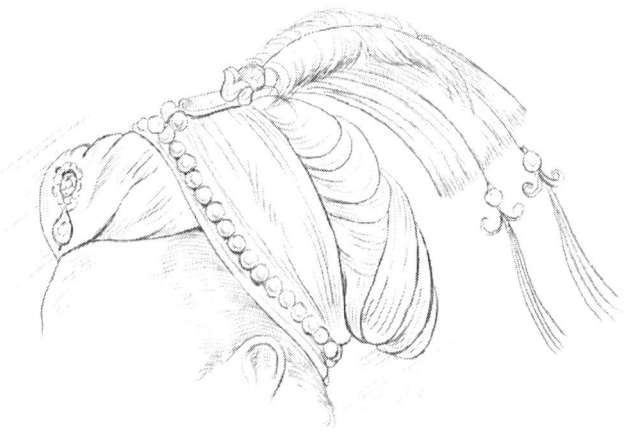

Male turban

ram motioned toward covered baskets filling much of the massive courtyard.

The moment he finished speaking, hundreds of servants, each carrying a wide, shallow basket, began approaching the base of the throne balcony where they each bowed and lowered the vessels for Jahangir to see.

This was the pomp and ceremony Jahangir loved. The seemingly endless procession of barefoot attendants in white turbans, short black shirts, and white billowing pants marched toward him, paused while their emperor saw what they carried, returned through the gawking crowd, then stood behind the observers. There were containers of valuable gems, bags of gold and silver, sari silk, fine golden cloth, and golden statues of Hindu gods.

Then animals were presented, the painted and decorated elephants first. A thousand of them trooped in, knelt, and bellowed on cue. Then came the horses, some sleek and well groomed, others saddled with riding gear. Camels adorned with saddles, blankets, and litters came next. It took four servants to carry each of the many caged cheetahs. Hooded falcons fiercely gripped the leather-protected arms of their trainers.

When the lengthy display was finished, Jahangir uncrossed his legs and stood. The audience gasped. Traditionally the monarch remained on his throne until he ended the durbar with his exit. Overcome with happiness for the outcome of the military campaign and love for his son, Jahangir stood in front of his throne, opened both arms toward Khurram, and spoke to him as he gestured with his hands. "Come, come, my son."

Khurram, hopeful but not knowing what to expect, turned to ascend the stairs leading to the throne balcony. When he appeared on the elevated level of the throne, the portly emperor continued to astonish both his son and the onlookers. He embraced Khurram warmly and spontaneously kissed his forehead. This was an exceptional gesture from an emperor who rarely touched anyone in public.

Khurram hugged his father in return. His heart soared with the hope that this was the sign he'd been awaiting—the sign proclaiming Jahangir would announce him the next to sit on this throne. The thought warmed Khurram's heart as much as his father's hug.

But Jahangir was not finished with his break from ritual. At his command, a basket of jewels he had ordered was brought to him. He bade his son to kneel, then gently tipped the basket's contents over the younger man's bowed head and smiled as the cascade of precious gems fell, touching Khurram's turban, then sliding down his coat and onto the floor of the balcony. Repeating the gesture made the day of the army's departure signified the emperor's great pleasure.

When Jahangir called for a jeweled and cushioned platform to be placed near his throne and indicated Khurram should sit upon it, the prince was speechless at the unprecedented honor and sat uneasily. His discomfort didn't come from the familiar cross-legged position but from the fact that he was sitting rather than standing in the presence of the emperor. He saw some of his own uneasiness reflected in the eyes of the men he was facing. None of them could remember such an invitation.

Although it was expected for an emperor to lavish his commanders with items of worth, Khurram was overwhelmed to receive a beautifully saddled horse in addition to the expected dress of honor. Eight burly men carried in a resplendent silver howdah that would shine during its public use by a Royal Prince. And heir apparent, Khurram hoped silently.

Seated on his black marble throne with his son beside him, Jahangir was happy beyond words. He had royal quantities of everything a man could want including a fine son who would sit upon this throne after he walked with Allah. He had decided this was to be so and waited for a perfect opportunity to make his decision public.

Khurram, sitting on his cushioned mini-throne and basking in the adulation of his father, again thought of his invisible Taj, and realized his pleasure was enhanced because he shared it with her.

❈ ❈ ❈

IN HER ALCOVE, MUMTAZ WAS BURSTING with pride for her beloved husband and delighted that he had sent her their secret sign. The Rajasthani treasures had obviously pleased the emperor. After the demonstration of Jahangir's feelings toward Khurram, there could be no question about who would wear the royal turban next. Her heart was full of happiness because Khurram was receiving his great desire.

Sitting near Mumtaz, Nur Jahan was not thrilled. She was in fact, increasingly disturbed at what she was watching. Even though she had promoted Khurram as Jahangir's obvious successor, she was no longer certain the prince was the best choice. The letters of advice she had sent to him in Rajasthan had been accepted more readily soon after he left Agra than later in the campaign. Now that she watched the Victory Durbar, Nur Jahan became aware of the difference between the malleable young man always open to her suggestions and the prince who stood with the emperor. The earlier prince was inexperienced and sometimes doubted his own potential. The man before her exuded self-confidence and assurance.

Even though he had grown up a favored son, Khurram had only recently come to show a stronger belief in his destiny to rule, a mature self-confidence. His victory in battle, today's then presentation of his contributions to the treasury, the unexpected and heartfelt attentions from Jahangir removed further doubt that he was his father's choice of heir.

This is not good. It is not what I want. Khurram is TOO self-confident to allow me dominion. I've promoted him for years, but now I must alter my plan or my own future is in jeopardy. Of course! This is it! This is exactly what Cobra was telling me. It had been right in front of my eyes but I'd been unable to see clearly.

Nur Jahan's face did not reveal her thoughts of Khurram's sudden unacceptability. The women around her assumed she must be very proud to have such a handsome, talented, and successful young man part of her family. They couldn't have known by her countenance that Nur Jahan was planning a fateful change not only for her own future but one that would affect the empire.

Mumtaz leaned over to share her happiness with her father's sister assuming they would share a look of pride. She was shocked by a thunderous turmoil emanating from her auntie for it brought to her mind the dark cloud she had seen earlier in the day.

But what else she saw had more affect on her than what she felt. Mumtaz stared as Nur Jahan unconsciously chewed her lower lip—a sure sign that all was not what it seemed. Although the empress maintained an otherwise composed face, Mumtaz knew that this woman who had been so friendly and helpful to her, her father's sister, the empress of the empire, the one called Nur Jahan, was no longer an ally.

14

Agra ~ Six months later

Normalcy began to return to the empire and Khurram's military victory went unmentioned for longer stretches of time. The married couple was able to return to the Moonlight Mahal and celebrate another full moon. Upon their return to Agra, the royal couple received a special invitation to join Mumtaz' father, Asaf Khan, for dinner. The only other guests would be Nur Jahan and Jahangir. Mumtaz was delighted.

"Your father has never asked us to his home before, Taj. Why now?" puzzled Khurram.

Mumtaz considered his question even as she held her thumb mirror up to better see her latest emerald and sapphire necklace. "I think it's an opportunity for Father to spend time with me." She lifted her thumb for a higher view. He will also honor his emperor and empress with his hospitality which will raise his prestige. It will be a relaxed family night for all of us, and I'm certain he's already stated the preparation of fine foods."

Mumtaz became more and more excited thinking about the upcoming food the evening would bring. "I do love kofta and I hope our cook, Muhktar, prepares it just as he used to. Although my digestion during pregnancy does make me more cautious with the spices…"

Khurram, who had been sitting next to Mumtaz, watched in

silent amusement as she rose from the divan and wandered out the doorway, muttering to herself and planning. "I'd like to wear something blue. Father always liked me to wear blue." Her voice grew faint as she continued walking. "Let me think...my pearl and ruby earrings from Jahangir. Those would please him. And..."

Trusting that Taj would return, Khurram explored the unusual and pleasant idea of an evening at Asaf Khan's with the four most royal Mughals. He stretched his legs and laced his fingers behind his neck comfortably as he waited for his wife.

When Mumtaz eventually reappeared, the faraway look she wore when she left had been replaced by a determination to speak. She stood in front of Khurram, leaned over, and took his face in both of her hands. Looking at him earnestly, Mumtaz said, "If Father serves kofta, ignore it. You won't like the way Muhktar prepares it."

As though she had spoken words of wisdom, Mumtaz again signed and drifted out of the room, leaving her husband slowly shaking his head.

❄ ❄ ❄

BECAUSE THE FEET OF THE ROYAL COUPLES must not touch the earth during the short walk to Asaf Khan's, their path was covered with crimson velvet shot with gold. This had been spread upon gold brocade which itself was spread upon a layer of unadorned red velvet. As they approached the fine mansion where they were to dine, three of the guests anticipated nothing more than a sumptuous meal and a relaxing evening among relatives. The fourth among them had planned much more.

At their arrival, they were greeted with music, gracious words of welcome, and Asaf Khan's teslim. They were ushered into a room had been prepared for royalty. The two women removed their face veils which were now unnecessary because the only men present were closely related to them. Nur Jahan proudly displayed a striking necklace. This latest gift from Jahangir was composed of nine precious jewels, each twice the size of a grape. The setting was pure gold and diamonds hung from below and a pearl was atop each of the colorful treasures. Wanting to choose jewelry that did not outdo that of the empress yet would uphold her husband's honor, Mumtaz had chosen a necklet of exquisite and valuable enamel work studded with gems and a pair of matching bangles.

Sitting on a bolstered platform higher than those of the others, Jahangir was situated in the place of greatest status. Asaf Khan gladly took his place next to the emperor.

As expected of a host to royalty, Asaf presented an expansive offering of gifts to his emperor. Delighted with presents, Jahangir looked at them all. The host and the emperor both knew Jahangir could decide to take all he saw, insult his host by selecting nothing, or select from the array before him. Tonight, he was fascinated by a unique tortoise shell bowl and allowed a relieved Asaf Khan to keep the rest of the offerings.

Three of the guests began the evening with sharbat, a traditional fruit drink enhanced with lime and spice. Jahangir's goblet was filled with wine.

Mumtaz enjoyed the flavors of the spiced meatballs, the chutneys, and the tiny pieces of pungent chicken. She was eating as much as she had while growing up in this household. Even though the food was similar in the palace where she now lived, and even though she could have anything she wanted from the royal kitchen, it soothed her to be eating the familiar food in her father's house. The returning daughter was nostalgic about her childhood home. The waterfall inside supplied a soothing sound and complimented the new lanterns. Persian carpets on the marble floor and the colorful tapestry hanging on the wall were as she remembered.

Absently taking a slice of onion that had been dipped in chickpea batter and fried to a delicate crispness, Nur Jahan was pleased with the relaxed and unsuspecting manner of the men around her, particularly Khurram. His mood would soon change if her plan worked.

Jahangir looked at his beautiful wife. By Allah, she was an

exciting woman. He could not stop enjoying the sight of her.

Khurram was settled into a satisfaction with the evening that dulled his normally sharp perception. He had led a successful force into Rajasthan, he was confident his father would choose him to rule, and he had recently returned from several idyllic days with his wife. This night was for relaxation, pleasuring his palate, and enjoying his family.

Mumtaz was aware of the increased intuition she possessed during the early months of her first four pregnancies. Tonight she was again aware that something unsaid was in the air, someone in the room was waiting. She looked at her husband. *No, she concluded, it wasn't him. Jahangir is jovial, too open for subterfuge. Father? Possibly. Auntie?* She recalled what she had seen the day of the Victory Durbar and her vow to be vigilant of Nur Jahan. *Of course! Auntie was up to something. Khurram was right after all—Father had a hidden reason for inviting us here. We should make up some good reason to leave right now before anything is allowed to happen. Maybe I can appeal to Jahangir's caring about my pregnancy so he won't be upset.*

"Khurram…" Mumtaz had spoken involuntarily, reacting to her sharpened awareness of nearby deception. Several faces turned toward her with questioning gazes. She locked eyes with her husband, willing him with her own intense look to be careful. When she realized his expression held no suspicions, she sighed.

"Do try the spicy cashews, Meerijan, they're wonderful." The comment about the nuts was the first thing that came to her mind. As she spoke, she popped one in her mouth, determined to be aware of all that was said or done that evening.

What DID Auntie have in mind?

15

Agra - 1617

With a double clap of his hands, Asaf Khan signaled for the waiting servants carefully holding a large metal vessel filled with hot charcoal to enter the room. The host inspected it to be certain that the flat stones had been properly heated by the coals before they had been covered by the iron grill. As the five diners watched from their cushions, servants grilled marinated pieces of lamb. The meat sizzled shortly, was deftly skewered onto long thin spikes, then pushed onto the plates which had been previously garnished with sliced onion, green chutney, and a wedge of lime. This preparation, muzbi, was a favorite appetizer of the royal family.

Khurram swallowed his first bite only to have Asaf Khan say, "Please honor me and have another," and served the lamb pieces himself. Tempted by the muzbi but knowing the evening was going to be filled with other delicious food, he refused politely and inoffensively, even though he knew their host would feign disappointment in what he called Khurram's "meager" portions.

There was nothing unusual about a servant bending to whisper into Asaf Khan's ear, so it went unnoticed by three of the guests. The fourth had been watching for this indication and when it arrived experienced a quickened heartbeat. Asaf Khan bowed gracefully, left the room, and returned a few moments later. Glancing at his sister, he nodded with the slightest head movement. Conversations stopped in the room for it was obvious the host waited to speak.

"Tonight, I've many dishes for you to enjoy. This you may have expected. But I have more than food and companionship. I have a surprise for you. Someone else will be joining us for the meal."

Khurram wondered idly about the identity of the guest. Assuming this unknown person was bound to pay homage to his father and himself as so many had lately, he remained relaxed. He expected a pleasant surprise; what he received was a jolt.

Shariyar, Khurram's usually ignored half brother, walked into the room wearing a brocade coat cut to camouflage the portliness of his body. He wore a chain of rubies around his neck, rubies on his wrist, and rubies embedded into the hilt of his cummerbund dagger.

Here in the high-ranking company of his father and Khurram was a person who'd never seemed to reach the manhood of his years. His somewhat prissy body, soft with fat, bulged under his fussy clothes. Shariyar, who didn't excel mentally or physically, had not been in the classrooms or the training fields where Khurram had spent so much of his younger life, so the half brothers knew each other only casually. Khurram knew of Shariyar mostly from the gossip focusing upon his half brother's love of parties, drinking, and boys. Because their lives were so totally different, it had been months since the two brothers had been together.

Khurram's mother was a Rajput princess and Shariyar's had been a mere concubine, which gave prestige to the older of the two sons and was part of the reason Shariyar had become more a royal afterthought than a person of value. A son of the emperor's concubine enjoyed more status than his own mother but less than the son of a queen. Because of this, Shariyar, and everyone else, had assumed that while the half brother would not inherit his father's royal turban, he could have anything else he wanted. Khurram didn't dislike Shariyar, he had simply dismissed him from his life so his presence puzzled him.

Khurram sat straighter against his oversized red and gold bolster, wondering at his own concern. Unconsciously, he smoothed his clothing and arranged his ropes of pearls to full coverage of his jama, knowing as he did so, his half brother's appearance was no accident. Even though his father-in-law had explained Shariyar was simply invited to partake in a family gathering, Khurram was uneasy. He became aware of a sense of menace in the room that hadn't existed before Shariyar had arrived.

"Shariyar! I'm so glad you were able to join us. Please come sit here." Nur Jahan filled the room with her husky voice. She pulled a pillow to one side of her seat and patted it in invitation. Shariyar sat. Nervous about this evening, Shariyar looked around the room, smiled at each of the guests, and quickly accepted the proffered wine.

Straightening even more, Khurram wondered if his nearly forgotten brother was being used. When his eyes fell upon the older woman across from him, he knew Nur Jahan was the reason for Shariyar's presence. Tonight was going to be more than an innocent family dinner. He watched his father's wife lean toward Shariyar, hang on his every word, and pat his arm while she laughed at something he had said.

Khurram kept his anger to himself but fumed inwardly. *This is the attention I should be getting, not do-nothing Shariyar! I'm the hero and the heir apparent, so I should be the one being flattered and touched. How can she do this in front of me? I'm willing to accept the responsibility of running the empire when father dies, so I should have her support. It's unfair that Shariyar is fawned over.*

Khurram calmed himself with the knowledge that Shariyar posed no threat. Jahangir was almost ignoring his chubby son even though Nur Jahan repeated everything he said. There was no reason to be jealous.

Mumtaz was increasingly certain that whatever happened wouldn't be good for Khurram. Ever since she'd seen the look pass between her aunt and her father she'd been particularly watchful. She noticed her husband's posture become increasingly alert even as Shariyar, warmed by the wine and attention, was noticeably relaxing. Nur Jahan was her most charming as she wove her web around this stepson.

Mumtaz was glad she had not left earlier in the evening. Now she could steer the conversation toward the events that made her husband so valuable to the empire.

"Father, while I was with Khurram in Rajasthan, I didn't have any of this delicious muzbi at all." Innocently taking another bite, she added, "We had to stay away for months to finally subdue the area our emperor wanted." She flashed a smile at Jahangir. "But it was worth it," she continued after she chewed the food in her mouth, "even though we both missed this exceptional food while we were gone."

She settled back on her bolsters content to hear 'Rajasthan' and 'Khurram' in the ensuing conversation.

Wanting to keep the banquet moving, Asaf Khan smoothly and gracefully brought everyone's attention to the next course. He ordered wondrous carpets to be covered with even more carpets, still beautiful but less precious. This now-raised pile was then draped with a leather shield that was in turn covered with a white linen cloth which was then covered with serving dishes heaped with foot fit for royalty.

Four women appeared with hand-washing water. Two of them held a golden bowl under the emperor's hands. The third poured water over his fingers from a matching golden ewer, and the fourth used her linen towel for drying. After Jahangir was finished, the other guests were likewise prepared for dining.

Lively music announced the arrival of the food. Asaf Khan's women brought dozens of dishes served in silver vessels. Their backs resting against bolsters, the guests were treated to an amazing assortment of foods.

Lamb, a favorite meat of the Mughals, was presented in four different guises. Biryani, an elegant and sophisticated dish of lamb pieces with rice, and shami kabab, grilled shapes made from minced lamb and chickpeas, were the first two. Nargesi kabab, another lamb dish, was named after the narcissus for its appearance when sliced: each thin piece revealed a mixture of spiced ground lamb wrapped around a hard-boiled egg.

Mumtaz' eyes lit up when she realized rogan josh, the fourth lamb dish, was in front of her. A servant, remembering her penchant for this rich and aromatic lamb curry, made certain it was among the selected dishes.

Even with an unsettled stomach, Khurram couldn't resist the array of food before him. He spotted his favorite side dish of cheese and peas served in a fragrant tomato sauce and enjoyed several servings, ignoring the heavier meat dishes.

Although Nur Jahan seemed to taste everything with enthusiastic delight, Khurram, who was watching her closely, noticed she ate little of anything. Her spiced chicken remained nearly untouched, and the assortment of vegetable dishes was simply moved around by naan. Long ago trained to use pieces of this bread as an eating instrument, the empress deftly kept her hands busy to give the impression of dining as she focused upon Shariyar.

Eating as heartily as his pregnant daughter energetically consumed her own food, Asaf Khan was unobtrusively watchful. He noticed Prince Khurram was barely putting food in his mouth. He smiled at his daughter's enthusiasm for the rogan josh. With a pang he realized how little he could do for this woman who used to be his little girl. Now that Mumtaz was married to the man who would most likely become king, as her father he could please her only by serving special foods. He smiled at the thought of her children, his grandchildren. It was now very likely that one of them would wear the royal turban and be the Great Mughal.

Shariyar and Jahangir were fully enjoying their food. They ate enormous piles of lamb and chicken dishes, vegetables, and mounds of rice and bread. Although neither of them paused to savor the food as their host would have preferred, their sensitive palates could accurately discern the various spices ground together to season each dish. They knew the rice was basmati, they appreciated that one was flavored with ginger, garlic, and onions while the other was steeped in saffron and apricot puree.

Taking a bit of yogurt mixed with crisp vegetables grown in her father's fields along the river, Mumtaz looked toward Khurram. When their eyes met, they shared the knowledge that Nur Jahan was up to something.

Finally, the satiated guests declined to try even another taste, and the dishes were quickly whisked away. The food-dappled cloth was quickly rolled up and replaced with a fresh white sheet of satin. Deftly, capable brown hands arranged an artistic pattern of flower petals on the cloth in preparation for the desserts. Much of the final course was covered with edible gold foil. When the sweets nestled among the colorful design, the elegant tableaux tempted the diners to take bites they had only recently declared they were too full to consider.

As his guests looked at the display before them, Asaf Khan was almost content. He had hosted the emperor, had been able to please his daughter, and he had helped his sister by including Shariyar. Still, the evening was not perfect. He was puzzled by the undercurrent of tension that even his own joviality and preparations couldn't dissipate. Perhaps Shariyar's presence had something to do with it. He couldn't see how, since Shariyar's inclusion didn't interfere with the rules of purdah. Nur Jahan hadn't given him much information, just requested he include Shariyar as a guest and she would do the rest.

His daughter seemed subdued, but women were sometimes quiet when they were with child. Khurram was the biggest puzzle. Usually outgoing, tonight he'd been strangely quiet. Unable to fathom Khurram being concerned with the likes of Shariyar, Asaf switched his thoughts back to the food before him.

"Come, come. Have a sweet to settle your stomachs." So saying, he moved to serve each guest himself. There was a sweet made with almonds and milk. Another was a halva, a thick, fudge-like mixture of milk and shredded carrot, artistically covered with pistachios and gold foil. There were four puddings, each identified with its own decoration: the almond and rice was topped with almonds, the banana with thin slices of bananas, the caramelized rice with pistachios, and the carrot with cardamom.

Throughout the entire evening, the empress continued to give Shariyar the bulk of her attention, flattering him with indications of her fascination. Flushed with the obvious success he was having with Nur Jahan, Shariyar became more and more relaxed and even wondered if he had sold himself short. Nur Jahan certainly thought he was worth her time and she didn't pay attention to men who were nobodies.

By the end of the evening, Nur Jahan had Jahangir leaning forward to hear what his son had to say. As Shariyar became more entertaining with the attention he was receiving, Khurram seemed to shrink and darken. Mumtaz looked at her obviously unhappy husband. *I must talk with him about these puzzling undercurrents I feel.*

Khurram was raging silently. *I won't have this! I'm the second most important man in this empire and I'm fuming about my stupid half brother for getting the attention I deserve. I'll make it clear he's never to be in attendance with me again. This evening was too much.*

16

Agra

Several days before the family dinner, unaware he was the subject of planning in another part of the palace, Shariyar talked with his friends. Reclining languidly on divans, they commented about the best cut of a robe, the color of a recently received gem, and the latest court gossip. Shariyar, assured by his parentage he'd live in luxury, knew in his heart that his "friends" were more fond of his lifestyle than of him. Because he enjoyed their presence and wanted their adoration, he accepted their thin loyalty.

"Your father is emperor, Shariyar. Think of how powerful you'd be if you wore the crown. Why don't you at least try to take it?" Mushkin, a relatively new arrival to the group of young men around Shariyar had asked today the same question nearly everyone had asked when they first became part of the circle.

"Mushkin, Mushkin, Mushkin," smiled the host, waving his arm in the air. "My older half brother, Khurram is much more fit to rule. I gladly leave to him the bother of making decisions on expansion, titles and rank, keeping the zenana supplied, dealing with the administration, attending durbars and weighings...not to mention the foreign entanglements and wars." Pausing, then repeating the words that hid his reluctance to compete with Khurram: "I'm happy with what I have."

"Look what is around me." Waving chubby fingers, Shariyar

continued to expound upon what had become his philosophy. "I'm content, more than content, to be waited upon and to give orders. I have the finest clothing, food, wine, and all of you to share it with. I'm pleased with this life of pleasure without the pressures of being emperor. I have everything I want." Except respect, he admitted silently.

Shariyar had understood what his birth meant early in his life. Even though Jahangir was his father, his mother, Nadira, had been a common concubine. As such, she received little affection from the other women of the zenana when it was known she was expecting a child. When she gave birth, the frostiness of her zenana sisters was even greater than it had been during the lovely young woman's pregnancy. During the months of Shariyar's infancy, even the lukewarm female friendships of her pregnancy diminished or transformed to animosity. Although she was shown great courtesy and respect when Jahangir was near or she was in public, Nadira otherwise was ignored by the women around her.

The new mother feared her pudgy, somewhat slow son would be treated no better than she had been. In loneliness, she and awaited the time he would be old enough to move from this den of jealousy and spite. She stayed alive in her glittering and friendless surroundings guarding herself and her son vigilantly for six years. She mysteriously died at the age of twenty-three.

Examining her body, the Royal Doctor sighed at the suspicious circumstances of Nadira's demise, and then wrote his unsurprising conclusion: death by natural causes. In truth, the causes were far from natural. A pregnancy, the desire of most zenana women and the reality of only a few, brought to life the worst emotions of those inclined to be spiteful. When Nadira gave birth to a healthy baby boy, a child who could possibly be an heir and provide lavish care for his mother, she was even more isolated by the women who could have offered warmth and companionship.

Many zenana women were able to create potions to disfigure a woman or cause her to lose a child. It had happened before that women who were healthy and full of life one day were unexplainably pallid the next. Even after the doctor was called, nothing changed. Women were plentiful and neither valuable nor irreplaceable.

When the doctor gazed at Nadira's lifeless body, he wondered briefly about the cause of her death. Perhaps it had been unnamed stresses within the zenana life, lack of freedom, loneliness for her relatives, or an inborn female frailty. Whatever the reason, he automatically filled out the death form and asked no more questions. The emperor wanted to believe all was well within his city of women. Any other truth would tamper with his idealistic fantasies.

After his mother's death, Shariyar continued to live in the zenana, ate the best foods and wore the finest clothing. His only lack was loving care. No woman paid attention to him privately, only publicly.

When he was old enough to move to his own quarters, though he was neither a student nor a warrior, was aware of what he had to look forward to in his future. Behind him now were the years of self-pity from being a motherless, pudgy boy who lived almost, but not quite, royally. Away from the unhappiness he had suffered in the zenana, Shariyar created the pampering and wealth fitting for the emperor's son. Turning deliberately away from the path his half brother had chosen, he embraced a hedonistic lifestyle. His friends were the first, and therefore the best, he had ever had. He had established himself as the focal point for other young men, preferring gossip to policy. From his own quarters in the men's mardana, Shariyar contentedly did his drinking, whispering, sometimes flaunting his sexual preferences.

The group of young men was interrupted by a soft knock on the door. When one of Shariyar's friends opened it, he found Almet, a veiled handmaiden to Nur Jahan standing before him. The prince rose quickly for all of his flabby bulk, and hastened to the door, motioning his friend to return to the divan.

"Welcome, Almet. I've not before had the pleasure of your company." Even though not interested in women, he noticed that her simply cut garment suggested a fine figure. "How can I help you?" His smile and pleasant voice masked the discomfort that surfaced whenever he came to the notice of a member of the royal family.

"My mistress requests that you join her this afternoon in the Jasmine Tower," her melodious voice answered. Her eyes, however, were trying to search beyond Shariyar into his unknown, therefore, intriguing apartment.

The prince knew, as did everyone else, that the empress' imperial edicts were not usually courteous requests, but he did not know why she wanted a meeting with him. Nothing he had would be of interest to Nur Jahan. Shariyar just stared, his bulk blocking the young woman's view into the rooms.

At length he spoke. "I'd be honored to meet with the empress in the Jasmine Tower. Is three hours past the horn acceptable?"

"Two hours past the horn would be better."

Choosing wisely not to displease the fearsome empress, Shariyar agreed. "Tell Her Majesty I'll be there at two hours past the horn." Shariyar quietly closed the door and slowly walked back into the room, sipping thoughtfully from his wine cup as he tried to understand what had just happened. The empress, who had everything the empire could offer, wanted a meeting with him. Any possible reason for the command eluded him. Sighing, he lifted his eyes and took in the scene before him: the overdeveloped luxury, his friends, and the wine. He smiled at these easily understood pleasures and gave up trying to comprehend possible scenarios until he faced them in the afternoon.

❊ ❊ ❊

LEAVING THE JASMINE TOWER after his meeting with Nur Jahan, Shariyar was no longer fearful of the empress, he was mesmerized by her. He chastised himself for not getting to know such a courteous and friendly woman earlier. He had been comfortable and, without hesitation, had answered her questions at length as they shared frosty glasses of sharbat and sesame biscuits. Nur Jahan asked about his life, his friends, his activities, and his thoughts on the empire. Shariyar had hungered for years to have a conversation with a woman interested in what he had to say, a woman who asked him questions about himself, and who even remembered his responses. The quickly infatuated prince privately vowed to support and obey Nur Jahan, for it was clear to him that doing so was the surest way to remain close to her now-important presence.

During their visit, Nur Jahan listened to the voice inside her head even as Shariyar spoke. The message she received confirmed her hunches. With a smile, she turned to Shariyar, looked into his eyes and nodded affirmation to her internal guidance.

"Shariyar, my son. May I call you my son? You're from the loins of my beloved husband, and I feel the two of us are connected in a special way. There's going to be a particularly elegant dinner in three days for members of the royal family. My brother will be our host, and I would like you to join us. You are a son of the emperor himself, and you would be welcome. My brother hopes you will be able to attend."

There was little for Shariyar to ponder. Would he spend an evening in the presence of this warm and mothering woman? Most certainly! Anything else he might have had planned was less important. Mentally visualizing the clothes he would wear, he was interrupted by Nur Jahan telling him not to bother deciding on his garments. She would choose something for him and have it delivered.

Her voice stopped him as he was about to leave. "Oh Shariyar," her tone remained casual, "the emperor has a fancy for rubies. He'd be pleased if you wore this chain when you arrive." So saying, she held out a rope of four dozen small but fine red rubies. His eyes bulged at the sight of the exquisite jewelry. He was nonchalantly being handed a treasure.

Nur Jahan walked out with Shariyar and nodded pleasantly to his bow. Still smiling, she congratulated herself. When his retreating back was beyond the reach of her voice, she whispered aloud to her internal Cobra Wisdom. "His mind is a blank slate ready to be written on, and he'd be pleased if I picked up my pen. He's perfect."

Shariyar had already put the rope of rubies around his neck.

17

Agra

Mumtaz sat on a silver-chained garden swing, enjoying Khurram's light pushes. She had discovered why Shariyar's inclusion at her father's dinner two days earlier had unsettled both of them. Now she was pondering how to share what she knew.

When the swing had arced fully away from Khurram, she began. "I heard something interesting today."

Khurram continued to push silently, giving his wife the time he'd learned she needed before she elaborated. "It's about the dinner at my father's."

Khurram immediately stopped the gentle pushes on her back and moved around to face Mumtaz. Taking the chains of the swing in his hands to stop her, he looked intently into her eyes, saying nothing, still waiting for her to continue.

It has to be about Shariyar. Khurram had thought about him often in the last two days, trying to understand why he even considered his almost laughable half brother was any sort of a menace.

Mumtaz took a deep breath. She knew her words would be a threat to his future, to their future, yet she couldn't postpone telling him.

"The empress is supporting Shariyar to become the next man to wear the royal turban."

The mildly spoken words reflected none of the anguish Mumtaz felt in saying them, nor none of the terrible impact they had on the listening Khurram. *One sentence,* thought Khurram as he stared without moving. *One sentence and everything I thought was mine is threatened. It's just like my father's wife to think she can take a bumbling man and transform him into an emperor.*

"My brother *knows* nothing, Taj. He could do nothing as emperor. He has none of the skills I have and none of the loyalty to our empire. Before two nights ago, his own father had almost forgotten him."

Dropping the chains of the swing, Khurram turned and stared into the garden. His jaw clenched and unclenched before he spoke again. "Shariyar is laughable, yet Nur Jahan wants to bring this family blemish out of wherever he lives and put him on the throne. But she's already chosen me."

Khurram was stunned, yet he had to admit this very fear had crossed his mind as he watched Nur Jahan with Shariyar. His eyes revealed the depth of his pain.

Mumtaz stood and slipped one arm around Khurram's waist. Together they strolled through the grand walks in the well-tended beds of jasmine and narcissus, trying to make sense of this news and to plan for their future.

In a lowered voice Mumtaz said, "She wants Shariyar to succeed Jahangir and is presenting her plan to the emperor in her own persuasive ways."

"But, why has she changed her mind? Why is she supporting someone else?" Khurram's voice was now full volume. "Shariyar has never made a decision in his life, and he's never even married and produced an heir. How could she possibly think he could rule an empire?"

Taj took a few more steps before she answered. "For all of the reasons you've just mentioned, Meerijan."

Her quiet words, almost whispered, calmed Khurram and allowed him to think. Gardeners working in the knee-high water, cleaning the many fountains in the pools looked up briefly at his voice then lowered their heads to give the prince privacy. Khurram knew Nur Jahan was smart enough to see that this almost forgotten son of Jahangir's couldn't lead. He knew there was some other reason she wanted him to rule.

The answer came to him as he stood in the garden with Taj. It did not arrive as a blinding flash but from small bits of awareness flying in ever tightening circles around a magnetic center. When the vagrant pieces of information were together, they revealed the answer he had been seeking.

"Nur Jahan wants to control me." Shaken by the revelation, Khurram shared what Taj already knew. "She realizes I'd fight her whenever we disagreed."

With increasing clarity, Khurram knew Shariyar would never disagree with Nur Jahan. The previously uninterested prince was now eager to assume the position of ruler of the Mughal Empire. She must have convinced him he would be happier being the emperor than not. Shaking his head, Khurram cursed a fate that had him sharing blood with such an inept man.

Mumtaz stopped walking and turned to her husband. "Auntie's primary concern is to rule after Jahangir is gone. She had to find a ruler who'd be content with the title and trappings and allow her to rule unhampered."

Events earlier that same day had shattered what was left of the trust she had in her father's sister. Mumtaz had admired her aunt's creative talents, her fertile mind, and her energy. She and the entire court knew of Nur Jahan's flair with women's crafts as well as her capable administrative talents. In addition, the two of them had shared the experience of coming from the same family and being royal in the Royal Zenana. Until earlier that day, Mumtaz had been unwilling to believe the whispered suggestions in the zenana and the swirling gossip insinuating Nur Jahan was no longer in support of Khurram. She had not been convinced of this change.

Now, after this morning, she could no longer avoid reality. Deciding spontaneously to visit her aunt, Mumtaz was told Nur Jahan had a visitor and was not to be disturbed. Thinking either Khurram or Jahangir must be with her, Mumtaz nodded and turned to leave. If the guest was Jahangir, it might be some time before her aunt was unoccupied. Even as Mumtaz turned to leave, the door to Nur Jahan's chambers opened and out stepped someone she had not expected to see.

It was Shariyar. Still facing Nur Jahan, he finished his last sentence loudly enough for Mumtaz to hear. "Thank you for making this possible." Then he turned and noticed Mumtaz not far away. Surprise and shock registered on both their faces as their eyes met.

Mumtaz gave a correctly polite nod of her head and Shariyar nodded back. His nod contained the confidence of a new status, different than a month earlier.

Moving her eyes, she met those of Nur Jahan who was still standing in her own doorway. Her aunt's look, Mumtaz realized, held a challenge rather than her usual affection. Mumtaz shuddered and turned away, suddenly aware of new dangers for her husband. She had been assuming Khurram would rule after Jahangir, yet today's chance meeting had challenged that belief. *True, Khurram might still be the next ruler; his father would be foolish to consider anyone else. But even if Khurram were to sit upon the throne, he would know his stepmother and his half brother had plotted against him. Would he banish them? Kill them? As terrible as Auntie can be, I wouldn't want Khurram kill her. But if Nur Jahan was an enemy…why not?*

"She's my blood, my family," she answered herself.

Putting her confusion into spoken words, she talked as she moved toward her apartment. "Why would she do this? Why would she turn against my husband and want Shariyar to be the next emperor? How dare she? It's obvious Khurram's the far better choice. Auntie scares me and…she usually gets what she wants.'

She continued to pace alongside a courtyard dominated by a rosewater fountain where her zenana sisters were playing Parcheesi using themselves as the pieces. She heard none of the happy chatter of the "piece" in blue being asked to dance forward two squares.

"If the worst happened and Shariyar were made emperor, Khurram would be a danger to the man on the throne. He'd contest Shariyar's right to rule and would have to be killed. And then it is well within the emperor's power to give the wife of a dead prince to another man. I'd have no say about it, and if Shariyar were so inclined, he could further insult the memory of his brother by giving me to a man of much lower rank. I know there are many men who'd be pleased to take a woman who'd shared a bed with Prince Khurram." She shivered slightly, then stopped as she considered a new idea.

"If Shariyar and Nur Jahan are successful, Nur Jahan could protect me from any retribution. I could beg mercy from Auntie, claim the bond of our shared blood, and I'd be spared. I could turn around right now and tell Auntie how unhappy I am with Khurram. To save my own life I could work with her against the man whose very presence and position could put me in mortal danger. Yes, I'd be much less vulnerable without him."

Nur Jahan had already told Mumtaz she would like to teach her to take the empress' position when the time came. Mumtaz had thought her auntie's suggestions had little meaning but now she changed her mind. Nur Jahan wanted and needed someone to follow her—a woman from her own family would be a logical choice.

A wicked chasm opened before her and shocked Mumtaz, making her see her own vulnerability. Her aunt had been successful in all she had ever attempted. Was this manipulation to choose Jahangir's heir any different? If Khurram weren't able to protect her, she was helpless. Where would she and her children find security if Nur Jahan was as successful as usual? As she asked the question, she thought of her husband, their father.

She slowed her step as memories came to her. Khurram's expression when he looked at her. The way a piece of his dark hair frequently escaped from the back of his turban. His touch when they were alone. His room-filling laughter. His playfulness and joy of living. The way he wrote poetry for her. His serious and thoughtful expression when he was working on a difficult problem. The way he had come to share his decisions with her. The tender way he held their babies.

Leaning against a column, Mumtaz whispered, "I can't imagine my life without Khurram. I love being his wife. I'd rather have him and my family than all of Nur Jahan's power." With this realization, she pushed herself away from the column and walked firmly toward her own rooms. Her decision seemed more correct with every determined step that took her farther away from Nur Jahan's protection

❋ ❋ ❋

MUMTAZ AND KHURRAM WERE THOUGHTFULLY re-circling the garden as they strolled and she felt the warmth and weight of his hand on her shoulder. She walked silently, knowing she had grappled with her own alternatives earlier. This was Khurram's time

When Khurram spoke, Mumtaz realized her husband had already moved past anger and hurt.

"Nur Jahan is right. She'd be unable to control me. Jahangir needs his wife to be strong where he's weak. Shariyar, who has had no power, would, of course, be willing to take the easy way out. He'll get his position and the respect he desires as emperor, while allowing Nur Jahan to create policy. We shouldn't be surprised. They're all behaving consistently with what we've known about them for years.

"But it won't work," he continued. "The country isn't better off with either Shariyar or Nur Jahan in this position. One is ineffectual and the other is power hungry."

Mumtaz agreed with a sound. "Although her plan isn't suitable," Khurram continued, "it isn't out of character. She has accomplished much and believes she'll always succeed. Her abilities and position are so powerful that her own father and brother hesitate to disagree with her. If she were a man, she'd stand with her sword out of its scabbard. Though she is a woman, her mind is equally defiant."

Khurram wondered why Nur Jahan wanted more than she already had. Other women would be content to be empress, the favored and loved queen of the Great Mughal. She, however, desired not only the riches and royal lifestyle her position afforded her, but also the control, power, and her strong and intelligent voice to be heard and obeyed. Because she could not be the emperor, she wanted to rule the emperor—and through him the empire.

Khurram dropped his hand from Mumtaz' shoulder and spun her around so they were face to face.

"Power. Absolute and complete power. That's what Nur Jahan wants!"

Mumtaz watched as her husband's words of understanding turned to stricken self-awareness. He whispered harshly, "The same could be said of me."

Bringing her hands up possessively to press the sides of his face, Mumtaz looked squarely into his eyes. "The most obvious difference between you and Auntie is you've been trained for years to head the empire. Neither Auntie nor Shariyar have."

Her words, her support, and her love touched Khurram. He covered her hands, still on the sides of his face, with his own and eventually replied, "Yes. When I'm ruler I'll make my own decisions, knowing all that I've learned and all that I've accomplished can't be taken from me. This will be my reign and I don't intend to share it."

Remembering Nur Jahan sitting next to Shariyar at the banquet, he whispered vehemently, "Not with anyone."

There was silence in the garden until Mumtaz spoke softly. "And that, Meerijan, is why Auntie has embarked on her difficult campaign. It didn't require much effort to promote you. You have been, and still are, Jahangir's logical choice for succession. We all know Shariyar's shortcomings and the empress may not be able to make him look presentable in his father's eyes after all of these years. Is it even possible for her to elevate your half brother to the glowing spot you now occupy in your father's heart?"

"Perhaps," mused Khurram. "Perhaps not."

18

Agra ~ 1617

"I'll win, you know."

Startled by the sudden appearance of the woman he'd been waiting for, Khurram jumped from the bench. Recovering quickly from his surprise, he began an automatic and fluid teslim, the gesture Jahangir now decreed necessary when greeting his wife.

Abruptly halting this obeisance with an impatient motion of her hand, Nur Jahan snapped, "We don't need that between us when we're alone, Khurram."

Her low, husky voice suited her well, as did the imperial lift of her chin. Her compelling good looks could not camouflage the strength and ambition flashing in her eyes.

Although Nur Jahan had always been determined to have her own way, Khurram was only now fully aware of his stepmother's fierce intention to have everything as she wanted. Because she no longer needed to weave her web of charm around him, Nur Jahan met him with a straightforward stance. Momentarily stunned by the force she emitted, Khurram took a deep breath and prepared himself for a verbal battle with his father's wife. He knew he had to wrest himself from the security of her support if he were to sit comfortably on the throne as he intended.

Nur Jahan raised her eyebrows slightly, waiting for his response to her initial words. At exactly the same moment, Khurram

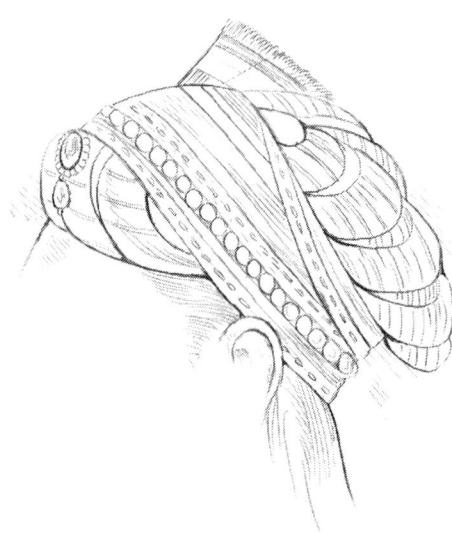
Female turban

swept his arm to offer her his place on the stone bench. She did not move. Rather, she folded her hands together at her waist, looked at him, and frowned.

"As Your Majesty pleases", remarked Khurram smoothly, accepting by his rising that their conversation would take place between standing participants.

Irritated, she scowled. "Khurram, if we're to continue talking, and if it's to be worth my while to meet you privately, we must drop the pretense of having a normal conversation. Use my name, not my title, or we'll have this talk in public rooms."

Thus, Nur Jahan deftly dismissed the deeply ingrained Mughal rituals Khurram had practiced since his youth. She had pointedly ignored, and even mocked, his gesture of respect, the use of her title, and his willingness to stand while she sat. She had discarded her advantages as the empress and faced him as his equal. Recognizing and admiring the confidence that enabled her to speak to him as a peer, Khurram also realized she was even a stronger adversary than he had assumed. Tensely facing each other, conscious of the importance of their meeting, they were each blind to the elegant, symmetrical gardens, clipped hedges, and marble pavilions surrounding them. Exquisite petal-sprinkled pools went unseen. Khurram spoke with princely authority, bringing their meeting immediately to the point he wanted to make.

"I am the most worthy of my father's sons to follow him onto the throne."

Nur Jahan remained silent.

"Surely, you agree."

Nur Jahan's eyes narrowed. Khurram waited. When Nur Jahan finally spoke, her tone was controlled, even icy. "What I know, Khurram, is that you used to be the most worthy. You used to be someone who'd listen to my advice."

"I still listen!" Khurram protested. "I value your ideas as I hope you value mine."

The beginning of a smile was on Nur Jahan's lips. "You've grown too self important, Khurram. You don't recognize the wisdom of one who's lived more years than you. There's much you can learn from me."

"Many people give me their thoughts, share their wisdom, and expect nothing in return. When you..." at this point, Khurram knew he was addressing the core of the difference between them. "When you share your thoughts," he continued, "it's with the expectation I'll obey them—not simply consider them."

As he said the words, Khurram knew he had just pinpointed his uneasiness with her support. She had become far too involved with braiding their futures together even though he was no longer the youthful man he had been when Nur Jahan had first become queen.

With sudden insight, Khurram saw, by Nur Jahan's criteria, that he had been overly successful in Rajasthan. Having been absent from Agra during those months, he had discovered that the machinations encircling him in the palace were but a small part of the larger world. He had also come to know that he would fight to be emperor, and that he would serve well the vast lands the Mughals controlled.

The campaign in Rajasthan had completed his preparation to rule begun with his studies and his court experience. Khurram remembered his frustration during the years of the palace training required of a royal prince. In classrooms he had learned science, medicine, grammar, math, astronomy, and geology. He spoke Arabic because it was the language of the Koran, and Persian because it was the language of the court.

Outside the classroom, he had practiced until he became a skilled rider, swordsman, falconer, and marksman. Public time with his father gave him familiarity with court life, dress, manners, language, and actions. He could discern truth from lies, use court intrigue to his advantage, and make quick decisions. He had learned how to write lyrical poetry, put it on paper in swirling calligraphy, and recite it smoothly. His grandfather, Akbar, had been an invaluable model as he dealt with the crucial balance between India's Hindus and its Muslim rulers.

As though she was reading his mind, Nur Jahan shrugged. "I don't need the same preparation as you've subjected yourself to, Khurram. My grasp of what needs to be done is intuitive…and right."

Khurram stared at her, amazed by her audacity. This woman was dismissing everything he'd already learned, and she was ready to take over. There was no doubt as they faced each other that the leadership of the post-Jahangir era would fall to one of them. The prize, the total control and shaping of the Mughal Empire, was worth the conflict they knew was inevitable.

Hindered by neither a judiciary system nor lawmakers, each wanted to have the Mughal's right to direct an army, put a person to death, grant titles and rank, and determine policy. The combined wealth of treasure and land would be at their disposal as much of India belonged to the head of the Empire. What the Great Mughal didn't own outright reverted back to him upon the death of the men who did. Nothing could be passed to family members at death, unless so decreed by the state—which happened to be, they were both aware, the Great Mughal.

Even though Jahangir's judgment and instincts were unreliable because of his addictions, Nur Jahan and Khurram had to be subtle in their dealings with him. The emperor's ability to imprison them, should he feel he'd been manipulated, was a real threat, particularly during the hours of each day when wine and opium influenced his thoughts.

"You've added confidence to your other skills and talents, Khurram," Nur Jahan conceded. "Your trip to Rajasthan matured you. But you made a grave mistake thinking you can rule without me. You're still too young to assume the leadership. Your father was thirty-six before he ruled, and you are only thirty now."

Rather than responding directly to Nur Jahan, Khurram made his own point. "Father thought he'd never be on the throne with Akbar ruling for so long. I can wait for my turn to rule, but I won't allow the opportunity to be taken from me by you or anyone else."

Ignoring the soft ultimatum of Khurram's words, Nur Jahan smiled menacingly and stepped toward him. Angrily she spat her words to him.

Female Mughal dress

"You think you know me well, dear Khurram. But all you know is that I've run this land for a long time. When I married your father, I foresaw a life without worry, an existence of ease and luxury. But it didn't turn out that way. I quickly became bored. At the same time, Jahangir was growing weary with the demands of the empire. He was less and less willing to carry the expected responsibility, and I began, slowly at first, advising him. Then I listened directly to the discussions with his counselors and guided him from behind the curtain. I'd slip my hand through an opening and place it carefully on his back so no one could see I was giving signals. He's now thought to be a wise ruler. These decisions—my decisions—have brought him much glory.

"Now I dictate and sign firmans in his name. Mine is the first woman's name to be minted on coins. The more I've run the empire, the more power I've been able to wield, the more I want what is not yet mine." Her face was flushed, and she was walking in circles with short determined steps, breathing quickly.

Nur Jahan halted, swirled around, then declared in her low, fierce voice, "I began my journey hesitantly, through love and duty. Now I embrace it and I will go further. The truth is, I'm already ruling." Putting her face close to his, she looked him right in the eyes, saying softly but very distinctly, "I'm not going to stop even when Jahangir walks with Allah."

The moment stretched again into silence. Khurram realized with dreadful clarity that Nur Jahan, the woman who'd previously been his admirer, had become his powerful enemy. It was clear that she'd do whatever it took to place Shariyar on the throne, to continue her rule.

Khurram's rank, the men he controlled, his position as a successful soldier, and his wealth were all reduced to mere obstacles to be overcome by Nur Jahan in her ferocity to destroy him as a rival. Khurram remained convinced of the probability of his success, but was disturbed by Nur Jahan's newest scheme.

Clearly, they couldn't rule together. Only one would rule and it would be without the other. If Shariyar were to be the next ruler, Nur Jahan would continue her domination for the rest of her life. If Jahangir continued to favor Khurram, Nur Jahan would become a widow overseeing the construction of her husband's tomb rather than a woman controlling an empire.

"I am the present and the future of India," spoke a more controlled Nur Jahan.

Khurram drew himself to his full height, pulled back his shoulders, and rested a warning hand on the dagger in his waist sash. "I will be the next Mughal ruler."

They looked at each other as adversaries, neither believing the other would prevail. Khurram remembered the Royal Tent he had used and the valuable property at Hissar that had been given to him. Both traditionally were received only by the chosen heir. There was no way this woman could overcome his advantages, even if she *had* survived the desert as an infant.

Their imaginary swords were crossed. Slowly, without words, they bowed to one another. When she raised her head, Nur Jahan paused, gave him a searching look, then pivoted on one golden sandal and walked away.

Khurram closed his eyes and mentally replaying what Nur Jahan had said. When he remembered the determination of her words and the strength of her passion, he heard a man's voice.

Speaking thoughtfully in the direction of her disappearing figure, Khurram was nodding his head. "You'd be a worthy foe if you were a man, Nur Jahan. It is lucky for me you are only a woman."

19

Agra - 1618

After the garden meeting with Nur Jahan, Khurram continued to support his father's policies, practice his marksmanship, appear at the required durbars at his father's side, hold meetings, and manage his financial affairs. Certain he would prevail over Nur Jahan, he spent time with his wife and family and attended to his religious requirements.

His first hint of change occurred one afternoon at the entrance to the emperor's private chambers. Lost in thought, Khurram reached the entrance before noticing an armed soldier standing in the middle of the archway, rather than to the side. Khurram nodded absently, thinking about the daily interlude with his father, one that they had both enjoyed for many years. Only when he became aware of the soldier drawing himself to attention did Khurram stop, puzzled.

"No one is to enter the emperor's chambers, Your Highness."

"You obviously know who I am by your address. Do you also know I come here daily?"

Rather than answering the question, the guard repeated, "No one is to enter the emperor's chambers."

Not particularly disturbed, Khurram returned to his own quarters. It was beneath him to argue with a lowly soldier simply following orders. If he had known his father was totally unaware of the directive given by Nur Jahan, he could have attended to the escalation of her influence against him.

When Khurram joined his father for wine and music at the evening session in the Diwan-i-Khas, Jahangir was jovial and friendly, but slightly less open than usual. Though neither man mentioned the afternoon, each wondered why the other had ignored their daily visit.

Slowly and subtly, Nur Jahan began corrupting her husband's devotion to his eldest son. Leaving orders to prohibit Khurram's visits she then reminded Jahangir how long it had been since the prince had come. When Khurram did visit, Nur Jahan was later casually scornful of his dependence upon his father.

The empress' swordless weapons were making themselves felt as they carefully cut single threads that had tightly bound the emperor to his son. Jahangir, who had never questioned Khurram's intentions, became critical of his actions and slowly began to doubt the motives of this previously unblemished source of pleasure. Jahangir's change of attitude from pride to criticism was slowed by his conviction of Khurram's unquestionable loyalty and love and his excellence as a dutiful son and soldier. Gradually, his love and trust in Khurram became pitted and suspicion replaced total acceptance.

Although Nur Jahan realized Jahangir no longer believed the sun rose and set at Khurram's command, her husband wasn't as disenchanted as she wanted him to be. Alone with him, she delicately picked away at Khurram's place in Jahangir's heart, and arranged frequent visits between Shariyar and Jahangir that each man thought had been instigated by the other.

Nur Jahan knew Shariyar wasn't the caliber of company Khurram was, but it pleased her that one prince was denied passage and the other was admitted. She mused about arranging to have them both arrive at the same time, so Khurram would know without question Shariyar had the access to Jahangir that was denied him.

Nur Jahan increased her attentions to Jahangir and coddled him, sand to him, and wrote him poetry. She tended to him lovingly even as she was taking over more and more of the administration and of the empire, reinforcing his reliance on her.

"As he grows to need me more," she spoke to her mirrored reflection, "he's less apt to interfere. It would be too risky for him to upset me, for I could withdraw my assistance. I've made him too comfortable to consider such a drastic move." Only the night before she had stroked Jahangir's forehead in her lap and said sympathetically, "Rest assured, my love, it means nothing that your son has stayed away for weeks."

"Has it really been so long?"

"I'd pay it no mind. I'm certain he respects you as much as he always has."

"Mmmm."

"And his love for you is as strong as ever."

"It should be. I've not changed. I've been overly kind and lavish."

Having planted another seed of doubt, she knew Jahangir would mull over her words when he was alone. It had been a while since Prince Khurram had visited. What was more important than seeing his father?

My, my, I must've forgotten to tell Jahangir his son was stopped by my orders and wasn't allowed to see his father. I'll mention it to him...some day.

Khurram felt the change of his relationship with Jahangir and immediately suspected Nur Jahan. His frustration increased as Jahangir's previous adoration of him became mistrust and suspicion. Still, Khurram remained silent knowing the emperor would listen to nothing against the wife he depended upon and trusted.

The single person who represented him to his father was the very person who was challenging him for the right to rule. With a sinking feeling, Khurram knew Nur Jahan's carefully crafted version of his activities and motives had been twisted to fit her own needs without regard for the truth.

At this time, the two most powerful women in the zenana decided, each for her own reasons, that Khurram should leave Agra. Nur Jahan was certain her chance of success would improve if Khurram were away. Mumtaz saw her husband's absence as a way to win the struggle he was having with her aunt.

Mumtaz moved first. She spoke as though the idea she had was spontaneous. "Perhaps it is time for you to leave the palace, Meerijan. When you returned victorious from Rajasthan, your father saw you as a hero. If you lead another military campaign, you will again be surrounded by the glorious light of victory. He's already mentioned a possible excursion to the Deccan. Consider requesting that you serve as the commander."

Khurram, pacing and glaring, seemed to be wrestling with indecision. Finally, he stopped his fitful movements and faced her. "I've thought about it, Taj, and I don't want to go. I've already received the highest honors a military commander could expect. I'm not certain I could be as successful as I was before. If I'm not, it would be held against me.

"Father is in poor health and it would be foolhardy to leave now. Nur Jahan would be unencumbered by my presence to ply my father with more lies about me."

Eventually, Mumtaz again spoke. "All you say is true, Meerijan. But I remember the look Jahangir gave you and how he honored you by standing, showering you with gems, and embracing you. Perhaps this trip will have a similar ending. It could remind him how valuable, how important you are."

"It doesn't feel right, Taj. I could risk much and not accomplish what I want. However" he continued after thinking through other options, "I can think of nothing else that has a better chance of success."

Speaking without inner conviction, Khurram put his decision into words. "I'll tell my father that I'll lead the army south. I feel certain he will be pleased to have me away."

Mumtaz wasn't certain if she should feel satisfied or not.

20

Deccan - 1619

India's arid high plateau, the Deccan, more southern than Rajasthan, swarmed with warlike, troublesome chiefs who fought among themselves at every opportunity. Khurram's mission was to bring them together in peace under the Mughal banner and extract a pledge to send tribute. If he were successful, he would again occupy his desired place in his father's esteem.

The low rugged Vindhya Mountain range that ran west to east approximately three hundred and fifty miles south of Agra delineated the historic boundary between northern and southern India. Hundreds of miles of difficult ranges formed a protective barrier to the northern entry of the Deccan's interior.

The campaign promised frustrating terrain. The triangular-shaped plateau called the Deccan was surrounded by three mountain ranges. In addition to the Vindhyas running across the "top," there were ranges, the Western Ghats and the Eastern Ghats, paralleling the coastlines. Tall enough to pierce the water-laden clouds from the Indian Ocean, these mountains divided the inner plateau from the coasts. The inland desert was dry while the lush coastal strips were tropical and fringed with palm trees growing close to the blue water.

Khurram could not clear his head of the uncertainty in Agra as he planned the warfare ahead. As he rejected the idea of repeating the previously used 'scorch and burn' technique, he couldn't keep his thoughts from wandering to Nur Jahan and what she would do in his absence from the palace. Thoughts of the conquest before him mingled with musings about Shariyar and Jahangir. His concentration on the upcoming struggle was lessened by his hopes that at his return there would be a prominent place for him in Agra.

The rituals of departure had been repeated with this campaign: Jahangir, dressed in fine raiment, stood on the jharoka balcony and was joined by Khurram. He performed the good luck ritual and bestowed gifts on his departing son, but this time with an undercurrent of restraint. The trays of jewels Jahangir spilled on Khurram's head were not quite so full, Jahangir's attention to the process of ensuring good luck on the mission didn't seem as complete, and the gifts were not equal to the quality and quantity of the gifts given when Khurram had left for Rajasthan.

"How could he do this?!" Khurram despaired to Taj when they were alone the first night of travel. As though by unspoken agreement, Mumtaz and Khurram both assumed she would accompany him on his travels. "How can my father dare to send me off to the far south and not even grant me the sincere protection and farewell his commander deserves? I've done nothing he can fault!"

"Meerijan, we are away from the Agra Fort with its intrigue. The weight you've been carrying has grown heavy on your shoulders. Allow it to melt away while you tackle the military situation in front of you." Her voice changed to an inviting tone Khurram rarely resisted. "Come, loosen your jama," she whispered, "that I might massage oil into your tight muscles." Khurram accepted Taj's wisdom. Military thought could wait until the morning. Right now, the feel of soft hands rubbing with a gentle firmness that loosened his shoulders was enough. He would think about other things later.

※ ※ ※

THE DECCAN WAS EVEN MORE inhospitable than the Rajasthani

Desert had been. Day after day, the army sweltered through gritty soil tufted with dried bushes, huge boulders, and deep depressions. The bluish heat haze of the jagged hills caused great fortresses to quiver from their position atop large outcroppings of stone, ruggedly protected by walls the same color as the surrounding land. The troops advanced south among great lumps of granite haphazardly strewn above the ground. Hindu legend described these as leftover building blocks, discarded by the gods after they created the world.

Khurram rode south toward his future with less enthusiasm than he rode away from his troubles in Agra. He had thought the almost impassable terrain of Rajasthan was difficult, but in contrast to the larger and more desolate Deccan, it seemed hospitable in memory. His task was somehow to bring this completely unmanageable portion of land between the two coastal mountain ranges under Mughal rule.

Unknown to him, fear began to grow in the hearts of the Deccanis when they became aware of the enormous might of the Mughal army they were to battle that was marching resolutely into their homeland. Remembering Khurram's techniques in Rajasthan, they fearfully discussed the possibility of his intentions to repeat those same actions in the Deccan. They assumed anyone dedicated enough to cross the usually protective mountains with an army must be contemplating unthinkable actions.

Fear became panic as they prepared to fight, ever willing to capitulate if they could do so with honor. In the end, the battles both sides had expected were not fought, and Mughal victory was assured by a series of treaties loosely bundling the differing principalities of the Deccan into a single entity that accepted Mughal sovereignty.

Khurram rapidly negotiated terms of surrender, thereby pulling off another brilliant campaign and the acquisition of vast wealth. Impatiently, he accepted the negotiated truce before returning to Agra.

Catching a glimpse of her relaxed husband riding on his fine horse, Mumtaz smiled. The months they'd been gone had been good for him. But more than that, she knew he would soon be with his father and nearer to the throne he hoped to inherit. Delighted with the results of the gamble Khurram had taken, Mumtaz had three reasons to anticipate the upcoming Victory Durbar. First, her husband was again a successful commander. Second, he had greatly increased the size of the Empire, and third, he was bringing home a larger fortune than before. Smiling to herself in the dimness of her howdah's interior, Mumtaz wondered if the emperor would repeat his emotional reaction and publicly embrace her husband. Better yet, Jahangir might officially proclaimed Khurram as his heir at this second Victory Durbar.

If she had been able to hear Nur Jahan's words, Mumtaz would have known how very wrong she was.

❋ ❋ ❋

"IT DOES SEEM AS THOUGH Khurram was inappropriately eager to leave his generous and loving father alone while he enhanced his own reputation," Nur Jahan had mentioned casually.

If Khurram had stayed in Agra, Nur Jahan would have shared opposite sentiments with Jahangir, such as, "I'd have thought Khurram would be eager to lead your armies again. He isn't cowardly is he? He isn't more interested in the comforts of Agra than the military life, is he? Surely, he's a finer man than that."

Drops of water. Plink. Plink. Plink. Over the weeks, with no contradictions about his son, the poison of Nur Jahan's words gradually began to enter Jahangir's consciousness

❋ ❋ ❋

ON HIS FIRST CAMPAIGN, scouts had met Khurram long before he had reached the palace. It was then he had given the Rana of Mewar's fabulous red ruby to Bokhari for delivery to Jahangir. When his procession reached the same area on their return from the Deccan, he looked across the plains for signs of a welcoming party and was satisfied when he saw their dust in the distance.

When the riders came close, Khurram frowned slightly at the small number of men. He recognized Bokhari, again the leading diplomat of the group, and changed his expression to one of genuine pleasure.

"Greetings, Prince Khurram," intoned the tall, white-haired Bokhari. "Welcome back from your military journey. The riders you sent ahead have already been to Agra to tell His Highness of your success in the Deccan. Their words have pleased him."

Khurram nodded, hiding the smile of pleasure he felt. He was returning in victory and knew his father, who always enjoyed celebrations, would be even now preparing for another.

Bokhari's next words confirmed his hopes. "His Highness expects you at a Victory Durbar in three days time, at the beginning of the third horn."

"Tell His Highness I shall be there, and I shall have treasures to show him. Take this to him now as a gift, an indication of what I'll be bringing with me." He handed a padded brocade box to Bokhari. When the diplomat had carefully packed it, Khurram resumed his travel to Agra.

Everything will be all right when I return, the prince tried to convince himself. But he knew that his determined optimism was competing with the knot in his stomach signaling something was wrong. Perhaps he was reading too much into the size of the diplomat's delegation; a successful general, much less a royal prince, should receive a larger welcome. Picturing the Victory Durbar, he visualized his father showering him with gold. Had Jahangir given anything to Shariyar in his absence? Although he wouldn't want to be Shariyar, he chaffed at the inequality of having to perform on the battlefield to receive what his half brother may have received for doing nothing. Lingering with these thoughts, Khurram predicted that he and his father would resume their strong relationship. He counted on Nur Jahan never breaking the bond he had as Jahangir's son.

❋ ❋ ❋

THE SPECTACULAR ROSARY of pearls and rubies Khurram had sent to his father in the padded brocade box had been tossed casually over its hinged container, and onto the rich coverlet which was draped on the divan where Jahangir and Nur Jahan sat. With mock sadness in her voice as her eyes stared at the rubies and pearls, Nur Jahan said, "It's a shame Khurram brought you this insignificant token from his military travels. I'd have thought he'd bring the Great Mughal a more valuable bauble."

Nur Jahan knew exactly what she was doing. Her comment had already been planned and would have been used no matter what Khurram had sent to his father. Adeptly, she again turned Khurram's actions and words into signs of disrespect. Respect, she knew, was so central a need of her husband's he wouldn't allow anyone, even his own son, to fail to honor him and the position he held.

❋ ❋ ❋

THE MORNING OF THE VICTORY DURBAR, Khurram awoke with a feeling of uneasiness. This perplexed him as he had planned today's Durbar as thoroughly as he had the successful one earlier. He tried to convince himself that it would be equally glorious, but his worrisome premonition that events would not unfold as he had hoped would not go away.

When he arrived at the Victory Durbar, Khurram saw a scene similar to the celebration of his first success. The courtyard was filled with many of the same faces and festival finery. The Diwan-i-Am had been again lavishly adorned with vibrant silk panels, white columns and carved arches sparkled in the morning sun, and colorful carpets covered the massive courtyard. Treasure-filled baskets were laid in neat rows waiting to be carried to Jahangir for his approval. Animals to be shown to their new owner waited in outer courtyards.

Jahangir arrived with his usual fanfare. He stepped from between the curtains and took his cross-legged place on his canopied and cushioned throne as the men assembled before him teslimed their allegiance. Khurram, tesliming with the rest, knew immediately from his tight stomach that something was wrong. When the greeting was finished and he heard the men behind him suck in their breaths, his fears were confirmed.

Jahangir's face was dark and his lips were pressed together in thin white lines. The emperor was not passive or neutral; his narrowed eyes and frown lines on his forehead reflected irritation. No one knew why Jahangir presented himself this way, least of all Khurram. The durbar would not go well.

What followed was a nightmare for Khurram. He had expected a repeat of the applause, the gifts, and the honors he had received in the past. But this time, his father was cold and impassive, accepting his victory tributes with cool silence. The nobles and courtiers were stunned by the lack of imperial happiness when Khurram gave his public report. They were aghast at how Jahangir treated his successful general—and son. Nevertheless, they uncomfortably emulated their absolute ruler and created an emotional silence that descended upon the Diwan-i-Am.

Jahangir had not asked Khurram to join him on the throne balcony, but left him miserable and confused on the courtyard level. Though the humiliated prince had no doubt the source of his father's displeasure stemmed from Nur Jahan's deceptions, his attempts to counter her domination of his father were consistently futile.

When Bokhari had met Khurram outside Agra, the diplomat had delivered the message that Jahangir would be going to bed early the night before the durbar and did not want to be disturbed when Khurram returned. Obeying what he had assumed was his father's request, unaware of the true source, Khurram had stayed away from the chambers of the emperor and unknowingly disappointed his father. His absence had also given Nur Jahan the opportunity to say, in silken and slightly sad tones, that it was regrettable Khurram had not taken the time to see his father after such a long absence. Had Khurram visited in spite of the message she had sent, Nur Jahan would have said to Jahangir that it had been pleasant to see Khurram, but it was a bit presumptuous of him to disturb the emperor when they would be together at the durbar in the morning.

Dismayed and puzzled at the Diwan-i-Am, Khurram knew none of this. Because he was standing at the front of the audience, looking upward at his father, the men behind him couldn't see his anguish, couldn't see the dismay on his usually cool and haughty face.

In his confusion and hurt, Khurram was not thinking of the invisible person who was taking great pleasure in his agony. Sitting behind a carved screen, Nur Jahan happily watched the wretchedness of the once proud and decisive Prince Khurram.

Disbelief and a growing sense of doom froze Mumtaz as she observed the painful scene. Too stunned to turn her head to observe her aunt, she empathized with her husband.

Nur Jahan's hard, unblinking eyes focused upon the deflated man before her. She could almost taste his fear but she wouldn't finish him yet. There was something else her prey must endure before she would strike the final blow.

21

Agra - 1620

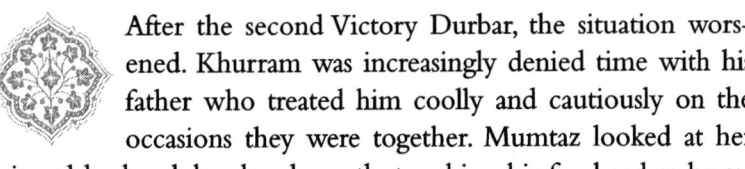

After the second Victory Durbar, the situation worsened. Khurram was increasingly denied time with his father who treated him coolly and cautiously on the occasions they were together. Mumtaz looked at her agitated husband, her hands gently touching his forehead as he sat on her terrace. Even the soothing sounds of the nearby water did not ease the pain in his voice, nor did it soften the wrinkles she felt beneath her caressing hands.

"The worst part of it is, Shariyar is taking my place in the affections of my father. Shariyar! That vacant puppet is hovering to sit on the throne."

Every day Shariyar was given a special gift or new privilege Khurram expected. His younger half brother was constantly with Jahangir, invited to evening festivities, and was taken on trips with his father. The prince fumed, knowing Nur Jahan was responsible for the change of both Shariyar's status and his own uncertain future.

Increasingly Khurram was edged out of the innermost circle in favor of the usurper who seemed to do no wrong. The court, famous for shifting allegiances, saw Shariyar as the current favorite and made it a habit of inviting him to their functions, offering him gifts, and currying his favor. Shariyar, presented by Nur Jahan and accepted by Jahangir, was steadily eroding loyalty that had previously belonged to Khurram.

As Mumtaz sympathized with Khurram, she was searching for a way to share the distressing news that she had just heard in the zenana. Hesitating only because of the pain she knew her words would cause, she felt the same heaviness that had been upon her when, not so long ago, she told her husband of Nur Jahan's new allegiance.

Mumtaz quietly gathered her courage, regretting her need to reveal more bad news. She silently appealed to Allah to quickly supply her with the right words. Knowing what she had to say wouldn't become easier with time. "Meerijan, do you know about the celebration to be held in the fort next month?" she began. Khurram did not move, and did not open his eyes. There were so many celebrations; they had little meaning to him.

"This is one you should know about." The tightening of her lap and the slight quiver in her voice transmitted to Khurram he was going to hear news of importance. He sat up and looked intently at Mumtaz.

"This one is a wedding. A royal wedding." Mumtaz held his gaze and recognized the moment he understood.

She was right. Khurram knew. Already Shariyar's rank had been raised as high as his own, new jagirs of land were given to him, royal drums played as he arrived, and his new standard flew when he was in public. Now there was to be a wedding.

"It's Shariyar, isn't it? Who is the poor girl chosen to become the wife of the fat, stupid favorite of Nur Jahan?"

There was a long pause before Mumtaz spoke. Khurram tried to convince himself it didn't matter who Shariyar married; all that mattered was the removal of another of his own advantages. Mumtaz took both of her husband's hands in hers, held them tight, and whispered only one word while she sent her love, strength, and support to him through her eyes and hands.

"Ladili."

❈ ❈ ❈

DURING THE REIGN OF AKBAR, Milhenrissa, now known as Nur

Jahan, had frequently been in the palace, the delightful daughter of the emperor's Chief Minister. As a gesture of high favor to Ghiyas Beg, Akbar found her a suitable husband. His choice was Sher Afghan, a powerfully built, handsome, fierce, and hot-tempered warrior from Afghanistan. Valuable to the throne but too volatile to have in Agra, Sher Afghan was sent east to Bengal, the empire's tropical land of great wealth, heat, and humidity. While there, the soldier and his young wife lived happily for several years and became parents to a daughter named Ladili.

Several months after the baby was born, soldiers arrived in Bengal and demanded to see Sher Afghan. During the heated discussion that followed, the Afghan felt his honesty was being doubted. Angered, he drew his sword to settle the matter. He attacked his armed visitors and was fatally struck down as he fought.

Milhenrissa, now a widow with a small daughter, returned to the city where she had been raised and took work as an attendant to a widow of Akbar's in the Royal Zenana. It was in his own zenana that Jahangir noticed the woman he eventually made his queen. During the years Nur Jahan was empress, Ladili had grown into marriageable age.

Shariyar needed a wife and Ladili needed a husband. Nur Jahan realized both situations could be solved with a single ceremony. With her own daughter married to the son of her husband, Shariyar's stature as well as Nur Jahan's own influence on the throne would be doubled. Taking for granted the bride and groom would agree with her decision, Nur Jahan began making the arrangements after manipulating Jahangir to her way of thinking.

※ ※ ※

KHURRAM UNDERSTOOD THE SIGNIFICANCE of the bride choice. He churned, watching his rival prepare to marry the daughter of a woman sworn to defeat him. His appetite diminished, the traces of his good humor in public vanished, and even in private, he was gently chided by Mumtaz' for his glumness.

❋ ❋ ❋

"You are planting trees in barren soil if you are trying to change my mind, Taj. The Deccan needs me. I was the man responsible for bringing it into the empire, and unless someone oversees what needs to be done there, it will do our empire little good to have this enormous area within our boundaries. I'm the logical person to oversee the standardization of their crops, their census, and even their measurement techniques. Right now, there's confusion.'

The real issue, not wanting to be in Agra during Shariyar's wedding, was understood but not spoken between them. Staying to be near his father would be An unnoticed gesture and less important to Khurram than his need to be away from Shariyar.

Khurram planned to use his father's Lunar Birthday Festival to ask for permission to move. They would be together at the Public Weighing to celebrate the twelve moon cycles since the emperor's last Lunar Birthday. Jahangir arrived wearing a costly white satin cape with hundreds of diamonds, rubies, and pearls sewn onto the cloth. Rich collars of jewels encircled his neck as he took his place to be weighed without removing any portion of his heavy garments.

He sat upon a huge pan suspended from a pulley until the opposite pan of the balance was filled with bags of gold to match his weight. The gold was then tallied and its value given to mendicants and the poor, thus pleasing the peasants and satisfying a religious requirement for Jahangir's good life after death. After the bags of gold, bags of different colors containing copper were piled upon the now-empty pan until they, too, weighed as much as Jahangir. Silk, perfumes, ghee, rice, and milk were all weighed against the emperor.

An even more elaborate version of this ceremony occurred every three hundred and sixty five days on the emperor's Solar Birthday. Both Weighings had been fixed customs since Akbar's reign, but their splendor had evolved along with other aspects of the Mughal lifestyle

Khurram was expected to attend the Weighing and the following feast. The emperor, as usual, threw silver baubles formed realistically in the shapes of fruits and nuts to the surrounding audience. While the men were scrabbling to pick up as many as they could, Khurram spoke in a voice low enough to be heard only by his father. "A magnificent cape you're wearing, Your Majesty." Khurram had chosen his father's formal title rather than the more intimate name he had used when in favor.

Not seeming to notice his son's formal address to him, Jahangir accepted the compliment and looked down at his jewel-encrusted cape, rubbing his fingers lovingly over the yards of gems. The garment was indeed splendid, and he did enjoy publicizing his wealth.

"I have to talk to you about the Deccan, Your Majesty."

"Well, what is it, Baba? Tell me quickly if you must speak now, for I have other things to do this day." Taking a deep breath, Khurram explained why a strong person was needed in the Deccan and why he was the most logical man to go.

Jahangir quickly considered the advantages to the empire of having Khurram's skills to oversee the transformation of the Deccan to the Mughal systems. He also recognized the increased peace he would enjoy in Agra with Khurram 500 miles away and far from both Shariyar and Nur Jahan.

"I shall have your appointment prepared in writing," he said in agreement. "Be ready to leave Agra in a month."

"Your Majesty, I can be ready much sooner than that."

"But you must be here for the festivities."

"You mean—"

"Of course." Jahangir turned to meet his son's eyes as he interrupted. "You must be here for your brother's wedding. It would not do at all, not at all, for you to leave earlier." Then he turned and was assisted toward the tantalizing aromas of the day's feast.

Khurram was frozen by his father's words. He was expected to stay until after the wedding. Hearing this, his feeling of success evaporated. He had no excuse to avoid watching Shariyar's marriage to Nur Jahan's daughter.

❊ ❊ ❊

KHURRAM DIDN'T REVEL in the idea of a royal wedding but his enthusiasm was hardly missed by those surrounding him. Nur Jahan, mother of the bride, made certain this ceremony was the grandest royal wedding ever seen. She saw to it that the gifts were the costliest, the henna ceremony where hands were painted with elaborate designs was the largest; and Shariyar's arrival the noisiest and most elaborate. In addition to horses, there were carts of hornblowing musicians, garlanded men, and kettledrums that were played enthusiastically along the mile of the lavish production.

Light punctuated the skies in the form of fireworks, flaming arrows sent through the night air, and thousands of small candles transforming the surface of the Jumna into a river of fire. The fort was a fairyland of lights, color, artificial waterfalls, flowers, scented air, and silk canopies held in place by golden pillars. The brocades, velvets, and jewels of the guests intimately guessed up the palace.

Throughout the weeks filled with excitement, planning, and rituals that culminated in the lavish wedding ceremony, Khurram's pain would have been unbearable if he had been alone. Together he and Mumtaz endured the festivities that spoke of their fall from prominence, and began to plan for life after their move.

Mumtaz knew Khurram was thinking about the weight of pearls hanging over Shariyar's face, the size of the dowry Ladili was bringing to the marriage, and the entire extravagance of the wedding. Her thoughts, much more personal, were memories of herself as a bride. How long ago it seemed when she feared her future and received the green bottle from her ayah.

As quickly after the wedding as possible, Khurram finalized the necessary arrangements and readied himself and his family to travel south. Unlike his departures to fight prestigious military battles, this leave-taking was a muted affair. Setting off to war, he noted wryly, was much nosier and more boisterous and more important than taking care of the land conquered.

In spite of his reasons for leaving Agra, Khurram's travel to the

Deccan suited him. He knew he must immerse himself in the Deccan in order to lessen his worries about Shariyar. He had grown to enjoy wide spaces of his new home and was soothed by the sand and clay-swept ground. As the highest-ranking man in the Deccan, he took pleasure in being surrounded with trained and loyal military men.

22

Deccan - 1621

The trio of tasks awaiting Khurram in the Deccan was more daunting than subduing the vast center of the subcontinent. The land needed to be methodically measured into the standard lengths recognized and used throughout the empire. The varied terrain of deserts, arid plains, mountains, alpine meadows, lakes, and forests created one of Khurram's greatest challenges. He ordered men to travel throughout the immense country using bamboo rods fitted with iron rings to get a more accurate reading than possible with the previously used ropes which tended to stretch or shrink.

Taxation was the second major issue but could be put in place only after the land had been sized and assessed. Vital to Mughal budgeting, taxes were levied in accordance to complex information including crop types, fallow or ploughed acreage, and potential diseases or other calamities that could befall the farmers. Khurram sought a workable balance between what he had to do to provide Mughal protection yet not overtax the farmers beyond what they would tolerate. Tax collectors all knew stories of entire villages that had relocated rather than pay what they considered to be unfair.

While land measurement and taxation were sufficient to divert Khurram's attention from Agra, he was additionally challenged to establish Mughal leadership through the Justice System. The only disputes that came to Khurram as Governor of the Deccan were those that remained undecided as they rose through the lower "courts." There was no civil law in the land, only religious scholars who based their decisions upon the Muslim Koran or the Hindu Shastras. The single remaining judge greater than Khurram was the emperor himself.

The brightest part of Khurram's life was the hours he spent with his wife and children. His family touched parts of his heart he had not known existed. The marble corridors frequently rang with the laughter of children as he chased them laughing into Mumtaz' arms. He participated in puppet shows, joined his children using toy swords and shields, rode stuffed horses, and told elaborate stories based on carved wooden figures of heroes and heroines. Looking at his children, he shook his head in amazement. "How can they be so different when they all have the same mother and father?"

"They *are* different, aren't they?" Mumtaz agreed.

Khurram looked at their eldest, a seven-year-old daughter, then at Mumtaz, then back to his daughter. "Jahanara has your fine looks," he remarked with satisfaction. Watching as the young girl played with their oldest son, Dara, six, Khurram smiled and added with pleasure, "She also has your gentle ways."

Dara was a quiet boy with a dreamy disposition who already preferred scrolls to swords. Affectionate and giving of his love, Dara was drawn to Jahanara as well as to his parents. Khurram wanted to see that this favored young boy received the education and training to prepare him for the throne in case he somehow became the Great Mughal himself. Khurram would go no further with his thoughts of Dara's future, ignoring the reality of what was most likely happening in Agra.

Shuja, their second son, was a particularly attractive child. At five years of age he was already fond of luxury. A charmer, Shuja received special attention and adoration from all who succumbed to his winning ways and sunny smile. Seeming from the moment of birth to enjoy the finest life had to offer, Shuja was happiest when he was being waited upon.

Rashanara, four years old, was a shadowy child in the growing family. Though a Mughal Princess, she would never marry, for if her father should succeed her grandfather, her husband could compete with her own brothers to be the heir. She lacked the cultural and emotional talents that abounded in her older sister. Her future was destined to be in the zenana.

It was Aurangzeb, also four years old but younger than Rashanara by only months, who was the most serious, the family's deepest thinker and a quiet observer of all that happened around him. His noticeably long narrow face and light coloring earned him the derogatory nickname of Snake. His self absorption and lack of need for others made him more difficult for Khurram to enjoy.

Suraiya Bano, one year old, was pudgy and lively for her age. She had had an older brother, Ummed Baksh, who had only been two years old when Allah had taken him to Paradise. Mumtaz understood that his siblings would eventually forget him, but she knew the love she had lavished upon him during his short life would remain within her mother's heart forever.

23

Agra/Deccan ~ 1622

Looking into her mirror, Nur Jahan smiled and hummed happily. While her maids oiled, combed, and arranged her long black hair, she delighted in reliving the recent events responsible for her fine mood.

First was her daughter's wedding. Although no longer current news, the marriage tied her more closely to Shariyar. Nur Jahan's smile revealed pleasure that now there was another marriage to tighten her position to the throne. She had chosen a son-in-law whose mind was no more intriguing than a stagnant pond, but it wouldn't matter when he became emperor, for she would be there to think for him. He only needed to act as the mouthpiece for decisions she would make. A small shrug of Nur Jahan's shoulders demonstrated the little concern she felt about the life she had decided for Ladili. Holding her mirror, Nur Jahan spoke to her hairdresser. "Pull it smoother around the sides of my face today," she ordered. When she again relaxed into the care of her attendants, she allowed her memories to continue.

The troubled relationship she had created between Khurram and Jahangir had prompted Khurram to move from Agra and allowed her greater freedom to organize her vision for the Mughal Empire. Last night, there had been a development that had the impact of both the marriage and the falling out between the two men. In terms of setting the stage for her own continued and increasing prominence, this development surpassed Khurram's departure. She could barely believe how quickly Cobra was bringing the crown ever closer to her. Shaking her head ruefully, she remembered she had not recognized the wonder of the situation at first, had even been upset by the news. Then Cobra had rearranged the pictures in her mind, adjusting them just a bit to reveal how the faraway circumstances she had just come to know, worked in her favor.

It began with the courier's harried delivery of a dispatch saying the Persians had captured the Afghan city of Khandahar. Although Khandahar was further north of Agra than the Deccan was south, events occurring in this distant, desolate, rocky area reverberated throughout the entire Mughal Empire. Far from being an ordinary city, Khandahar was a large, fort-dominated area, controlled and protected by the Mughals and strategically positioned on the trade route between India and Persia. As long as Khandahar was in their control, Mughals were assured that Persia wouldn't invade from the north. Shah Abbas of Persia, even as he professed eternal friendship and the desire for peace with his "brother" Jahangir, had ordered his army to lay siege to the important city. After only forty-five days, the Persians took Khandahar.

The grim news prompted Jahangir and his advisors to conclude Mughal troops must be mobilized to recapture the fallen city. But who would lead the army against the Persians? Which commander carried the loyalty, strategy, and the powerful instincts of a true leader? Names flew among the gathered military advisors. They stopped speaking when the choice was clear to each of them: Khurram.

The men held their collective breaths and looked toward Jahangir, unable to predict his response to their choice of his distant son. The emperor took his time before he answered while dozens of conflicting images of Khurram flashed through his mind. Eventually separating the knowledge as an emperor from his sensitivity as a father, he nodded his assent.

"Yes, Khurram is the best man, one who will certainly recapture this important land for us." He hoped Nur Jahan would agree with him particularly now that she was so close to Shariyar.

When Nur Jahan heard of the decision, she was very still. It was wrong, she thought to give this potentially glorious command to Khurram. He should stay in the Deccan while her dear Jahangir became increasingly frail and Shariyar learned to take his place on the throne. Then she felt the Cobra hiss inside of her and the empress saw events differently. By the time her husband had finished with a defense of his selection, Nur Jahan smiled.

"You're right as usual, my husband. Your idea is brilliant." Secretly she was even more confident of her own victory. Encouraging Jahangir to place Khurram in charge of the Imperial Army in Khandahar was exactly what should be done. She wondered why the perfection of the choice had initially escaped her.

Her mind was working quickly, for she knew that before Jahangir wrote to Khurram, she had to see to it that her unsuspecting spouse would question, even a bit, that Khurram's response would be immediately favorable.

"No doubt your son will willingly obey you, My Love," she smiled. "After all, you're not only his father but also his emperor. He'll be happy to lead your army northward. It will be another honor for him to reflect your glory and pleasure."

"What's your meaning, my dear?" he asked.

"I'm simply agreeing with you." Nur Jahan deliberately looked away from Jahangir and toward the wine she was pouring for him. She knew he felt particularly pampered when she served him, and she also knew the wine distorted his reactions. "Your son is obedient and willing to do anything you suggest. If it were any different, you'd have to order him to march north, rather than suggest it. You know your son better than I do. After all, he's of your own blood."

Swallowing his wine, Jahangir suddenly wondered how far he could trust his son. Was Khurram's love and devotion for him based on politics or parentage? This internal argument between his warring egotism and insecurity continued.

How could Khurram love me?

Of course Khurram loves me.
Khurram will disagree with me if I ask him to go to Khandahar.
There's no question Khurram will do anything I ask.
Perhaps, I'll ORDER Khurram into Khandahar as his emperor. No one, not even a royal prince, would dare disobey a firman.

Nur Jahan watched the emperor's face reflect his conflicting thoughts. Holding her own golden goblet to her lips and pretending to sip her wine, she suspected Jahangir's communication to his son would be an order rather than a request. Khurram would surely realize who was behind the words and feel her daggers as he read them.

Now watching her hair being arranged, she recalled the beauty of the agonizing choice she had just presented to her enemy. With whatever choice Khurram made, to go north or not, his position would be weakened.

❊ ❊ ❊

KHURRAM TRIED TO TURN HIS ATTENTION to the day's concerns, but his heart was not in the reconfiguration of the Deccan that hot morning. Although it was true the area was significant to the empire as well as important to him, this was not where he wanted to be now. His place was in Agra. Perhaps his home city was prominently on his mind more than usual because his scouts had reported an entourage riding toward him with a message meant for Khurram alone to receive. Their pace assured Khurram his father was alive, for if the emperor had died, the riders would have pushed their horses to a lather. Whatever the message, it rated a hand delivery.

When the men from Agra arrived, a dignified Prince Khurram entered the throne room and found the man waiting there was none other than Abdul Bokhari, the man Jahangir had sent to greet Khurram on the outskirts of Agra both times he returned from his military campaigns. Khurram had known this tall, thin, hooked-nose man with piercing dark eyes for many years. Not only had Bokhari's experience and proven abilities qualified him to be a trusted diplomat, he remained a friend to both Khurram and his father. The emissary's head was covered with yards of fabric the shade of green indicating he was officially in the employ of Jahangir.

Although Bokhari was older, he remained standing in the presence of royalty as the two men engaged in the ritualistic banter that their rank required. Both knew there was an important message not yet shared, even as they proffered and received the expected hospitality before they proceeded. After the pleasantries, Bokhari handed Khurram a leather envelope. The prince broke the wax seal and removed the paper inside. It was a firman, an order from the emperor. Khurram felt his stomach begin to churn again as it had when he first heard of the envoy coming his way. Quickly running his eyes to the bottom of the page, Khurram noted Jahangir's handprint.

Rereading the entire message, Khurram allowed no reaction to show on his face. He had known Bokhari long enough to be fully aware of the consummate skill with which the older man could discern emotions and reactions from the tightening of jaws, narrowing of eyes, or deepening of breaths. The prince remained inscrutable, keeping his thoughts private and not allowing the man before him anything to read.

The prince rested the firman on his crossed knee and looked up to the face of the still-standing Bokhari. There was much more he needed to understand before he could decide upon his response.

"Bokhari, you've brought an important message from my father. I assume that your knowledge of events in Agra and the northern lands exceeds what is written on this page. Will you sit with me while we talk beyond what is in this message?" Immediately, cushions were placed for Bokhari to sit in comfort. Wine and light food were brought to the room.

Khurram indicated they wanted to be alone and waited until they had the room to themselves. With genuine affection, both Bokhari and Khurram settled in for what they realized would be a lengthy conversation.

"Khandahar?" said Khurram, making a question of the single word.

"Khandahar," nodded Bokhari in answer.

"In the firman, my father orders me to lead the army north and recapture the fort there and all the lands controlled from it."

Bokhari, assuming correctly Khurram's awareness of Khandahar's location and strategic value, added nothing to the prince's accurate statement.

For a moment, neither spoke. During this stillness they took measure of one another. Khurram faced a man who'd taught him much about diplomacy. This man had listened to Khurram's frustration with his father and understood the competitive love binding the two men. Bokhari, grand and impressive in his magenta brocade jama, was dearer to him than any man other than his father.

As he looked at the prince, Bokhari was remembering Khurram as a youth, delighted with the world's marvels. It saddened him to witness that joy replaced with the solemn responsibilities of the adult now in front of him.

"The firman orders immediate speed in this matter, an quick return to Agra where you'll receive the command of the army and depart for the north as soon as you are ready. Because so much is resting on the battle for Khandahar, the emperor will pledge many chests of gold coin for you to use for salaries and equipment."

Betraying no emotion as he listened to the words of his friend, Khurram sat impassively. When Bokhari had finished, Khurram considered the consequences of leading his own army, as well as that of the entire Imperial Army, to Khandahar.

When he spoke, it was in questions. He paused to hear Bokhari's response before he asked another.

"What was the nature of the correspondence between Shah Abbas and my father?

"How many men and what equipment will be available?

"How long should it take the army to reach Khandahar?

"Have efforts already begun to prepare this force?

"How did you find my illustrious father and his equally illustrious wife?"

This last question caught Bokhari by surprise. He had never heard Khurram come this close to admitting his awareness of Nur Jahan's influence. Although it was common knowledge, it was seldom mentioned aloud. Throughout their conversation, Bokhari had given Khurram the open, honest answers the prince knew he would. He had elaborated when he knew further details and admitted when he lacked knowledge. His response to the questions about Jahangir and Nur Jahan, however, came only after a considered pause. His eventual and thoughtful reply was, "When we are through with the other matters before us, Prince Khurram, I would like to speak to you of your father and his wife."

Bokhari's intention became clear when, still seated, he bowed deeply toward Khurram. When he sat up, he was holding his large gold and topaz ring in his hand, having slipped it off his finger when his lowered head had hidden it from Khurram.

The ring represented his office, his position as Jahangir's representative. Without the ring, he was no longer speaking for the man who employed him. Without the ring, he was speaking to Khurram unofficially, as a friend. Khurram nodded, quickly understanding the symbolism of the action.

"I've come this long distance to let you know the gravity of the situation. The Persian monarch has moved his forces into Khandahar. He sent forays into our territories to the south—the protective buffer. His agents supply tribesmen, and he is expecting to stay in control. If Mughal troops are not quickly sent to Khandahar, the worst could happen.

"But the other matter is personal. It concerns your ailing father. He needs to go to the cooler climate of Kashmir for his health, but he'll not leave the heated plains of Agra until this matter is settled. His wife and doctors are greatly concerned.

"Both the emperor and the empress believe a fierce, quick strike from you is the best offense for countering the aggressive military movement of Shah Abbas. You may be our only hope in restoring peace and tranquillity to this troubled area."

Pausing to inhale and exhale slowly while he searched Khurram's face for understanding, Bokhari spoke to the young man with a personal plea. "Your empire needs you more now than ever Khurram, and I pray you consider moving at once."

He lowered his voice even further. "Some things are no different in Agra. The emperor spends increasing hours with his wife and the son that is also a son-in-law. There is no news of an upcoming royal birth, but there is grumbling about how distant Jahangir is becoming from the court that serves him. I don't know if he's even aware of the noose his wife has around his neck, but others are.

"A victory in Khandahar would be good for the country and for your father. I feel some of his ailments are caused by a lack of excitement. He may be tiring of the gilded trappings of his office and eager to find greater significance to his life. If not, there's fear he won't be with us for long.

"Kashmir has always been good for him because he is out of his stifling routines. He doesn't build buildings, he doesn't order his armies into new territories, and he's not an avid reader. What does he have to live for beyond his wife, his jewels, and the rituals of being emperor? His daily wine and opium help fill this emptiness...but they are not enough."

When he had finished, there was another silence. Bokhari solemnly slipped his ring back on his finger and as the emissary of the emperor rather than a personal friend, he rose. Leaving Khurram with many thoughts to ponder, Bokhari respectfully bowed, then backed out of the royal presence.

Khurram absently fingered the paper resting on his lap. There was no command from an emperor that held more authority than a royal firman. Adding to its impact was its personal delivery by a man trusted and respected by both the emperor and the prince. The prince, no less than any other Mughal subject, was expected to obey or risk punishment. When he read between the lines, Khurram heard his stepmother's voice communicating her thoughts to him as clearly as if she'd written them herself.

The same moment the prince realized he needed his wife, Mumtaz appeared in the throne room. She had never been there but had suddenly known he wanted her. No audible request for help had been made, simply an awareness between two people who shared their thoughts. She had risen from where she had been listening to women singing, used her secret exit from the zenana, and arrived to answer her husband's silent need.

Smiling at her as she removed her veil, Khurram's first words told her the content of the message. "She's ordered me to go to Khandahar!"

"She?"

"Nur Jahan."

"But she can't order you to do anything."

"The words in the firman are hers. I know my father, and without her influence, he'd never have *ordered* me, he'd have *asked* me to go."

"Your father is sending you to Khandahar? Meerijan, that's wonderful! You've done so well as commander of his army." When Mumtaz saw anxiety where she expected to see pleasure on her husband's face, her mind raced until she touched upon the problem.

Slowly she spoke. "You'd be in Khandahar if something should happen to your father."

"Shah Abbas' troops can be predicted to keep my forces engaged for an extended time. In addition, there are warring tribes living in the hills around the fort who'd delight at shooting us. The empire's supply line extends only to Kabul, not all the way to Khandahar. Laying siege to the fort brings up two more worries. The first is our inadequate artillery. The second is the casualties most likely to be inflicted upon us when we have the fort surrounded."

Mumtaz saw another difficulty for Khurram. "If you weren't successful against the Persian forces *and* the local tribes, it would further hurt your chance of succession."

Being free to voice his frustration with a woman who loved him regardless, Khurram continued, "I don't believe the conclusion to the conflict would come quickly. Khandahar is far, unfamiliar, and inhospitable. The Deccani rulers would fight for me—but not for a long time and not so far from their homes."

"If Jahangir died, what would Nur Jahan do?"

Khurram had already thought about this.

Leaning his chin on his fist, he coldly predicted the moves he had already imagined. "She'd fortify the position of emperor for Shariyar and see that he was crowned before I could return from Khandahar. He'd obey your auntie who probably would have already swayed critical nobles to her side with promises of riches and advancement. As a grieving widow, she'd be even more difficult to refuse. To take the crown myself, I'd have to battle the very forces I've been leading in my father's name.

"I know the Deccan, and I'd be much more effective here than in Khandahar which is an entirely different terrain—and weather. My command in Afghanistan would undoubtedly be difficult, and I'm uncertain I'm up to the rigors it requires."

"Why don't you tell your father you won't go?"

Khurram stared at his wife. "Taj," he spoke slowly, "Father sent his command to me as a firman. There's no way to refuse. Yet, if I accept the honor of fighting in a distant territory at the head of my father's troops, I sacrifice my security and any chance of being in Agra to claim my birthright."

"But," repeated Mumtaz softly, "you can't refuse his command."

"That's exactly my quandary. I can't go. I can't stay. I must obey the firman, yet to do so goes against all common sense."

After Mumtaz left, Khurram continued to pace and mutter. Trying to work his mind around the two disastrous choices before him, he asked Allah for guidance. Then he stopped, stood for a moment, and smiled. He had the glimmer of an idea. Talking to himself, jabbing his finger absently as he paced, Khurram came to a halt, grinned in satisfaction at the empty room, and stretched.

Striding to Mumtaz' quarters, he found her sleeping. After briefly adoring her peaceful face, he awakened her .

Mumtaz started out of her sleep, saw who it was, and smiled at him sleepily. He watched as her eyes blinked and then opened wide, remembering his quandary and asking without words to be told of his decision.

"We'll be leaving the Deccan shortly and heading north," he told his wife. Khurram knew what he had to do and do quickly. Already a message had been sent to Bokhari stating his own infinite respect and loyalty to his emperor and agreeing to travel north. Bokhari would reach Agra faster than he could, and Jahangir would soon be pleased to know his son was in motion.

24

India - 1623

Although he'd quickly ridden north as he had promised, Khurram had never intended to make the entire trip. Stopping partway at Mandu, he sent a messenger to Agra, and then announced to those who traveled with him that they would be staying until he received a reply.

Khurram wanted to avoid going to Khandahar as intensely as he had wanted to march south to Rajasthan years before. There was nothing to prove now, he was older and he had experienced the costs of long military campaigns. He did not need to ride, fight, and kill to carve out an empire. Although Khurram felt the pull of adventure, he was clear this was neither the time nor the place for him to have one.

"Why are we staying here, Meerijan?"

"I've sent a messenger to Bapu telling him I'll serve him well in the task of thwarting Shah Abbas' transgression. I pointed out the rainy season was only two months away, and my troops are too tired to march to Khandahar before then. They're reluctant to face the downpours, the floods, and the high winds of the monsoon in addition to the hardships of battle. I humbly requested we be permitted to stay here in Mandu until the rains are over."

Mumtaz recognized all of what she just heard as Khurram's plan to avoid Khandahar. Suspecting there might have been more to the message than her husband had shared, she asked, "Did you write anything else, Khurram?"

Use of his name, rather than the usual endearment, told him her question was serious. He sighed in recognition of her infallible instincts and knew he would be unsuccessful if he tried to keep his plan from her.

"I said I wanted complete control of the army and the sole ability to promote and demote as I decide."

"Hasn't the emperor always promoted and demoted officers himself?"

"Yes."

"Do you think he'll change his mind and give you the authority you request?"

He would, thought Khurram glumly, but Nur Jahan will never let me get away with it. Aloud he said simply, "Perhaps."

"Khurram …was there anything else?"

"The Fort at Ranthambor," he admitted. "It's a lovely and spacious fort within our empire, and I'd like to have it for my family."

Trying to erase the look of disbelief on his wife's face after the admission, Khurram hurried on. "There are spacious areas for us there and room for much of the army. It's strongly built." His final comment had been spoken as though pleading with her to throw her enthusiasm behind his plan.

"But we've always lived comfortably. We don't need to own a fort."

Khurram explained to Mumtaz who had rarely been unable to follow his reasoning. "I don't really want the fort. It's simply another reason my father might release me from going to Khandahar."

Understanding finally washed across Mumtaz' face. "So the story about the monsoon, the promotions, and the fort are nothing but ploys? You're hoping if you agree to obey your father and his firman, but then make a list of conditions that Jahangir will replace you?" She stared at him. "Is there anything else?"

Khurram, decisive and positive when leading his troops, found it difficult to meet the eyes of the woman who could read his heart, the woman who dared to differ with him.

"Yes." There was a short pause. "But only one more request." Even though he knew he did not *have* to tell her anything, he knew he would. "I also made it a condition that the Punjab be added to my lands."

"The Punjab?" Mumtaz threw her hands in the air in surprise. "That's one of the richest farmlands in the entire empire."

"Exactly," Khurram beamed. "He'll never agree. We'll soon be returning to the Deccan. Even I wouldn't pay my price if I were in my father's shoes, Taj. Surely, he'll find someone else for his campaign, and we can remain in India. With time, the memory of this event will fade, and I'll regain my former prestige because I've proven my loyalty by obeying the firman."

Mumtaz was thinking that the plan was far too risky. Simultaneously she was delighted. It was daring, courageous, and, yes, slippery. It could be the very answer they sought. The plan could work only if Jahangir didn't share the letter with Nur Jahan. If his wife discovered the contents, her view would certainly be different than her husband's. Even so, what could Nur Jahan do? Khurram would either stay in Mandu during the monsoon or, as he hoped, be ordered to return to his duties in the Deccan.

He smiled reassuringly. "Don't worry, Taj. Father has been distant, but he understands me well enough to see through my words as he's always done."

But Mumtaz wasn't as sure as her husband that his scheme would play out the way he visualized.

Khurram, unworried, slept well that night.

❋ ❋ ❋

WHEN KHURRAM'S TERMS WERE READ in Agra, Jahangir was disappointed that his son would not be leaving before the monsoon, but Nur Jahan raged with fury. "How dare he! How dare he!" she repeated over and over. Even as she strode forcefully, with tightly fisted hands, she knew her husband was puzzled at her reaction. Although she could read between the lines of the letter from Khurram with the same awareness that enabled Khurram to know her thoughts when he had received the firman, Jahangir was not privy to the full scale of their rivalry.

Controlling her exasperation, Nur Jahan had to interpret her stepson's request in a way that would convince Jahangir of his Khurram's deviousness while increasing her husband's reliance on her.

She stepped close to Jahangir and stared into his eyes. "Don't you understand, My Love. He's defying you. This brazen son of yours is making up reasons he can't lead the army now. The idea of someone, anyone, ignoring a royal firman is unthinkable. It's never been done before, and it shouldn't be allowed now. He is showing no respect for your direct orders."

Her vehemence was again too much to contain. Nur Jahan moved from Jahangir, needing additional space between them to deal with her anger. "He's getting too smug for his own good and is beginning to take matters of the empire into his own hands. His concerns are for himself only, and there's no regard for you." Her words were meant to strike Jahangir where he was the most vulnerable.

"Nor is Khurram considering your empire," she continued. "He's being deliberately defiant to you as both his emperor and father. No," she continued, beginning to see the impact of her words on Jahangir's face, "he's more than being defiant, even though defiance would be bad enough. He's ungrateful. That's it. He's ungrateful even after all the trust, rank, and support you've given him."

"This ungratefulness to you, my gentle, loving husband," she lowered her voice and looked at him with great tenderness, "is worse than anything else. It's worse than lying, vanity, and even drunkenness."

Slowly, responding to the power of his wife's conviction, Jahangir was led to agree that Khurram should be reprimanded for his insulting list of demands. "This letter displeases me," he finally said, nodding vigorously to placate his seriously distraught wife.

"Displeases you!" shouted Nur Jahan, feeling her internal fire flame.

Jahangir asked with genuine consternation, "What else should I do?"

Deciding to bring Jahangir quickly into line with her thinking, Nur Jahan seized the opportunity before her. She would completely eliminate the possibility of Khurram on the throne if she chose her words carefully. With Jahangir's full attention, her determination, and a bit of help from Cobra, she would have what she wanted. She had posed this very question to herself earlier and had hoped her husband would give her the opportunity to lay out her plan. Remaining quiet, as if she were in deep thought, Nur Jahan waited to give her response.

She had already concluded Khurram's popularity and leadership were a double threat. But if he was not going to use the trained and equipped men under his command to join with the Imperial forces, she reasoned, he had no need for them. Further, if Khurram had no attacking force, her own success would be assured.

"There's only one thing to do," she said slowly when she had deemed enough time had passed to give the illusion of contemplation. "He doesn't expect you to give in to his demands. He probably thinks you'll allow him to return to the Deccan, which is neither useful to the empire nor does it obey your orders.

"We..." she corrected herself, "you...must act quickly." Her plan sounded even better to her as she spoke, the words gaining volume and force as she outlined her thoughts. "His vain demands need to be slashed with your swift action. His disobedience is an indication of the evil soul he's managed to keep hidden from you until now. He must be quickly brought back to a position of loyalty, or the empire could well be lost." She paused, using silence to imbue her next words with the power to inspire Jahangir to action.

The room was filled with a calculated and dramatic stillness.

Then Nur Jahan uttered the words that had been in her mind since the Cobra had fed them to her. "You must strip your ungrateful and temperamental son of his army. Order him to send it to you at Agra. Immediately."

Jahangir gasped. Fully aware that the next move was his, his mind filled with unaccustomed and conflicting thoughts. He sat slowly lifting his wine cup to his lips again and again, as though seeking guidance from the red liquid.

I've always believed Khurram has been loyal and supportive. But if that's true, why would Nur Jahan say he must be brought back to the path of loyalty if he hasn't already strayed? Maybe my wife doesn't realize how severe it is to take an army from a prince. The shock of being without men to command could crumple my son. I don't want that. I only want Khurram to obey his orders from me.

But if I don't do what my wife feels so passionately about, I could lose her... How can it be that a man should have to choose between his wife and his son?

Engrossed in his own mental turmoil, Jahangir was unaware of Nur Jahan's careful observation of him. Watching his face, wanting to read his mind, she sat without movement, her hands bunched into tight fists in her lap. *If Jahangir calls his son's army to Agra, my struggle against Khurram will be over and my desired future will move more swiftly toward me. My enemy would be without support, and helpless. I've given Jahangir my plan and now I have to wait to see if he will accept it.*

Jahangir finally raised his eyes, looked at his wife, and nodded with a heaviness he did not try to conceal. Nur Jahan immediately called for scroll and brush. In spite of his lack of conviction, Jahangir composed a letter to his son with words stronger than the feelings in his heart. Even as he felt his breath become shallow and raspy, he wrote to proud, passionate Khurram that he was to be stripped of his army. By the time Nur Jahan began to dictate, he was beyond reacting and dutifully wrote what she said.

※ ※ ※

DAYS LATER, IN MANDU, Khurram sat in stunned belief at the words his father had written. ..."send army immediately to Agra," "demands rooted in ambition and vanity," "not your time yet to wear the crown."

Khurram paced and talked in his distress. "He would've respected my decision as one he himself might make if Nur Jahan hadn't been with him. Father and I shouldn't be exchanging harmful letters. If this had happened without Nur Jahan he would have asked, not commanded, me to go north. My list of demands would have been seen for the smokescreen they are; and I'd be returning to the Deccan with my father's blessings. Father has been even more strongly influenced by Nur Jahan than I've realized. He and I have been pushed apart by her, and it's time for one of us to make it clear the distance must be repaired."

He stopped his pacing and picked up a favorite likeness of his father. He remembered the kindness, the generosity, and the love he had known from this man. He would never forget the first Victory Durbar when the depth of the emperor's feeling radiated through the arms that surrounded him with the public embrace.

"I'll do what I should have done, earlier," he spoke aloud. "I'll write a personal letter to him, explaining why I've come to Mandu rather than Agra. When he receives the words written with my own hand, his love and affection for me shall be rekindled." Speaking to the painting he held in both of his hands, he whispered to it, "We won't let this new gulf between us widen, Father."

Mumtaz appeared at his side during his midday meal. She had been informed the dispatch had arrived and knew Khurram would want to discuss it. Seeing him take only small servings of favorite dishes and decline other special food she had ordered for him, she prepared for bad news.

Toying with her golden bangles, Mumtaz asked, "What did your father say?" When Khurram shared what had been in the letter, she was equally angry at the humiliating loss of his army.

"What's next, Meerijan?"

Khurram pushed his plate away, motioned the serving woman to leave, and turned to his trusted wife. "I'm willing to fight my stepmother, but not ready to stand against my father. I must separate the two in my mind by letting my father know I'm still the worthy son I've always been."

A Tartar guard slipped into the dining area and apologetically handed Khurram a scroll. It said that a second messenger had arrived from Agra and insisted that what he carried should be delivered immediately to the prince.

Khurram turned the rolled paper in his hands noticing the seal of the empress. As he broke the seal and unrolled the scroll, he wondered if her words would contain an antidote to his father's harsh message. They did not.

In bold writing, Nur Jahan declared Shah Abbas and the Persians wouldn't wait until the rains ended, so Khurram needed to go to Khandahar right away. If the prince found it offensive to brave the rains, the emperor would find a leader less timorous. She repeated the words of his father saying, "If you are not inclined to take your army to Khandahar, you are to send it immediately to Agra where it will then go farther north under a different commander." Her letter inflamed the sense of loss that Khurram had been fighting since his father's message had arrived.

Abruptly Nur Jahan's written words and tone changed. She told Khurram his reluctance to obey the earlier firman was a cause of serious concern to Jahangir. She requested him to change his unfortunate decision even at this late date and reminded him piously that unquestioning obedience was the hallmark of loyalty. The consequences of his ill-advised demands could be physically harmful to his father.

Khurram and Mumtaz looked at one another after Khurram read the words aloud. "She sent this to rub salt into the gash she herself has inflicted," he said in unbelieving tones. "How does she think she'll get away with rebuking me, even as she gives me another order? She's gone too far this time. Dispatch my army?

Never! Allow myself to become undefended? Never!" He jumped to his feet and crumpled the message in his hand.

Khurram wanted desperately to prevent the clash he feared would come if he did not act quickly. Calling for paper and brush as soon as he arrived in his own quarters, he began to write. Eloquent words of his love and loyalty filled the paper. He swore he was the honest and loyal son Jahangir had always assumed. He reiterated that he would never disobey his father and hoped Jahangir believed him. When he was finally satisfied with the wording, he called his most trusted courier, Allami Azal Khan, to deliver the emotional message he had just written to his father. He had committed a portion of his heart on paper.

Allami, knowing the value of the words he carried, traveled quickly to the Imperial Court in Agra, assuming he would be ushered at once into the presence of Jahangir. He imagined the emperor would read the message, allow the words to seep into his core, shed a few loving tears for his son and immediately write a reply of forgiveness. His vision was similar to the one held by Khurram.

It didn't happen as either had expected. When Allami appeared with a message to Jahangir from Prince Khurram, he was affronted by the lowliness of the room where he was told to wait. After waiting for hours, he was not led to Jahangir's quarters as expected, but told to give the scroll to a servant who would deliver it to Nur Jahan. The empress would then take it to Jahangir.

Diplomatic arguments were to no avail. Seeing he had no choice but to pass Khurram's personal message to Nur Jahan's servant, Allami did so. An even longer wait ensued during which he was treated scornfully and coldly by all who came into the room. Allami, a man who had served many years in the complex maze of Mughal machinations, had been unable to perform the task given to him. He returned to Mandu empty handed and reported to Khurram of his degrading treatment and his opinion that Jahangir had never seen the letter.

Listening to Allami, Khurram knew Nur Jahan had finally

done it. She had pushed him over the edge he had tried to avoid. His fury was so overwhelming, he could not move other than to drum the fingers of his right hand on his knee and to shake his head at her insulting treatment of his exalted messenger. *Her handling of Allami revealed the arrogance of a crafty queen being deliberately rude, not only to the courier, but to the royal prince he represented. Does she think I am merely a nameless soldier in the vast Imperial Army? I'll show her I am the son of the emperor, a man who'd inherited royal blood from both parents, a contender for the throne, a successful commander, and the leader of my own armed force. f there is to be a war between us, I intend to win.*

That night the light in Khurram's room cast shadows that paced, stopped, and paced again. Absentmindedly twisting the pearls he wore around his neck. He was no longer the loving son wanting to maintain a intimacy with his father. He was Prince Khurram, a soldier fighting for his birthright. Although publicly his fight was against his father, privately he knew the person he had to defeat was his stepmother.

He was being drawn toward a conflict he no longer tried to resist. Allah had ordained he sit on the throne, and Khurram would see to it. His heavenly will would be aided by the prince's own earthly force. The successes he had earned in past battles, his gunpowder, horses, and brave army, would all be put to good use. Having come to his decision, Khurram was resolute. From his mother's blood, he was a Rajput, eager for a fight, a warrior who enjoyed battlefield action. In addition to the armor he wore, he was protected by a strong sense of righteousness and an eagerness to grab this opportunity to defeat Nur Jahan.

When the morning dawned, Khurram was fresh and ready to face his troops even though he had been awake many hours planning his attack against the Imperial Army. Filled with confidence, he had accepted the seriousness of his planned actions as the only option open to a proud man.

In a stirring speech, Khurram asked each man to stand by his side and defend him as they attacked Agra Fort. Optimism was high in the prince's camp, and even though the Imperial Army was much larger and experienced, his dedicated soldiers swore allegiance. Knowing Jahangir was ill, they wondered if this might be the only battle to fight before their leader was crowned the Great Mughal. In their minds, many of them began spending their unearned but expected reward from Khurram even as they readied themselves to attack.

25

Three days after Khurram's attack on Agra

Mumtaz shivered with excitement. Alert with the fear of being found out, she moved toward her midnight rendezvous. The following morning, she and Khurram would leave to continue the rebellion against the Nur Jahan-influenced Jahangir which had not been, as he had hoped, conclusively decided in the initial battle three days earlier.

She felt her elephant stop even as the sound of two low male voices came through the protective curtains. The large animal below her knelt, lowering the howdah forward, rocked back, and then leveled its back and remained down on all four knees. Two mahouts were whispering in the night. Then silence. Footsteps. Suddenly, the darkness of her howdah was sliced with the brilliance coming from a lantern held by the man leaning toward her.

"Bapu!"

"Arjumand!"

Father and daughter looked at one another with both happiness and sorrow, for this may be the last time they saw each other. He loved his beautiful daughter and the joy she and her family had brought into his life. In turn, she cherished this man who had tossed her in the air when she was very young. When she was older, Mumtaz had listened to him and her grandfather speak of their involvement with the empire, absorbing valuable political astuteness from their examples and wisdom.

"You're leaving in the morning?' he asked.

"As soon as it's light, we'll be on our way."

"Which direction are you heading?"

She looked at him sadly, took his hand in both of hers, and, with her eyes lowered, replied, "Bapu, even if I knew, which I don't, I couldn't tell you."

"Of course, Arjumand. Forgive me for asking." Mumtaz heard the childhood name she had almost forgotten spoken tenderly by her father and ached for the loss he was facing.

Mumtaz knew of the closeness between her father and his sister, Nur Jahan, the very woman Khurram was fighting. For years, Mumtaz had watched Auntie bring Asaf Khan into her increasingly powerful position at Jahangir's side. Although confident that her father would have risen to his current rank on his own, she assumed his progress had been speeded by his prominent sister.

In spite of his obligations to Nur Jahan, Asaf Khan didn't want to say goodbye to this woman and her family. He had long ignored the rift between Nur Jahan and Khurram, hoping he would never have to choose between his powerful sister and his daughter.

With Khurram's failure to speedily snatch his father's throne, Asaf Khan knew he must make a decision. After much soul searching, he had come to a conclusion. Unaware of the great extent to which Nur Jahan was responsible for the rebellion and believing in the importance of the Mughal Empire, Asaf Khan remained loyal to Jahangir and his sister. He would not harm the empire.

When Khurram rebelled, Mumtaz had to accept drastic changes in her relationships with Jahangir, Nur Jahan, and most sadly, her father. After his son chose to attack him for the crown, could Jahangir ever welcome his daughter-in-law back into the royal circle? There were many harsh and evil things about her Auntie but Mumtaz could remember many times when she had helped her. Knowing she would keep the bright memories of these people and not review the dark ones, Mumtaz had to be content with their place in her heart. Her recent loss of another baby boy, one who hadn't lived long enough to be named, filled her with a need to reach out, cling to the living people she held dear.

"I can't accept that you and I are on opposite sides of this battle, Bapu."

"It's also difficult for me to realize you are leaving in the morning."

Asaf Khan's voice lowered, "When you leave with Khurram, you take my grandchildren." His eyes watered as he asked her to keep their memories of him alive.

Mumtaz knew that her children loved their grandfather as much as he adored them. His joy with them was evident when they were on his lap, singly or doubly. It wasn't unusual to see the children hanging onto his body, holding a leg, or draped over his shoulder. He removed his jewelry so it wouldn't cause injuries or be pulled out of his ears as they wrestled and played. He'd even allowed Dara to unwind his turban.

Mumtaz felt a wave of her father's pain at losing his daughter, his son-in-law, and his grandchildren. She couldn't be harsh with him nor, she realized, could she change his mind—even though she had to try.

"Bapu, can you come with us?"

He looked at her for a very long time before he spoke. "You know I cannot. No, Arjumand, I've sworn an oath of loyalty to Jahangir, and I'll stay beside him even as you stay with Khurram"

"We're on separate paths. I believe my husband is right, I love him, and I'll be at his side as he travels to fight for the position he deserves. Your choice saddens me, but it doesn't surprise me."

Then she smiled, hoping to raise his spirits with a compliment. "Perhaps, I learned my loyalty from you."

"Perhaps," he whispered sadly.

26

Two years later ~ 1625

The rebellion between the proud and clever personalities lasted more than two years. Without Nur Jahan, Khurram would have been quickly victorious, but the empress' instincts and the powerful Imperial Army she controlled through Jahangir were more than the prince could defeat.

The moon oscillated from crescent to fullness many times as the weary prince won one decisive battle only to lose the next. The size of his army fluctuated with the outcome of the battles and his continuing ability to pay the men who fought for him. Receiving no money from Agra, Khurram depended solely upon his personal treasure and what he took from his victories.

The beleaguered prince found both gratification and disappointment among the kings in India. Those willing to pledge themselves and their treasury to his support were outnumbered by others who refused to assist him, offering only gracious but short-lived hospitality. They took no chance that their friendship to Khurram would bring Jahangir's Imperial Army to their land.

After two years of being a rebel in the land he thought he would rule, dragging his homeless wife and children with him, and beginning to lose more battles than he won, Khurram sued for peace. It was 1625 and he had exhausted his health, his men, and his money while being chased in a full circle around the empire.

"I've nothing left, Taj. I've no wealth, army, or even hope to become emperor. If I'd continued to fight, I'd have harmed everyone who's been loyal to me." Because he was a prince, Khurram was not killed. On this point, Jahangir stood firmly against Nur Jahan's desire for Khurram's death. Jahangir adhered to the Timurid Code which forbade the killing of royalty. Instead, Khurram was forced to live permanently within the borders of the Deccan without an army.

Mumtaz hoped the calm life in the Deccan would heal her exhausted and stressed husband. As she listened to him, she massaged his temples, trying to relieve his tension and hopelessness about never becoming the emperor. Again he felt the humiliation and distress as he had in Agra when he watched Shariyar being favored. It was the heavy defeat of a man whose lengthy attempt to fulfill what he felt was his destiny had failed.

"I can't return to my former home in Agra. I've only a token number of soldiers under my command. The Red Tent is no longer mine and the lands I used to own now belong to Shariyar." Even Mumtaz' gentle circles on his temples gave him none of the pleasure he usually felt. "Father used to praise me," he continued glumly," but now when he refers to me in his journals, he doesn't write my name, only used the word 'wretch' instead."

"Remember what the astrologer said, Meerijan. My destiny is to marry an emperor."

He simply looked at her, only a weak belief in his eyes.

Khurram sat up to face Mumtaz. "Why has fortune forsaken me? There seems to be no harmony, no order left in creation. If there were, surely I'd be sitting on the throne in Agra."

With all of his lamenting, Khurram hadn't spoken of a matter that deeply concerned him, the choice of crown or coffin. If he didn't receive the crown, his future was the coffin. If he were the Great Mughal, he would see that his competition was taken out of the world. Even if Shariyar didn't think of the gruesome deed himself, there was no question in his mind that Nur Jahan would suggest it.

Khurram needed a plan to ensure a future for Mumtaz and their children. He knew he couldn't allow his family to die for him and his elusive destiny.

One evening he glanced toward Taj and was aware of the resilience she had shown during the last two years. When they had been moving throughout the empire from one battle to another, Mumtaz had lived with few servants, clothes she didn't change all day, and only a portion of her sumptuous jewelry. In addition, she had given birth to a son, Maurad, and was again pregnant. *She should have a home of the finest marble, hundreds of attendants, and rare and beautiful treasures surrounding her befitting her strength, loyalty, and love. I wanted to do better for her.*

Mumtaz, now laughing at 2-year-old Maurad's delight when her husband pulled the noisy stringed toy horse for him, remembered the last years differently than her husband did. Her thoughts were of admiration for Khurram who had made certain his family was cared for even as he was enmeshed in his fight for the crown. *It would have been a family adventure if we were not being pursued. I relished the time without palace duties, found I didn't need more help than I had, and cherished being with the children. It was a time I remember fondly except for the heaviness it brought to Khurram.*

Khurram's face was relaxed and happy this night, but Mumtaz' face clouded as she recalled the physical and mental collapse he had suffered. It was one of the reasons he had ended the rebellion. When they were alone, Mumtaz looked up from her embroidery and asked, "Meerijan, do you remember our island stay?"

Appreciating her attempt to convert memories of his rebellion into memories of sights and places, he answered thoughtfully. "The one in Rajasthan? Yes, I remember it well." Not only did he recall the visit, but he knew it would have been impossible several years earlier. The island Mumtaz referred to belonged to none other than the Rana of Mewar, the very man who had surrendered after Khurram's campaign in his desert land.

This rana had several homes in Udaipur, his city in central Rajasthan, which included an imposing City Palace and a hillside Monsoon Palace. His third palace, for use during the summer months, was a breathtaking white marble palace floating in the middle of Lake Pichola.

When he realized Khurram was heading toward Udaipur, the rana had pondered his options. To offer him hospitality would be both fitting and foolish. Fitting because of the rana's admiration and respect for his military acumen and his princely status, foolish because allowing a rebellious prince to live in his palace would anger Jahangir.

The rana's solution was to ensconce Khurram and his family on a smaller island that shared the same lake as his floating palace. This island, Jag Mandir, offered total privacy though it was less grand than the Floating Palace.

"I remember the life-sized carved elephants standing in a row with their trunks in the air," smiled Mumtaz.s

"And the elaborate black marble gazebo I had built in the garden."

"Remember the City Palace across the lake? It was so beautiful at sunset when it became the color of the setting sun."

"We were safe there with the entire lake as our moat," Khurram remembered.

Their memories of the white marble, the uncluttered spaces, and the entrancing garden watered by the surrounding lake would be of greater importance than they suspected in the future that only one of them would live to see.

27

Deccan – 1625

The hot wind and the rising temperatures in the Deccan, where he was required to live, swept Khurram's thoughts toward the more comfortable north. He remembered how his father, when the chilly but welcome coolness of winter was finished in the plains of Agra, often planned the perilous trip to Kashmir. This month-long journey was possible only when the weather allowed him to cross the high, cold, and treacherous mountains guarding the Vale of Kashmir.

Summer in the plains of Agra was a season of dry, blistering air filled with dust. In the excessive heat, the earth was parched, trees became leafless, and energy-sapped animals moved only when necessary. Wind scorched lungs and heated walls making them too hot to touch. People lay in the open air without coverings: in the city they were in the streets, in villages they were on stringed beds. Those lucky enough to have gardens went to them even though the air was not cool, only less stifling.

In June the relentlessly blue sky would host a wisp of a cloud. Gradually, it would multiply and become enlarged with the moisture drawn from the land by the upward-traveling heat. With great anticipation, the inhabitants of the plains watched as the clouds continued to darken and cover the land. Finally, they were joined by wind, thunder, and lightning and at last the release of torrents of beloved rain. The monsoon had arrived.

This was a joyous season of ten to twenty rainbursts a day with pleasant weather in between. To Jahangir, however, nothing was more delightful than being in the mountains of Kashmir where he vacationed as often as possible during this time of the year.

Khurram had learned that Jahangir would again be traveling north accompanied by Nur Jahan, Shariyar, and Ladili. He ached to be there as well for he shared his father's obsession for the precious jewel of northern land filled with fruit, flowers, and rushing water.

Even the luxury of the royal camp could not completely protect the travelers from the physical and mental hardships of the cold, bitter winds, snow, and treacherous footings on the road to Kashmir. Though it was called a road, the ground underfoot that led the visitors over the Pir Panchal Mountains bore little resemblance to the smooth thoroughfares of the plains.

Khurram smiled as he thought of the months he spent in the Kashmir paradise. It began with a first dramatic sight of the valley below and ended with a departing look as they turned to the mountains they would climb on their return to the Plains. The valley was fringed by snow-topped mountains and decorated with masses of wildflowers. Hillsides of green, terraced grasslands and lengthy narrow trails combined with breathtaking waterfalls to welcome travelers to the idyllic vacation grounds. Mughal ingenuity along with the natural beauty of the mountainous vale had created Khurram's favorite delight of all, the gardens.

Inspired by descriptions of gardens in the Koran, Mughals faithfully included all four features mentioned in the book when they created their oases. First was a surrounding wall, tall enough to keep the world away from the thoughtful beauty inside. This also served as a physical barrier between the secular and spiritual world. Second, the entire garden was divided into equal quadrants representing four, a powerful number. The third essential was water, a symbol of well-being in an arid world. Water was usually contained in channels to divide the garden into quarters and then again to divide each of these smaller quadrants into four sections, resulting in sixteen equal spaces. The fourth feature was a multitude of flowers, bushes, and trees planted in regular and symmetrical lines repeated exactly in every square.

Before visiting Kashmir, Khurram had known gardens only on the level plains where the four elements designed within the walls were in vivid contrast to the arid land outside. The thick barriers became an important separation between the garden and the rest of the world. Moving water was sedately pumped within channels as it flowed in the flat garden.

The geography of Kashmir required each of the four requirements to be dramatically adapted. The wall was not needed because the native plants and trees that grew on the steep slopes kept the terraces private. The gardens rose steeply, water cascaded down terraces, chutes, and channels into Dal Lake below. Pavilions, thrones, and terraces were built beside and over the rushing water. Flowers of yellow, orange, purple, and white were planted along either side of the gurgling flow. Beginning sleepily at the highest levels, the water came to life as it raced, danced, skipped, and chortled to the bottom.

Plantings of the pleasure gardens allowed those who strolled the paths to breathe deeply of the flowers' perfume, to cool themselves in the fountain spray, and to view the lush growth around them. Khurram allowed the memories to flood his mind: floating houseboats bedecked with lights…music…enchanting lakeside parties…the cool water on his fingertips as he was paddled across the lake while reclining in a shikara.

His pleasant reverie extended for hours until the multitude off stars appeared over the Deccan. They were the same ones he had viewed in Kashmir. Leaning back on his elbows for a more direct view of the heavens, Khurram contemplated his future.

Does one of these twinkling lights control my destiny?. I've always though I'd become emperor. Why would Allah deceive me all these years if the light from my Star of Destiny wasn't going to reach me?

Absently pulling the grass growing around his cushion, Khurram continued to muse.

I'd soon be emperor if it weren't for Nur Jahan. Allah, who knows about everything, must know about her. Must know she would be part of the Mughal royalty. Must have known her threat.

Striking his open hand forcefully with his curled fist, he began speaking to the stars above him. "I should be at my father's side. I should be his admired son, not a wretch. Nur Jahan has poisoned his mind against me." His voice began softly, but got louder as his emotions reflected his building anger and frustration. "I should hate Nur Jahan. She is taking my birthright—everything I've been trained for, studied for, expected."

Both clenched fists were at his temples, his bowed head was filled with thoughts of the woman who had caused him to feel such rage. *She* decides who will become the Great Mughal, he thought. Surely, Father had already chosen me. Yet, here I am in the Deccan, hundreds of miles from them together in Kashmir.

Khurram's dark thoughts reflected none of the sky's beauty.

28

Kashmir ~ 1627

Of all the people struggling up the mountains that surrounded the Vale of Kashmir, Jahangir was the happiest. Behind him were the plains of Agra with its browning grass, hot air, and flowers past their prime. He was filled with the anticipation of seeing his beloved sanctuary once again.

Jahangir reveled in the crisp air, thin sun, and the sights of spring's harbingers growing fresh and proud through the snow. He exulted in the indentations snowy hares had left in the pristine white fields and the sound of the gurgling streams swollen by melted ice. Jahangir no longer noticed the sudden loud cracks of iced limbs falling as he endured the stinging rains, snowy days, and biting cold for the pleasure of vacationing in Kashmir.

Excited as a youngster at a party, Jahangir seemed to drop years from his age as the summit was reached. Eagerly, he urged his horse up the last incline and stopped, thrilled as he always was, at the sight before him. His heart beat faster as his eyes took in the fields of vibrant flowers that painted the valleys and the hillsides. Huge trees surrounded terraced green fields of rice. Gigantic natural gardens bloomed with almond and peach blossoms, violets, narcissus, and blue jasmine. Irises and tulips carpeted rooftops. After the chill mountain air, the caressing breeze tinged with only a light scent of distant snow was a welcome change. The aromatic flowers held none of the dust and heaviness of the plains.

The promise of the enchanting sight before him pushed unpleasant thoughts from Jahangir's head. He had left Agra feeling anger toward his wretch of a son who dared to rebel against him, puzzlement over the flabby son his wife seemed to favor, and the suspicion that Nur Jahan was a different woman with others than she was with him. He would deal with these and other issues when he returned, but not now.

He had left summer behind him in Agra, had traveled through the mountainous winter, and was now refreshed by the joyful air of a burgeoning spring. He, and those who traveled with him, would stay through spring and summer and leave only because the snows in autumn made their return impossible any later in the year. The exhilaration Jahangir felt was contagious and soon nearly everyone was smiling, laughing, and relaxing as the tensions of mountain travel slipped away.

When he passed a large meadow filled with colorful flowers he bellowed, "Guards!" The trained men wheeled around and with quickly-executed maneuvers protectively surrounded their emperor. Jahangir, appreciative of their readiness, explained he was in no danger but wanted them to perform a task for him. Soon, they were picking flowers in the meadows. Grumbling, the stalwart men wondered how Jahangir planned to use the flowers before they wilted. Soon enough they found out. They were ordered to tuck the flowers they'd gathered into their turbans, then remount. The delighted Jahangir rode the rest of the afternoon enjoying his own meadow of bobbing flowers ahead of him.

With pauses for artists to sketch new plants and flowers for the books Jahangir was constantly compiling, the party finally reached Dal Lake, ringed with snowy mountain peaks. Drops of water sparkled on lily pads floating on its surface.

Invigorated by the increase of pleasure and the decrease of responsibility found in Kashmir, Jahangir took in the spectacular braiding of Allah's natural and unfettered beauty with the carefully controlled gardens he and his ancestors had created.

Sitting at one of these gardens days later, Nur Jahan patted her forehead daintily at the cool fountain and spoke to Shariyar of his life as it would be when he was emperor. Her son-in-law was hungry for the respect Nur Jahan emphasized, and became her even more willing follower as she continued to talk.

Sitting nearby, Ladili sighed softly so her mother could not hear. Nur Jahan was the best of mothers. Then she looked at the man she had married at Nur Jahan's insistence, and Ladili had to admit Nur Jahan was sometimes the worst of mothers.

29

Kashmir - 1627

Nur Jahan heard Ladili's light footstep coming down the hallway, turned her head from the vision outside her window, and watched as her daughter arrived for her morning visit. This hd become a routine to keep the bonds between mother and daughter sweet and strong. It also enabled Nur Jahan to stay abreast of Shariyar's life.

Ladili hadn't inherited Nur Jahan's striking appearance. Only through her eyes could she be recognized as a relative, for they were similar in size and color and framed with lush lashes as were her mother's. Tall, slender almost to the point of bony, Ladili needed additional age to develop the lovely curves she inherited. As a young woman, she was angular where her mother was soft. No one was more aware of the comparison than Ladili herself, the gawky daughter of a famously beautiful empress.

Nur Jahan noticed her daughter wasn't looking well. Even as she took Ladili by the shoulders and leaned forward to touch cheeks, she felt a twinge of guilt for saddling her with the overweight and stupid Shariyar. Then she remembered Ladili's future as an empress, and how fortunate it was that Shariyar was not offended by Ladili's less than exciting looks. Should Shariyar perform his duty as a husband and her daughter conceive, pregnancy might enhance her attractiveness.

"How is your husband?" Nur Jahan asked. She hadn't seen him

for several days. To herself she admitted the only reason she spent time with her uninteresting son-in-law was to continue weaving their lives more closely. She was using their time together to explain her positions on policies of the empire as well as her personal agenda. She was also improving his court etiquette and his knowledge of Mughal history. She still needed to teach Shariyar to function according to her wishes even when she was not present.

Believing everything was going well for her, Nur Jahan ignored a fleeting sense of danger. Her influence on the emperor was so complete she even had the option to choose the successor who perfectly fit her need to rule. Khurram, the greatest threat to her plan, had failed to take the throne in his rebellion and was now contained in the Deccan. As a bonus, all three of the players in the drama of succession were together in Kashmir. Nothing could go wrong now.

Quite unexpectedly, Ladili blurted, "Mother, my husband is afflicted with a terrible illness and it's getting worse."

The fear flickered again, this time it was more pronounced. Something unknown... Ignoring the panic in her daughter's voice, Nur Jahan pulled herself inward toward her central core where Cobra resided.

"What are Shariyar's symptoms?" she asked in a sharp voice that matched her look toward Ladili. "What do you see?" She had to know the details and learn as much as she could before she and Cobra could make the right decision. Even now, she felt the uncoiling presence preparing to assist her.

"It has to do with..." she began, embarrassed and hesitant. "It seems...well, his pillow... Oh mother, Shariyar is losing his hair!" wailed Ladili.

Nur Jahan smiled indulgently and relaxed. Such a simple thing. Not a symptom a woman, like herself, would find upsetting. A receding hairline was more disastrous to the young than to anyone else.

"No, Mother, it is much more than his hairline," cried Ladili when Nur Jahan tried to comfort her. "He's losing all the hair

Mughal necklace

from his body. He no longer has a beard, eyebrows, or even eyelashes."

This could be more than she'd originally thought. "Call the Royal Doctor to have him look at Shariyar immediately. Tell him the order comes from me." Nur Jahan found comfort in action. The response conveyed to her trembling daughter that, as usual, mother would take care of the problem.

After examining the hairless prince, Jahangir's doctor joined Nur Jahan outside the bedchamber. "I've only seen two other cases of this sort. Actually, I haven't personally seen even those, but I've heard about them from other doctors. His condition is a rare and relatively benign form of leprosy. No telling how it came to affect him, but we have to deal with the fact he does have a dreadful affliction that could become worse if not treated speedily. The scales that have formed on his skin will continue to spread if we don't move him to a warmer climate. Heated air seems to counteract the spread of his problem."

The empress furrowed her brow and bit her lower lip as she

thought. It was imperative that Shariyar, Jahangir, and she be together.

"May I speak frankly, Empress?"

"Of course."

"I've treated Jahangir for many years and I know the cooler climate of Kashmir is much better for him than the plains would be at this time of the year. The air is thinner and clearer here and it eases his breathing. He's not a strong man, and it makes no medical sense to send him on a long arduous journey to a lower elevation. Though his secondary capital, Lahore, is much closer than Delhi from here, Kashmir is by far more beneficial to his health"

His words reminded Nur Jahan, as he was sure they would, of the main reason for the trip to Kashmir—Jahangir's health. The air refreshed his weak lungs and eased his sometimes-labored breathing. Kashmir was the best place for her husband and the worst place for the man she was grooming to succeed him.

Because of the threat of additional symptoms if Shariyar weren't attended to in warmer surroundings, he and his entourage left the very next day for Lahore. Flat on a litter and moaning with the inconvenience and embarrassment of it all, Shariyar gave himself over to being taken from Kashmir. Watching the departing figures grow smaller and smaller, Nur Jahan wondered if the separation of Shariyar and Jahangir might be significant.

Uncomfortable about the unexpected change in her plans, Nur Jahan tried to turn her mind toward designing a new garden. Many moments passed before she realized she had been staring at the plans thinking not about the color and shape of plants but about her life should Jahangir not live to see his palace in Lahore.

30

Kashmir - 1627

When Shariyar and Ladili were gone, the Vale of Kashmir was different for Nur Jahan. The gardens were as lovely as they had always been, boat rides on the placid lakes were still as calming, and festivals continued to be delightful. But through the remaining months her heart was no longer calm because Shariyar and Jahangir were so far apart. She could feel Cobra's restlessness but could do nothing about the turn of events, for Jahangir ignored her usually successful tactics and refused to leave his cherished Kashmir earlier than planned. He was not breathing easily, even in Kashmir, and was determined to absorb as much of his adored mountains as possible and would not consider departing before the threat of snow.

Spring, summer, and early autumn were wonderful in Kashmir, but the white winters were cruel. Even when the warmest months had passed and the aroma of saffron perfumed the air, the wheat had turned golden, and the trees flamed with color, Jahangir wouldn't seriously think of leaving. He relished these mild days of autumn and, from his carpeted seat in the garden, savored the sight of tall sunshine-colored poplars and the large copper-colored chenar trees. But he couldn't ignore the growing chill in the air, that announced the beginning of winter. Soon he would have to leave.

It was only when the sky darkened, temperatures dropped, and a light snow fell in the foothills that a saddened Jahangir agreed to begin the journey to the plains before their dream in Kashmir became a frozen nightmare.

An atmosphere of uneasiness and confusion surrounded those readying to march back across the mountains. Rumors swirled about the meaning of Shariyar's mysterious departure, Nur Jahan was preoccupied, and Jahangir clearly wasn't well. Staying in the high altitude during a bitterly cold winter was not an option for their ailing emperor. Neither was a long journey to the plains of India. The choice between these two unsatisfactory plans was in the hands of the empress who concluded they would travel only as far as Lahore where her husband would spend the winter. He would be in the more comfortable plains, Shariyar was there, and the trip would be shorter than returning to Agra.

Although only sixty years old, Jahangir, who had mistreated his body often and dangerously during much of his life, was now paying the price for his earlier indulgences. Despite this, travel through the mountains seemed to revive him. He surprised the travelers when he commanded a stop to once again enjoy his passion for a hunt,

Camp was set and beaters encircled an area abundant with deer, and then walked their circle smaller and smaller to increase the concentration of animals in the center. The finest buck of all was cut from the herd and driven toward the waiting emperor. On neither his usual saddle or howdah, Jahangir was hunting from a cushioned platform with his rifle primed and resting on a tripod. Though unable to ride as before, he held the same treasured sporting gun with the ebony stock he had used many times. He waited, wrapped warmly in several Kashmiri shawls—including one twisted around his turban.

The bushes in front of him swayed, and he heard the approaching sounds of running hooves and the labored breathing of the buck. Jahangir, refusing to accept that his strong arm, sharp vision, and dependable accuracy were gone, brushed away all offers of help. Only after the errant bullet left his gun did he realize how poorly he had shot, totally missing the vital region of the animal where its hide covered his heart and lungs. Instead he bloodied the animal in the haunches but didn't drop it. With an adrenaline response instinctive to his breed, the buck lunged crookedly in his heroic attempt to leave this place of pain and return to his does.

Even as the Royal Runner, Diljar, darted to follow the deer's trail of blood, Jahangir slumped in his chair, knowing he'd never hunt again. Allah had given him many hunts and many animals, and he accepted the cherished activity was part of his past.

Astonishingly, the deer ran quickly in spite of the spurting blood pulsing from his wound. Dilijar ran quickly to keep him in sight. He planned to pursue the deer and drive it back toward the emperor, giving the aging man an opportunity to shoot again, surely more accurately the second time.

Although young, Dilijar was well respected. The son of a man who had been Jahangir's Royal Beater for twenty-seven years, Dilijar's ability to understand the animals he chased, his love for his job, and his loyalty to Jahangir had earned him the prestigious position of Royal Runner. He had run animals to Jahangir before, and it was assumed that his speedy legs and keen eyes would again prevail.

Swiftly following the deer through the brush and branches, Dilijar did not know, even if the buck did, that their path ran alongside a cliff. Eight hundred feet of sheer vertical drop was only one step to the side. The deer was moving painfully, following the familiarity of the terrain and responding to his steady supply of adrenaline. Dilijar was running in a darkening and unknown area, watching the deer in front of him more than he watched the trail. He noticed the deer favoring the back left leg below his wound, and hoped he could turn the animal toward Jahangir before it bled to death.

A drifting mist now covered the path with whiffs of whiteness. The innocent softness was thick enough to hide the tree root growing slightly above the level of the path. Not seeing the root before his toe hit it, Dilijar stumbled. Recovery from such a lurch was not a problem for him. If he had been running at a moderate pace, or if he had somewhere to place his feet, the stumble would have done nothing but cause a split-second falter. It was Dilijar's fate that he was running at full speed when his foot came down on nothing but space.

His screams as he fell attracted the other beaters to the spot where he had left the path. Realizing they could do nothing to save him, they prayed collectively before readying themselves to recover what remained of Dilijar.

Later, when Jahangir saw Dilijar's bleeding and broken body, he knew the Angel of Death was near to take him to Allah. The emperor closed his eyes and put his fingertips together, then placed his hands in his lap. He had seen death many times in his lifetime but this broken body of his loyal Runner was a personal omen. He believed he would be with Allah soon.

Thoughts of his own mortality had entered his consciousness when he had wounded the deer, convincing him he had seen a vision of his own death. Jahangir was awake much of the night with fearful dreams and hallucinations. In spite of his lack of sleep, he ordered, and heroically survived, several more days of progress. But the dying man could not escape his fate.

Asaf Khan, accepting his sister's request to join her and her husband, gasped when he saw Jahangir so close to death. Although he was sitting up, Jahangir's skin was white and sweaty, his eyes were glazed, and he had lost much weight. With incoherent words, he made it plain he wanted to toast his own survival.

Nur Jahan ordered wine to be poured into three goblets. She carefully helped her husband raise the cup to his lips because he could no longer do it himself. Jahangir, the emperor who'd had countless cups of wine in his life, the man who'd enjoyed the feel, the taste, and the effect of the liquid of fermented grapes, couldn't swallow even one mouthful.

Nur Jahan chose to stay by his bedside that evening. She alone watched his last night of fretful tossing, turning, and flailing.

31

Kashmir ~ 1627

Only Nur Jahan heard Jahangir's gasping and tortured breaths as she laid her head on his chest with her ear above his laboring heart. Her tears were real as she waited for his death of the man she loved and who had loved her. The last words she spoke as she lay close to him were tender and grateful.

Even after she could no longer hear his heart and knew he was gone, Nur Jahan didn't move. She savored these last moments alone with him, knowing as soon as she moved, she would become the decisive and focused woman of her reputation. She held her husband close, softly emotional with the memory of their love.

Eventually she sat up, placed Jahangir's hands on his chest, leaned forward and gently touched her lips to his forehead.

"The Great Mughal is dead. Long live the Great Mughal," she whispered. She held his face in her hands one last time, lengthening the moment before she would leave.

Standing, she turned her body slowly, leaving her eyes on Jahangir's face as long as she could, hovering between her past as Jahangir's wife and the arrival of her well-planned future. Turning, she stepped hesitantly. Her strides gradually became more resolute by the time she reached the door. Her first words to those waiting outside the door were a brisk announcement and two commands.

"The Emperor Jahangir is dead. When he's readied for viewing, you may pay your final respects." The quiet men in the hallway absorbed the enormity of this news. Though they had been expecting the announcement, their silence reflected respect for the man who had just passed away.

"Asaf," she spoke to her nearby brother, "have the Royal Physician prepare the body for funeral rites to be held here as soon as possible. There should be the usual four days of mourning and alms. When the passes are open this spring, I'll return for his body and have it properly interred in Lahore, the place of his choice."

She searched the cluster of people gathered outside Jahangir's door until she saw Mashtar, a man she'd hired to attend to business she did not want known. Mashtar had already received her closed and waxed message packet. He knew nothing of its content or destination, only that he was to carry it until given further orders by Nur Jahan.

In a low voice the emperor's widow said, "Deliver the message you hold with all speed to Shariyar in Lahore. Tell him I will follow as quickly as I can." Further instructions to Shariyar were inside the packet.

Confident that Mashtar would obey her orders, Nur Jahan swept to her room to prepare for an immediate departure to the city on the plains where she would join the man she had chosen to become the next emperor. She wanted to be by Shariyar's side as quickly as possible, preferably before he declared himself ruler. She was still thinking about the details for the formal coronation to be held after the mourning period when her thoughts were interrupted by an unexpected visitor: Asaf Khan.

Assuming her brother came to offer solace before he obeyed her recent command to him, Nur Jahan acknowledged his presence with a nod, then turned away to continue dictating to the Packing Servants what to prepare for her journey. The brother and sister had been particularly close during the days of the influential Persian Junta, and she assumed their goals remained ccongruent.

Completing her decisions concerning her immediate packing, she turned and held out her hands to her brother. "Asaf, it's good of you to come." She continued speaking in a rush of words. "There are many things we need to do right now. I've sent a message to Lahore, so Shariyar will prepare himself to be crowned emperor. Before that happens…"

Her voice trailed off as she looked at her brother. He had not taken her hands as usual and he was looking at her with a new expression on his face. There was impatience and, yes, dissatisfaction in his eyes where before there had only been agreement. She had seen this same look from him before but never had it been directed toward her as it was now. Certainly, his expression was neither respectful of her position as the emperor's widow nor was it brotherly.

She sharpened her tone. "Asaf, I'm going to leave here within the hour to go to Lahore. See to it my personal belongings follow me as quickly as possible. You are also to take care of the arrangements for Jahangir as I've already described. Be certain they are in strict adherence to Muslim law. Jahangir must be buried with all the rituals worthy of the highest reigning Mughal in the land.

"Meanwhile," she continued, wrapping a warm shawl around her shoulders, "I shall meet you in Lahore when you've finished overseeing these details and are free to travel. By that time, I'll have prepared for Shariyar's coronation. It will be short and solemn because of mourning, with the full celebration later. I need to see the royal turban on his head and the sword of Humayan cinched around his waist to know he is truly the emperor."

Nur Jahan had turned to collect a few items she would carry with her when she was stopped by of her brother's words.

"It will not be so."

His low, deliberate sentence was delivered with a strength that caused her to turn slowly to face him again. His eyes had not changed, but he had. His shoulders were straighter and he stood taller than before, no longer in a subservient posture. His hands, usually together and below his waist, were now apart, the right one resting on the hilt of the sword he didn't usually carry.

Nur Jahan knew Asaf wasn't going to harm her with this sword, but he could brandish it threateningly. Not believing she was in physical danger, but recognizing the need to bring him out of his strange and frightening attitude, she knew she had to act quickly. This was a different brother than the one she'd known, but he was still her brother and she knew what to do.

Ordering her servants from the room so the two of them would be alone, she changed her tone and asked sweetly, "What did you say, Brother?" Emphasizing the word that reminded him of their family bond, she paused, confident she could diffuse the potential threat he posed. After all, they were siblings, and she had paved his way to great power.

He must want something, she thought, her mind racing to deal with this unexpected situation. *Of course! His posturing was only an act. He wants assurance that he will still be in power with Shariyar on the throne. I will see that he remains Army Chief. In fact, I will see that he has the position our father held as Chief Minister.*

Breaking the silence following her question to Asaf, Nur Jahan spoke, offering her brother what she was certain he wanted. "Shariyar needs wise counsel at his side, Asaf. He's had little experience with administering a large and complex land. You'll have more power and wealth than you do now You'll exert even greater influence on the young and inexperienced Shariyar than you did upon Jahangir."

She smiled, assuming her offer would be irresistible to Asaf.

Behind his impassive face, Asaf was thinking about his family and the Mughal Empire. Both were important to him. Both needed Khurram. Not only was his son-in-law a caring father and husband, he was the man who would be the most able person to keep the empire strong. *As much as Nur Jahan has done for him, she mustn't be allowed to choose a dull-witted and uninterested Shariyar for the throne.*

Looking at her he said, "There are other plans, Sister." Asaf spoke this last word using the same tone and pause Nur Jahan herself had utilized only moments ago.

His voice froze Nur Jahan until she remembered who she was.

When that happened, her anger overcame her and she wondered how her brother dared to speak to her in such a way. Filling herself with royal hauteur, she stepped toward him, close enough to see the individual hairs in his moustache.

"There are no other plans. There is no other course of action," she glared.

"You have told me what *you* expect to happen." His voice wasn't loud, but it resonated icily. "Sit down," he commanded, "and I'll tell you what *will* happen."

Stunned, Nur Jahan stepped back, almost stumbling on an ornamented stool behind her. Uncharacteristically awkward, she sat while keeping her eyes raised to the face of her authoritative brother. She could not believe her ears as she listened to his version of how the next few days would develop.

"I'll put the turban of royalty on the head of Dewar Bakash as soon as I leave you. Yes, a royal nephew. Dewar thinks he's been chosen because of his abilities and his place in the royal family. He'll find out later that his head is simply being used to keep the turban warm for Prince Khurram."

Clasping his hands behind his back and stepping toward his sister while shaking his head, he went on. "No that's not entirely true. He will, as emperor, be the rallying point for the imperial troops when they fight against any usurpers who might want to wear the turban."

Asaf could tell by his sister's face she understood this reference to Shariyar. If Shariyar had to muster an army in Lahore to fight the imperial troops, he'd most surely be humiliated by his total absence of military training. Asaf, able military man that he was, could easily defeat him with the army already moving from Agra.

Before Nur Jahan could even begin to prepare a counterplan, Asaf resumed his explanation, appreciating that his sibling appreciated its thoroughness.

"You understand the problem Khurram would have if the imperial troops were fighting *for* Shariyar as their emperor. The difficulty will be even greater for that same inexperienced man to wrest a victory from the army that will be fighting for the newly crowned Dewar, Winter King, who assumes he'll have many years to rule."

All too clearly, Nur Jahan saw the cleverness of the plan. Poor bald Shariyar had no skill for leading men into battle. He had always intended to rely upon a willing Nur Jahan for military thinking, but Nur Jahan suspected Asaf had plans for her not to be in Lahore to offer her essential guidance.

Careful to keep her face passive, Nur Jahan willed herself to travel to her core, to the source of her success—Cobra. Her brother was no match for what was waiting to be uncurled within her. Long seconds passed before she felt the initial stirrings, the sinewy movements that preceded Cobra's advice. But wait, the feelings were becoming fainter rather than more vigorous. What was happening? Nur Jahan sensed a void where she had come to expect fullness. Concerned, she received a faint message: "His strength is greater than mine." Then total stillness.

Cobra wasn't there. Dead? Sleeping? Did it matter if she could receive no advice? Fury and rage exploded in her as she realized the depth of her loss. Before she spoke, she paused to take a long look at her brother. The strength Cobra mentioned was not discernable to Jahangir's widow. She saw a mortal man and wondered why Cobra had been defeated by him. Yes, Asaf was trained to use the sword hanging by his side; yes, he could fight well even without that particular weapon; and, yes, he was protected by the two armed men who stood at the door. But she had never considered him greater than the force that had guided her. What had Cobra meant?

Then, unwillingly, she understood. Asaf Khan had not overpowered her physically but with his belief in the tradition of the Mughal Empire. A soft murmuring inside her head increased until she fairly vibrated with the hum of one unyielding word: ENDED...

Fighting the inevitable, Nur Jahan fortified herself with memories of all she had done, the changes she had made in the empire, the buildings and gardens she had commissioned, and the money she had multiplied. Why, she had married an emperor and had altered the course of many lives. She was beautiful, talented, and—where did this unwanted thought come from?—defeated.

With rare self-examination, Nur Jahan reluctantly discovered that far under her drive for self supremacy, she shared her brother's strong sense of tradition. Sighing deeply, something she had not done since she had been a very young girl, Nur Jahan accepted her fate as she had lived her life by releasing her thoughts of ruling the Mughal Empire and determining to create another role for herself.

Her regal bearing gave no hint of the remarkably calm acceptance of her changed status. Standing tall and holding her head high, she heard her brother call to the doorway soldiers.

"Guards! The former empress has decided it would be most appropriate for her to stay with her husband's body. After Jahangir has been properly interred, she'll continue to stay in her rooms in mourning to become used to widowhood. No one will enter or leave her quarters other than the necessary attendants, and they shall remain silent. She will be sending no messages. Do you understand?"

The men nodded as though it was natural to be obeying commands from Asaf in the presence of Nur Jahan. She thought she saw a flicker of satisfaction in their faces and wondered if they had harbored resentment for the years she had been in charge. Or perhaps they were simply surprised that the woman who had even recently inspired much quaking offered no resistance to the orders.

※ ※ ※

THE DAYS AFTER JAHANGIR'S DEATH swirled with intrigue that would have delighted Nur Jahan and brought forth her greatest talents had she not been confined to her quarters. Asaf Khan learned that his sister, in what had been her last political action, had sent a letter to Lahore immediately after Jahangir's death. He assumed Shariyar would desperately gather troops to fight Asaf Khan and the Army in a last effort to become the Great Mughal.

Asaf Khan had to move immediately in three directions, each centered on a different person essential to one part of the plan. The first, immobilization of Nur Jahan, had already been done. She would not be able to direct the military march of Shariyar from her gentle imprisonment.

Second, Dewar Bakash needed to be convinced he should place the turban on his head. He had given Nur Jahan the impression the young man was already persuaded, but it was not yet true. Dewar's acceptance was necessary to give him the right to battle the forces of Shariyar in Lahore but he was hesitant to agree with Asaf Khan's plan for fear his reign would be a short one followed by an early dath. He was convinced otherwise and, after a hasty coronation, took up the banner of the army and headed the troops to Lahore where Shariyar was gathering his own army. The clash of armed men outside the city was, to Asaf's thinking, inevitable as Shariyar would surely fight for the prize he'd already thought was his.

The third part of Asaf's plan involved Khurram. He sent Royal Runners to take word to him in the Deccan. There was no time to write details, but he had included his own ring in the messenger's wallet as a sign of authenticity.

Three miles outside Lahore, the imperial forces met Shariyar's large but inexperienced army. The pretender to the throne had grabbed the treasury of Lahore and spent it on men to fight for him. He marched proudly with his army that spread far over the plains. He led cavalry, musketeers, war elephants, and camel artillery. Even though they wore glitter and gold and were heavily armed, his men knew nothing of war. They were experienced not as soldiers but as butchers, carpenters, tailors, and bakers who had been recruited by Shariyar, lured into donning fine uniforms, and well paid.

The battle was, as Asaf had predicted, over quickly. The hodgepodge army was routed, the "soldiers" fleeing behind Shariyar who lead the retreat. Trembling, Shariyar hid himself in the zenana where he was later found rolled in a carpet. He spent the next days solitarily imprisoned in a sunless cell just below the sumptuous quarters he'd enjoyed earlier.

32

Deccan - 1627

Months after the night Khurram had been sweltering in the Deccan and recalling the coolness of Kashmir, an attendant burst into the room as he dealt with paperwork. Although the attendant had immediately shown obeisance to the prince, muttered the correct verbal greeting, and profusely apologized for his rush, Khurram was irritated by the rude disruption before he realized the urgency of the attendant's manner could mean only one thing.

"A runner, Your Highness, a Royal Runner has just arrived." Since the time of Akbar, runners had swiftly covered the length of the empire, being used only for important messages between the royal family members. Filled with bhang, a mild preparation of cannabis, and wearing a belt of bells, each man quickly covered many miles a day in his leg of the relay.

"He's carrying a message…"

"Of course, he's carrying a message. That's what they *do!*"

His snappish response to the attendant covered his nervousness. *It's about my father,* he thought. *Either he died or he is close to death and wants to see me before he ascends to Allah's mansion. Or perhaps he is no longer on this earth and Shariyar is emperor.*

Suddenly aware of what must be done before he met the messenger, Khurram commanded, "Write a note for me."

"Your Highness?"

"Write a note for me. I will see it sent before I speak with the runner."

"But Your Highness, he's a Royal Runner and doesn't expect to wait."

"Either write a note or send someone here who will," Khurram demanded.

Embarrassed to keep the exhausted and sweating runner waiting, Asadbillah spoke a few forceful words over his shoulder and almost immediately a small man, spry for his years, appeared with his paper, brush, and ink in hand.

"This note goes to Her Highness, Mumtaz Mahal. It is to say, 'Taj, prepare to go to the Moonlight Mahal.'"

The Writer had gracefully brushed Khurram's words on the page almost as soon as they had been spoken. When he looked up to see what else Khurram would dictate, the prince waved his hand indicating he was finished.

"Have it delivered immediately." Khurram did not move until the messenger left, then he ordered himself to be finely dressed. If this was, as he suspected, to be his last appearance as a ruler, he would look royal.

❉ ❉ ❉

MUMTAZ FELT THE SADNESS emanating from the paper she held in her hand. She had dreaded the thought of receiving this innocuous code even as Khurram must have been reluctant to write it. Not only did it admit the end of her husband's hopes, but it dashed her own as well. She had believed in Khurram's destiny absolutely, and was dedicated to supporting his belief that he would become emperor.

"You cannot be kept from your destiny for it seeks you even as you seek it. No man can alter what Allah has apportioned for him." She wholeheartedly accepted this phrase of her grandfather's and had often repeated it to her husband. She briefly mourned the loss of the dream briefly, then urgently called her servant. She summoned the children and made packing decisions. She moved swiftly, not knowing how much time she had before the assassins would arrive.

She removed her personal dagger from its hiding place. The gold mounts on the velvet sheath sparkled and the ivory discs that were attached with red tassels fit her hand. She held it and knew if anyone threatened her, or one of her children, she would use it.

There was no question in her mind Khurram would have been a majestic ruler. He would have been strong, compassionate, and cultured. The beautiful buildings of his dreams would have graced the empire. Turning her attention to the matters at hand, Mumtaz sadly accepted it was not to be after all.

※ ※ ※

THE MESSENGER, HAVING WAITED long enough to be breathing regularly, bowed to Khurram and handed him a dusty leather pouch. The first runner in the relay had received this same pouch twenty days earlier in Kashmir. A head above the tallest palace guard, this one stood with his long thin runner's legs protruding from the cloth wrapped around his groin. He was barefoot, having removed his buffalo hide footwear before he entered the august chamber.

With a sense of finality, Khurram took the wallet and broke the wax seal. When he tipped the opened pouch, a ring fell into his hand. He recognized the golden ring with an unusual heart-shaped sapphire as a prized possession of Taj's father. How very long ago it seemed since he had dined at this man's home. It was the first time he had been with Shariyar and his father together. And now...

So Asaf Khan has sent a message to me, he thought as he felt the heavy ring in his palm. No doubt he is doing so to provide advanced warning that will allow his daughter and family to flee to safety.

There was a single sheet of paper in the pouch. With every eye in the room watching him, Khurram silently read the short, handwritten message: *Your father is dead. Come immediately to Agra to be crowned Emperor.*

The implication of the message staggered Khurram. How was it that even though Shariyar and Nur Jahan had been in Kashmir with Jahangir, Shariyar had not been crowned?

Is this a hoax to lure me to my death? The heft of this ring from Taj's father reminds me that he would not have sent it unless he was serious. It could be a trick. It could be real. I have to choose and I have to do it now.

With a dazed voice he announced, "My father is dead." He allowed the stunned silence that followed his announcement to lengthen before he turned to his aide. "Have twenty men ready to ride with me to Agra after four days of mourning."

He had already risen when he stopped and pointed to the runner. "See that this man is well fed and has a comfortable place to rest."

After another step he stopped again and smiled at the attendant who had brought him the news of the runner's arrival. "Tell my wife she no longer needs to make preparations for Moonlight Mahal."

33

Deccan/Agra - 1628

Four days after Khurram had received the news of his father's death, he and twenty chosen men departed for Agra, leaving the rest to follow at a slower pace. Just before departure Khurram gathered his men together and spoke to them in his most commanding tone.

"We will ride with determination and purpose but without unseemly haste. This is no ordinary ride and each man must reflect in his posture and manner that he is escorting a future king to his coronation. We will be dignified rather than military men on a rampage." Emulating their leader, his bodyguards rode proudly.

Only two days north, a horseman carrying another wallet stamped with Asaf Khan's seal met them. Anxiously, Khurram dismounted and found a comfortable spot along the road to open it. His face and body relaxed when he finished reading.

Dewar Bakash, the interim emperor, had led the army that defeated Shariyar and was the only person that now stood between Khurram and the throne. His hands clasped behind him as he paced, Khurram recalled his warm feelings for his nephew.

The repetitive pacing continued even as his eyes narrowed and his lips changed from a smile to a grimace. *Dewar*, Khurram thought, *now considers himself the Great Mughal. He's worn the Royal Turban and has tasted the power of the throne because of the Army's victory. Even if he agrees to relinquish his title to me, can I allow him to remain at* large? Surely, he would always be a threat to my reign. He can't be allowed to live. But could I become the very first Mughal to murder his way to the throne? If I leave him alive, I risk a rebellion. To remove Dewar Bakash would be despicable. I'm so near to the full realization of my dreams, and I'll surely have everything I'll ever want if I'm emperor. Perhaps, the glory of my reign will compensate for taking it from another man.*

No, I can't do it. It is too repugnant for me to think of harming this young man. My mind is made up, I won't break the Timurid Code with murder. Then Khurram had a new thought and stopped before he returned to his men. *Is Allah testing me to see if I'm worthy of the destiny he has for me? Must I order Dewar's death to show I'm worthy of being the Great Mughal?*

While still filled with righteousness, Khurram grimly penned a quick letter to Asaf Khan. Until he actually wrote the words to send Dewar, the Winter King to the spiritual world, he was uncertain of his ability to do so. Even though Khurram touched no knife or neck wire, he knew he had as good as murdered Dewar Bakash with his written command. Pausing only a moment, Khurram added Shariyar's name to the list of those to be assassinated before he rolled the paper back into the pouch. Feeling he had only done what he was forced by circumstances to do, Khurram watched with diminishing regret as the rider swiftly took his order northward to Asaf Khan.

Unaware of the intense grief that would come to him in the future through one of his own sons because of the decision he had just made, he remounted and rode even taller in his ornate saddle as growing crowds lined the road to glimpse the man who would become their emperor.

❊ ❊ ❊

WHILE KHURRAM RODE toward his coronation, Asaf Khan was spending his days and nights insuring that glorious event would indeed happen. Following orders from the man he supported, Asaf Khan removed the royal turban from Dewar Bakash's young head—and had him killed. Shariyar also was sent out of this world. Now Asaf had to accomplish one more task, something that could only be done on a Friday.

He would have Prince Khurram's name read in the mosque during the weekly public prayer. The khutba, a short message read by the imam, would mention the new emperor's name to the Muslims congregated there. The worshippers would give their implied consent to be this man's subjects if they remained. Though the Muslim leaders agreed that Nur Jahan's rule through Jahangir had benefited the empire, they believed a country ruled by a woman was doomed. With a ringing voice, the imam shouted the name of Khurram.

❋ ❋ ❋

HAVING CHANGED THE COURSE of the Mughal Empire both through his own plans and his obedience to the commands of the man who was now emperor, Asaf rode to Agra. Though his desire to see Khurram and his daughter and his grandchildren in Agra had influenced his actions, it was his conviction of being right that drove him to contain Nur Jahan, defeat Shariyar, order the deaths of two men, and have Khurram's name read in the mosque.

Officially, Khurram was emperor the moment the khutba was read in Lahore after the battle with Shariyar. Because Agra was where he would live, rule, and build, messages were sent throughout the land to proclaim Shah Jahan's coronation and four days of festivities in that city. Abdul Muzaffar Shihabuddin Mohammed Sahib Qirau Save Shah Badshah, formerly known as Prince Khurram took Shah Jahan, King of the World, as his regnal name.

The imperial magnificence and generosity satisfied everyone. Religious leaders prayed for the king at the crowded mosques. The wealthy and influential displayed their most adorned garments and bedecked animals. Noblemen, sheiks, Hindu Rajput chiefs, and Moslem khans streamed into the capital. Eminent writers, astrologers, and sages flavored the air with their words. Artists painted

Shah Jahan in his splendor, poets wrote odes to him, and singers sang them.

Peasants, not caring who was on the throne or what he chose to call himself, enjoyed the entertainment and food. The air throbbed with continuous music provided by drummers, horn players, and singers. The jingling bells of the dancers added lightness to the intensity of the drums. Jugglers, wrestlers, and animals performed. Animal fights elicited impassioned cheers. The river carried barges of musicians whose music became louder as they approached, then diminished as they floated past the city. Peasants consumed imported fruits and exotically flavored dishes usually unavailable in their villages.

One night, the walls of the fort were covered from top to bottom with lanterns and candles while thousands of spinning wheels and artificial trees were filled with exploding rockets and twenty thousand small burning earthen oil lamps rivaled the stars in the sky.

None of the tensions of the last few years showed on the thirty-six-year-old face of Shah Jahan as he kept his date with destiny. He stood contentedly in his shining robes and flashing jewels amongst the glittering trappings of royalty.

The new emperor lavished his family with gifts, starting with bequeathing to Mumtaz 200,000 gold pieces, 600,000 rupees, and an annual allowance of a million rupees a year. Their six living children surrounded her as they each received an endowment in addition to their annual allowance. Though she was missing the five children who had not lived to see their father crowned, she would not mar her husband's pleasure in this day dwelling upon thoughts of them.

❋ ❋ ❋

ON THE THIRD DAY of the celebrations, Shah Jahan stood at the jharoka window and looked below. A living sea of people cheered again and again, each wave of sound louder than the one before.

His subjects saluted him with their voices as he stood proudly, wearing the royal turban and the symbolic sword. Cheers rose even higher when his sons, Dara, Shuja, Aurangzeb, and little Maurad were escorted to the balcony. The two princesses and Mumtaz remained, as usual, out of sight. Shah Jahan's sons were lifted high enough to pour trays of gems over their father's head.

The revelry and celebrations continued to blare and reverberate well after Shah Jahan departed. Desiring a respite from the noise around him, Shah Jahan headed toward the zenana. He should have known, he realized as he entered the female space, that his women would be creating their own noise. Against the rules of the zenana, as well as the even stricter rules of Islam, they were drinking wine. Their laughter could be heard as they ate, played games, waved sparklers, and lounged casually. Never before had he seen women smoking the water pipe customarily enjoyed only by men. They were inhaling bubbly tobacco from the tube of the jade bowl nestled in a matching ring around the bottom to keep it upright.

He scanned the large rooms until he saw the woman he sought wearing a dazzling bodice of gold brocade designed with paisleys of pearls. Mumtaz was speaking to their beautiful fourteen-year-old daughter. He regretted the child would not be allowed to have a husband and children of her own

When he met Taj's eyes, she gave her husband a secret hand signal. The message in her slight movement told him she would meet him alone. *Again,* he mused as he signaled back, *she understands my desire for quiet after the exhilaration of the day.* Within minutes, they'd made their separate ways to one another. Sitting close enough to touch, they started talking at the same time.

"We've succeeded, Taj!"

"It was always your destiny, Meerijan."

Surrounded by the muted blasts, whistles, and music of the outside clamor, Shah Jahan took the hand of his wife. "The celebration is sweeter and has more meaning for me because of you, Taj." Responding to the quizzical rise of her graceful dark eyebrow, he went on. "If we'd not shared the last years, I wouldn't have survived to become emperor."

He held up his hand to quiet the comment she was about to make before he finished. "There have been times in the past, and there will doubtless be times again in the future, when your challenges to my thoughts will frustrate me." He put his finger gently on her lips as she opened them to protest. "You know this is true. It's also true that I listen to you, although it may not appear I do so. I'm proud of what you do…even when it makes me angry or uncomfortable."

Putting aside her usual humility, Mumtaz truly listened to her husband as he again told her she was as essential to him as he was to her. She smiled at his words and put her hands on either side of his face.

"You're a complex man, Meerijan. At your greatest triumph, you are here alone with me rather than receiving the cheers of the empire. It's one of the things I love about you." She rolled her hands down his dark beard and gently brought her fingertips together under his chin. Looking at him with soft seriousness, Mumtaz said, "I will love you, Meerijan, until the end of my life. I will care for you, listen to you, and help you any way I can. You are my husband and the love of my heart."

34

Agra ~ 1628

Nur Jahan had been detained in Kashmir until after the coronation. When she was finally escorted to Lahore, she listened as Ladili described the battle, Shariyar's capture and then his death. Shariyar was dead, Khurram was on the throne, and she had no army. That she was still alive was due to the fact that killing a royal woman, even a powerless one, was not done. It was the first time she could recall her gender working in her favor.

Abruptly summoned to appear before Shah Jahan, she traveled the tree-lined road between Lahore and Agra wearing the plain white linen of widowhood. She walked fearlessly into Shah Jahan's throne room to face her former enemy and looked boldly into his eyes. She fully understood her action could cause her to be ordered to die. Though he was the victor, both the woman standing and the man on the throne knew the outcome of their clash could have easily been different

The next move was Shah Jahan's. Before him was the woman who had turned his father against him, chosen his half brother to become the Great Mughal, given her only daughter to a doomed marriage, and caused a destructive rebellion. All of this so that she could rule the empire.

"You've used your skills against me, Nur Jahan." His voice was low and his look was stern. "For this, you could easily die." The atmosphere in the room grew tense as some of the onlookers feared Shah Jahan would carry out this threat. Others feared he wouldn't.

Even simply dressed, Nur Jahan had the regal bearing of a queen. She stood tall, her arms relaxed at her sides as she awaited his next words. Her face was turned slightly upward and she stared back at her stepson as he gazed down from his elevated position. Although she stood alone, they both knew guards remained only a few feet behind her. The moment belonged to Shah Jahan and his former rival.

Hookah

If I were in your position, I'd get rid of me. I'd erase an enemy. But it's more complicated for you because I'm a woman and your father's widow. I've felt since our conversation in the garden that your instinct to kill me would falter.

Shah Jahan was also thinking about the meeting with Nur Jahan in the garden and understood that he had won only because of unexpected help. However it had happened, he had become the Great Mughal and was now sitting on the throne in a position to decide her future. He had already removed reminders of her from the palace and ordered a recall of the coins Jahangir had minted with her name upon them. Agreeing that predecessor's money should remain in circulation, Shah Jahan justified his move because this woman before him had *not* been a ruler.

I could hang her upside down until she died, but death by tiger would be more exciting to watch. I know I won't do that either for Taj wouldn't want me to order her aunt's death. I won't allow Nur Jahan to haunt my wife even in nightmares.

Aloud, he said, "We could discuss the past, Nur Jahan, but it will change nothing. However, we can arrange the future. We both know your power no longer exists. Rather than send you to Allah, I will give you a task. You've built the tomb of your father, and now I want you to build a fitting and final resting-place for your late husband. You'll be given the money you need as well as a personal pension."

Nur Jahan said nothing.

"Go now." Shah Jahan's words combined command and farewell.

Nur Jahan teslimed to her emperor, then turned her back to him and, with imperial dignity, walked away in deliberate defiance of custom.

The onlookers were aghast at such audacious behavior. Surely he would have her head for this, or perhaps some other gruesome punishment. Perhaps, she would be put into a dungeon and fed poust until that mixture of water and opium made her lethargic and stupid before it killed her.

Shah Jahan's initial response to the insult of Nur Jahan's back was to strike her down. But he paused, and when he did, he reconsidered. He had been insulted by a defeated enemy, one to whom he had given clemency. The absurdity of Nur Jahan's act prodded the emperor to do something totally unexpected. He chuckled. Shah Jahan was amused at the audacity of this woman who had fought him so well. He admired her, did not want to see her again, but would give her this last gesture.

Guards were watching his face, waiting to receive their order to grab the arms of the woman in white who was walking away from the emperor. When Shah Jahan motioned to them, they, surprised but obedient, pivoted and created a pathway allowing Nur Jahan to proceed untouched.

Before turning to the next matter, Shah Jahan concluded his dealings with Nur Jahan by dictating to a scribe: "She is to receive 20,000 rupees a month more than the rupees she spends for mausoleum materials." Remembering the distress he felt when he was banished from the royal city, he gave Nur Jahan the same ache by adding: "She's not allowed to return to Agra. Ever."

35

Indian village - 1629

"Tell us again, Papa." The many people gathered in his crowded hut repeated Chundar's youngest son's request. "Hahn! Hahn! Hahn!" they chorused. Yes. Yes. Yes. "Tell us again."

"But I've told you the entire story from beginning to end twice. Surely you're as tired of hearing it as I am of telling it!" Chundar, his round face flushed with recent fame, fibbed. Although not a handsome man, Chundar's broad face was kind and his smile revealed strong white teeth—a rarity in his village where chewing cane had left most teeth pitted and stained.

The cloth over the door was pulled aside and the voices in the small room subsided as they recognized the newcomer. Someone quickly gave up his space on the mud floor, reverently motioning for the ancient and respected elder of the village to take his place.

The old man stopped his shuffling walk and motioned with his gnarled hand toward Chundar, "Don't bother to stand up." In his shaky voice, he added, "I've come to hear of your journey to Agra." As he took a deep breath to continue, the room remained silent. "Tell me so my ears, my eyes, and my heart will feel they were there with you." He looked down at his frail body and smiled toothlessly. "It is unlikely I'll ever travel so far myself."

Flattered to be asked to share his story once more, Chundar began. "I've lived in this village and even on this same piece of land all of my years, as did my father and his father before him. My grandfather began planting his fields too many years ago to count. I grew to know what to expect from the soil...and from my wife." Affectionately ruffling the hair of the bright-eyed boy at his side he smiled and added, "My children, however, can still surprise me. I have three sons and more than enough land for my needs. Each of my boys will have a large plot of their own when they're old enough to take brides. The gods have been good to me.

"One planting ago my wife, my sons, and I attended a camel fair for a week. The sights were the most memorable we'd ever seen. Little did I know I'd be seeing even greater things soon after.

"Returning to our home, I went to my fields." He caught his wife's eye and lowered his head and voice. "My wife has said I love my land more than I love her." There were murmurs of understanding from the farmers hunkering in the room with their feet flat on the floor and their knees under their chins. Then, lifting both voice and head, he continued loud enough for all to hear.

"I wanted to see the growth during my absence." Heads in the room were nodding, affirming once more to Chundar that he was among people who understood the strong pull of the earth that affected the predominantly Hindu villagers of India..

"But this time something was wrong. My fence had been carefully moved to decrease my lands and the signs of this change had been carefully erased. I wasn't angry. I knew immediately that my neighbor, a great trickster, had done this."

The man Chundar was referring to was more than simply his neighbor. Chundar and Malador had grown up together, eaten at each other's homes, and had shared as brothers for more than twenty-five years. Rarely a day went by, even after their marriages, without the two of them being together. When they became fathers, their deep friendship continued. Chundar was blessed with three healthy sons and Malador had fathered three daughters.

These two men lightened the hard-working lives of the villagers with their pranks. One time, a goat had been tethered atop Malador's hut. Another time, Chundar came home to find everything from his small home moved outside and set up exactly as it had been arranged inside. Another time Malador and the entire village had served Chundar as though he were a rich man for a full day.

"Knowing a good joke when I saw one, I meandered to Malador's house to speak with him. I wanted to ask about how and when he was going to move the fence back. I'd help him undo his labor because I knew he did it just to make me laugh. I looked forward to sharing his practical joke, and I assumed we'd slap each other's backs and share a glass of beer."

Here Chundar stopped and everyone watching could see he still felt the disbelief of what happened next.

"When I got to his house and called out I had to wait longer than usual. Finally, his daughter Sharia came to the door and told me her father was gone. She disappeared again. I was surprised at her behavior because I've been like her uncle since the day she was born. I suspected Sharia was upset because of Malador's moodiness. He'd recently confided in me his concerns about finding husbands for his much-loved daughters now that the eldest was getting close to marriageable age. He worried about providing not one but three dowries without having to bear heavy debt. He also didn't want his daughters to have to settle for the poor quality of husbands available to village girls who had nothing of value to bring to their marriages.

Chundar paused to light a bidi and inhaled the inexpensive tobacco deeply before he continued. "A week later, I was delighted to see Malador when I went to the field. I put down my hoe and walked toward him, but he was uncharacteristically gruff. Still assuming we were friends, I told him I got his joke and asked him when the fence would be back to its right place. You can imagine my surprise when he simply looked at me seriously and said, 'It is in the right place.'

'No, really,' I protested lightly, 'the fence is too close to my stream.'

'The fence has always been where it is now. Your property is on one side and mine is on the other.'

"I was stunned. I'd truly thought he was only pulling a prank and had been waiting for me to discover the trick, then we'd laugh, and that would be the end of it. But this wasn't to be. My friend's worry had become so desperate his mind had snapped. Instead of asking me, his blood brother, to help, he'd resorted to taking land from me. Did he think I'd say nothing? It was the land I would give to my sons.

"I don't know how long the situation would have continued if my wife hadn't gone to the panchyat with the story." This group of five elders of the village judged local disputes giving the village itself the first opportunity to settle disagreements. "The only issue to her was how much land would go to her sons, so she was clear. Because of my many years of friendship with Malador, I was more muddled.

"The two of us told our story to the panchyat. Because there was an uneven number of listeners, we assumed there couldn't be a tie. I was certain the decision would be in my favor, I'd get my fields back, my sons would again be assured of the inheritance they'd always expected, and my life would resume as usual.

"But a strange thing happened. After they heard our stories, and voted, one of the members was undecided and didn't have an opinion. The other two were split. It was the first time in our village that a dispute had to be heard beyond the panchyat.

"We had to travel to another court that heard only the cases that the panchyats couldn't decide. Our friendship cooled, as was to be expected, because Malador continued to insist there had been no theft.

"My anger and irritation grew every day I was away from my fields. I knew they were my fields, yet here I was riding in a cart for two hours wasting my time talking to another group of men about something that shouldn't have happened. It must be that a father's need to provide for his daughters touched deep sympathy in the men who heard our stories that Malador's plight was in some way accepted. Like us, they each knew families who'd fallen into lifelong debt to the moneylenders, while paying for large dowries and wedding celebrations beyond their means. For the second time, the men who heard our stories were unable to decide, and we were sent to the final judge—The Great Mughal in Agra at his Justice Durbar."

Disputes within the boundaries of the empire were handled by a judicial system serving both Hindus and Muslims leaving Shah Jahan only a few cases that were unsolved by the lower courts. When Chundar and Malador traveled to Agra they were to come face-to-face with the man who ruled supreme. They would meet the absolute judge who would settle their dispute with finality. There was no recourse on earth higher than Shah Jahan.

"This ruler lives one hundred and twenty miles away in a palace by the Jumna River," explained Chundar. "I'd never been to Agra, and I had no desire to leave my village again. Yet, because of Malador's theft I unhappily prepared to travel to the grandest palace of all.

"The cart trip from our village to Agra was slow, dusty, and surprisingly interesting. I'd been Malador's friend for so many years that spending time with him without working in the fields wasn't totally unpleasant. Even though we were traveling to have our disagreement settled, our deep friendship was a comfort in this foreign territory."

"Agra," croaked the old man in the room when it seemed Chundar was pausing too long. With an impatient wave of his hand, he demanded, "Get to the part about the palace and the Great Mughal."

Clearing his throat and giving himself time to mentally organize the vast array of images and sensations that had assailed him when he entered the looming red walls of the fabled fort, Chundar continued in a voice filled with awe at the memory.

"We got out of our bullock cart and walked to the entrance of the fort and were immediately jostled by people, fancy palanquins, horses, and elephants streaming toward the loudest drums I've ever heard. My best pants and shirt, silk though they were, had been washed many times and had become smooth and light colored. I was dressed better than the very poorest in the crowd who wore clothes that were no more than layers of rough cloth but I was much plainer than the city men who wore brilliantly colored silks.

"I wondered what was behind the walls we were moving toward. Where did all of these crowding people go when they were inside? Did they have business with the Mughal as we did? Would the emperor have time to hear our story today?

"I wanted to remember everything—the wide moat, drawbridge, the mountain-high entrance, and the ramp inside the walls—so I could tell you about them when I returned." The natural storyteller in Chundar continued, embellishing his descriptions and enlivening his tale with dramatic and sweeping hand gestures.

"When I reached the top of the ramp, I stopped so quickly I was bumped from behind. The tiled courtyard stretching before me was as large as my field here in the village. I was used to tilling an area this size, not to seeing it as a gathering spot. Scalloped arches enclosed three walls of the enormous space. Under each of these archways was an armed soldier wearing magnificent boots and carrying a long-barreled gun. Even the soldiers wore colors I've seen only at village weddings.

"I walked slowly, noticing the huge silk canopy held up with silver poles. Men wore complex and unusual turbans and bold sashes with daggers. Flags and banners fluttered in the slightest breeze.

"I love our beautiful village, but now I see that except for our leaves and the paint that has been applied to some of our walls, everything is some shade of brown. The palace is a universe of colors, and only the poor seem to think brown is good enough to wear.

"The men closest to the throne platform were under a roof, all facing a wall as though they were ready to pray in a mosque. There was a balcony against that wall where Shah Jahan would soon be sitting."

Chundar told them of the jewelry on the men who took their places near the front, and of carpets designed with flowers so realistic he initially stepped carefully so he wouldn't crush a petal. Through his telling, Chundar brought to his fellow villagers the glories and lavishness of the sights at the Agra palace.

"Everywhere I looked, there was something wonderful to see. When attendants sprinkled rose water over the heads of those who waited, the container wasn't brass as it is here but silver encrusted with amber." He didn't share his thought that the perfumed water might have been used to kill the scent of unwashed feet.

"I had no idea what to do or how long we'd be standing on the carpeted courtyard before it was our turn to present our stories. Despite the wonders of Agra, I ached to be working in my own fields. Malador was to blame for my distance from home. How foolish I'd been to think moving my fence was a joke. I was angrier with Malador at that moment than I'd been since our problems started.

"The music coming from a room atop the entrance arch was so loud it added to the noise and confusion of the great press of people, keeping us all a bit more jittery and anxious than we already were. When the musicians suddenly stopped playing, the atmosphere immediately changed. A hush swept through the courtyard, then a crash of drums and blaring of trumpets announced the arrival of the man we'd been waiting for.

"This musical flourish coincided with Shah Jahan's arrival and continued until he sat cross-legged on his throne. We copied those around us and folded our hands in front of us below our waist," he automatically repeated the gesture as he talked, "and teslimed with our bodies and right arms." Chundar tried to sound as though he had spontaneously performed this movement. In fact, he had practiced the sweeping motion frequently on the trip to Agra.

"We were barely able to see or hear what was happening in front of us, so great was our distance from the throne balcony. My gaze wandered about the scene in front of me for at least an hour before I began to feel comfortable. Finally, a servant came toward us and motioned for Malador and me to follow him, and I was again nervous. We edged our way slowly up the side toward the shade canopy. When we reached its edge, I could see the roofed and columnar pavilion all the way to the throne balcony on the far wall.

"We continued to the sandstone barrier where the foot soldiers, servants, and villagers had been standing. Ahead of us, behind a silver railing, stood dignitaries and diplomats. Closest to the throne wall, those of the highest rank stood behind a golden rail. The emperor's sons were standing behind their father on the balcony.

"We walked until we were in the shade under the canopy, but the man we were following kept going and didn't stop until he was at the very edge of the pavilion itself. I suddenly felt sick and couldn't breathe. I was confused, and for several moments I didn't know where I was or what I was supposed to do. My mind had stopped and I couldn't talk. The sights before me blurred and began to spin. I was gasping like a fish pulled from the water.

"I was overwhelmed with the conviction that my being there wasn't worth my feelings. I wanted to leave and not have to come back to that place with its overpowering noise and grand sights. I felt nothing good happening there for me.

"And I wondered why Shah Jahan should be the one to decide our boundaries. He'd never planted a crop, scanned the sky for signs of rain, or felt the hot sun on his bare back as he toiled in a field. He'd never been on our land, slept in a hut with a floor of cow dung, nor gone into debt for a dowry or a wedding. Yet, because of his birth, he had the power to make decisions about my life—and your lives—that include all of these things. But I saw no escape when our guide moved resolutely ahead, beckoning us to follow. I mutely obeyed.

"We walked up two marble steps to the floor of the great Diwan-i-Am where I could tell through my bare feet that the carpet I'd stood on far from the throne was much thinner than this luxurious rug under the canopy near the Great Mughal. I moved forward to tell again the story of my disputed property.

"Even with my eyes down, I could feel the man who'd decide my future looking at me from his throne above. Hesitantly, I lifted my eyes and for a moment I stared into the deep brown eyes of my emperor. This was the famed Shah Jahan. His regal posture as well as his sumptuous clothing and jewels left no question in my mind. On his sleeve he wore a ruby armband surrounded by two large pearls. He also wore pearls scattered with emeralds and rubies around his neck. It must have been a pearl day for he had them on his turban, around his wrists, and on his fingers.

"He looked deep into my mind, then turned his head slightly and looked at Malador. He simply said Malador's name followed by mine. He sounded intelligent, interested and used to being obeyed. I felt there was nothing more important to him at that moment than to hear our stories. As wildly different as our lives were, I knew that Shah Jahan would be fair.

"Malador was beckoned to tell his story first. I expected him to tell his lie about seizing my land and planning to sell it for his daughters' dowries and weddings. As before, he'd weep and plead for the land to be clearly his with no mention he had taken it illegally.

"But he surprised me. Perhaps the same awe had touched us both when we came to Agra. Maybe, he'd realized he'd gone too far. Whatever it was, his story was similar to the one I had been telling and he admitted he had moved the fence to increase the size of his fields. I believe he finally awakened to the seriousness of his present surroundings. He told the Great Mughal that he'd done so to provide for his daughters. His predicament had elicited sympathy in the past, and he must have assumed Shah Jahan would judge him as others had.

"Shah Jahan listened carefully. When Malador had finished, there was no sound, not even a rustle behind the carved screens hiding the women of the zenana. There was no need for me to speak, as there was now no difference in our stories. I simply shrugged my shoulders when Shah Jahan turned toward me with his eyebrows raised to indicate I was to speak. For a moment the peacock-feather fan silently moved the air surrounding the thoughtful emperor while he decided our fate. His face relaxed.

"'Malador,' he finally said, 'your concern for your daughters touches me greatly.' 'I understand the burden you face. By the very fact you've come all this way to tell me your story demonstrates your daughters are very dear to you. Because of this, I bequeath the sum of two thousand rupees to each of them for their dowries and weddings. That should be enough to see they each attract a fine husband.'

"Malador's grin revealed his happiness. The emperor continued with the expected comment: 'The land you stole shall be returned to Chundar.'

"We thought he was finished. We both thought we'd be free to return home and live the rest of our lives as we always had. I even hoped that we'd again be friends. All was well now because I had my full lands, and my good friend had the money he needed for his daughters."

Chundar brushed his work-hardened hand across his simple eyes, trying unsuccessfully to remove the memory of what followed. His audience waited quietly, noting his lowered voice when he continued.

"But we were mistaken. Shah Jahan wasn't finished. 'Malador, your daughters will not be punished because of your theft. Unlike you, they are blameless. They will have ample dowries, but you will not be at their weddings.'

"It was only then I noticed the two hooded men carrying large hatchets on their shoulders, standing at the side of the emperor, waiting to carry out his orders. They moved slowly toward us, grabbed Malador and half carried, half dragged him away, as he nearly swooned in their grip."

Chundar paused at this point, lost in the memory of watching his dearest friend being hauled toward certain death. His audience watched him struggle through this part of his story, not realizing Chundar's roiling stomach was constricting and churning beneath his khurta.

No one waiting for him to continue knew the true events of the day in Agra. They'd been told Shah Jahan had only meant to scare Malador and before any damage could be done he'd waved his hand and stopped the hatchetmen. But Chundar knew differently. He recalled the moment and his deep instinctive reaction to the horror of losing his lifelong friend. Throwing his arms wide and falling to the ground in a position of supplication, he shouted, 'No!'

Shah Jahan heard the cry so filled with fear for the life of a loved friend, and it touched the emperor as cries rarely did. Although he had heard the screams of countless battlefield deaths and had impersonally ended hundreds of lives, Shah Jahan heard something different in Chundar's wail. The man before him was obviously tortured by the idea that his friend, a proven cheat, was going to be taken from the world. He had seldom seen devotion of this level and raised his hand to stay the executioners.

He repeated his condemnation of Malador to Chundar. 'The man is a thief and a liar. I won't have such people in my empire. You are fortunate to be rid of such a neighbor.'

As he raised himself, Chundar was not remembering the betrayal of the last few months. His mind dwelt upon the happiness he had known when he and Malador had each other in their lives. Now Malador was sobbing in the clutches of executioners. Chundar knew without question what his decision would be if he were able to choose between the acreage he had promised his sons or the life of Malador

Chundar thought he was putting his feelings into words, but was uuttering only garbled gasps and stutters. Unaware he'd risked his life when he countered a command given by the Great Mughal, he continued trying to talk, hoping frantically that some sense would eventually come out of his mouth.

The obvious anguish of the man before him, pleading for the life of a condemned friend touched Shah Jahan even as it created a quandary. Though he had, through Chundar's act of desperate courage, become aware of the deep feeling between the two men, he *was* the Great Mughal whose commands were not ignored.

Shah Jahan asked Chundar, 'What would you have me do?'

Even in his agitated state, Chundar understood his next few sentences would determine Malador's fate. Taking a deep breath he began hesitantly.

"'Majesty, my humble suggestion is that you award the land to Malador. Let him sell it and use the money as he needs. I will accept this decision and the two of us can return to our village and resume the life we have lived for so long.'

"'I hear what you say, Chundar, but I have already ruled. What will become of my command?'

Chundar would never know where he got the audacity to suggest to the Great Mughal that he reverse a public judgment. 'Your Majesty, the wisest of men is known to change when new information is presented. You ruled most fairly when you returned the land to me and bequeathed money for Malador's daughters. Now that you…and I…understand that his life is more important than the land we've fought over, I pray Allah will provide you with the compassion to exchange one for the other.'

During a long silence, the emperor remembered how proud he had been of the conclusion he was now reconsidering. But this obvious depth of feeling the one peasant had for the other went beyond simple justice.

Brushing aside the reasons why he should not listen to his heart, Shah Jahan suddenly spoke. "Let him go."

Surprised, the two men who had been holding Malador let him go and propelled him forward with a push.

Looking at Chundar, Shah Jahan continued. 'Your bravery and loyalty will be rewarded with ownership of the land in question, dowries for Malador's daughters, and one hundred rupees for yourself.'

Aware of the danger of setting a precedent of changing his mind, Shah Jahan raised his voice so all could hear. "No one," he looked around the crowded courtyard seeming to connect with each pair of eyes looking at him, "no one shall speak of what has happened today."

Chundar heartily agreed. He didn't want the villagers to know the truth as Malador's family would be disgraced if the original command became known.

Chundar and Malador were dismissed so Shah Jahan could attend to another case. It was a shaken pair of men who walked away from the courtyard, the fort, and into their cart for the journey home.

Chundar worried that the day's trauma would cause his friend to remain speechless. Momentarily, he himself was drained of words after his courageous and unplanned plea for Malador's life, so neither spoke. When their cart turned off the main road and began bumping down the track toward their village, Malador turned his tear-covered face toward his friend. Chundar noticed that behind the tears Malador's eyes were clear and no longer touched by the madness that had recently clouded them.

Chundar gripped Malador's shoulders, then pulled him into a great hug, conveying with his entire body that he would never speak of the true events of the Justice Durbar. The accurate ending of their greatest story would remain untold.

The storyteller shook himself and mentally returned to the group waiting expectantly for him to finish recounting the Agra adventure. "At that moment, Shah Jahan, the wisest of all rulers, ordered the execution to stop. He'd just wanted to show Malador how our case could have ended if someone else had been on the throne."

For Malador's sake, Chundar forgave himself this lie he had told so many times.

36

Agra - 1630

The soldier's report Shah Jahan received upset him greatly and he made no effort to hide his regal displeasure. The scroll in his hands described the challenge the Mughals were facing in the Deccan. He couldn't think of that dry and rocky section of the empire without negative memories. When he returned victorious from the Deccan, he had been met with his father's indifference, he had gone to the Deccan to avoid witnessing Shariyar's rising star and then again when he had lost the rebellion. No, the Deccan didn't hold happy thought for him. Now, it had to be dealt with yet again.

"Are the rebels organized? Do they have a leader?" The sharp tone of his questions revealed his attitude.

"Yes, Your Majesty."

"Do I know the man?"

"Yes, it is Khan Jahan Lodi."

Khan Jahan Lodi. Angered but not surprised, Shah Jahan realized many of the men surrounding him also knew Khan Jahan Lodi. They were probably remembering the wealthy man who had spent most of his life among them in Agra.

Khan Jahan Lodi had been a noble in the Mughal Court since Jahangir had been emperor. His dashing good looks, bravery, and flair for living well had made him highly popular. Enjoying his company and his counsel, Jahangir had rewarded him with high rank and counted him a personal friend. His robes of honor, horses with jeweled saddles and fine weapons from Shah Jahan's father were part of his lavish estate. Shah Jahan had assumed that Lodi would be loyal to him because he had followed his father onto the throne. He had been so certain the friendship was reciprocated that he had girded him with a sword traditionally bestowed only upon members of the royal family. He had anticipated a close future with the witty and charming Afghan.

Lodi had different ideas. No longer satisfied being a man who only treated himself as a king, he was now in a position to become a ruler himself. His change in attitude was easier since Jahangir, the man who had originally held his loyalty, was no longer on the throne. He wanted more than terraced gardens in Kashmir and feasts of fifty dishes.

He had become receptive to the whispers of Afghans who had been wooing him for many years. These serious men from the north were rougher, more brooding, and sometimes more explosive than other courtiers. Afghans were frequently in attendance at Shah Jahan's court, but many grumbled that they were not fairly represented. Considering themselves courageous warriors and therefore deserving a greater presence, they had approached Lodi to be their king. They wanted him to raise their banner and lead them against the empire that was not giving them enough respect.

At first Lodi ignored them, but gradually their words overcame his resistance, and he began to listen more seriously. Flattered to think he had been chosen as a leader, he eventually agreed it was fitting for him to wear a crown. He accepted the banner of his Afghan countrymen and in so doing became a threat to Shah Jahan's empire. Learning of his former friend's switch of allegiance, Shah Jahan gave the order to have him arrested. Alerted by his palace spies, Lodi acted quickly. Except for the few jewels he had stitched into his clothing, he left his immense wealth and swiftly escaped into the night.

Before reading this most recent report, Shah Jahan did not

know the Afghan had gone to the interior of the subcontinent. A confederacy of the southern powers led by Lodi was a threat to his own rule. It was difficult to retain the fractious Deccan, and with the Afghans banding various tribes and clans together, even more so.

"Lodi must be stopped in this conflict between his Afghan vanity and my Mughal prestige." Shah Jahan spoke unwaveringly. "At this time, our troops are without question stronger than him, but we can't count on that in the future. We will put a final and decisive end to his plans." Shah Jahan polled the men around him for the name of a man to command the army.

Even as he asked, an idea came to him. Slowly and thoughtfully, he turned his choice around in his mind. Aloud he added, "We need a man who knows the country well. Someone who is willing to smother Lodi completely, so there are no sparks left to ignite a future fire."

A smile slightly upturned the corners of his lips. "I know who we shall send." There was a pause while the men around him waited to hear his choice. "I will go myself."

Aghast at the thought, his advisors spoke simultaneously in a tumble of sentences.

"It is not worthy of your prestige."

"We have others we can assign."

"You are needed here in Agra."

Shah Jahan knew the victory would be more significant and longer lasting if he commanded from the field rather than from the throne in Agra. There was another reason he wanted to go himself. He had been the emperor for two years and longed to leave the stultifying routines that controlled his days as well as the fawning of the court.

The predictable routine of his days had begun to chafe him. Before every sunrise that did not herald a holiday, Shah Jahan woke, completed his ablutions, and said private prayers in his personal mosque. At sunrise he stepped onto the jharoka balcony to receive the adulation from below as he basked in the first rays of the sun. Next he sat in command at the public durbar, followed by the smaller, more intimate durbar on the south side of the open terrace that overlooked the Jumna. From there he went to an even more private spot, the Shah Burj, where he met with only the most senior officers.

It was not until these three audiences were finished was he able to seek the privacy of the zenana. Even there, he could not escape being a judge. At least during the monthly Zenana Durbars he had the luxury of lounging in softness, rather than sitting in his usual upright and cross-legged position of the morning, as he assigned dowries, awarded money for medical attention, and approved marriage matches. Though many petitions had already been heard and decided by Mumtaz, the highest-ranking woman in the zenana, there were always cases for him to hear.

After his zenana respite, he was expected back at the Shah Burj, then more hours at the smaller audience location for less formal gatherings and matters of lighter importance. Because he drank only moderately, and because he would be up again early in the morning, he usually left before the others.

In bed he would listen to relaxing musicians until ten o'clock when, from behind a screen, a smooth-voiced reader lulled him to sleep. When she noticed the emperor was no longer awake, she would whisper, "May your awakening be perfumed with the scent of violets" before she slipped away.

This was the life of the emperor, a life he had aspired to for decades. Knowing he would want to return to it, Shah Jahan nevertheless anticipated changing his daily routine long enough to subdue Khan Jahan Lodi.

The Great Mughal was unaware of the grief that awaited him in the Deccan was greater than any he had previously experienced in the unlucky region.

37

Moonlight Mahal ~ 1630

Trust me, Taj. You'll soon understand.

Mumtaz stared at the note sent by her husband and said to Sattisima, her attendant in the howdah, "I have no idea what he is talking about." Was he referring in some way to how he had tried to dissuade her from leaving the palace because she was again with child? She had justified her insistence that she come travel with him because of her history of doing so. Snuggling further into her cushions she spoke to Sattisima, "I'm in the early stages of this pregnancy, and we will arrive long before howdah travel becomes too uncomfortable."

Sattisima, who had never been away from Agra, barely heard the empress. She was peeking between the curtains of their elephant-top conveyance as Mumtaz had done on her first journey. "Oh, look at the long-legged birds standing in the river. There is some sort of a building I can barely see far back in the trees." Her dark eyes sparkled with delight to notice what she assumed no one else had seen before.

"What an unusual grouping of tree," she continued. "It looks as if they were all planted in the form of a square. There are even sharp corners."

Mumtaz had been listening nonchalantly to Sattisima's comments. When she heard mention the "square" of trees, she hurriedly opened the curtains herself.

There they were. She knew those trees. They were planted slightly past the point where the road divided, one track heading south and the other to...Moonlight Mahal. With a twist of her head, she could see her elephant and one other had separated from the long cavalcade that had left Agra and were now alone on the road leading to the place where she and Khurram had spent so many wonderful times.

Laughing aloud with the glee of a young girl presented with a surprise, Mumtaz finally understood the note she had received. She and Khurram were heading to her favorite place in the entire world. She reveled in the memory of their last visit and her enchantment not only with its physical beauty but how their own special garden encouraged them to grow spiritually, emotionally, and, when pregnancies had not been too advanced, physically.

When Mumtaz climbed out of her howdah, Shah Jahan was waiting for her. She would have responded to the gladness within her and rushed into his arms if she had not learned to forgo such undignified behavior. In private he was Meerijan, but where others could see them, he was the emperor and she was the empress

A servant began to open the gate, but with enthusiasm breaking through her previous restraint, Mumtaz held out her hand, and the startled gateman dropped the key into it. Slowed by an eagerness that caused her to tremble slightly, Mumtaz fumblingly fit the key into the lock and pushed the gate open with her small hands.

Before she stepped into the Moonlight Mahal, she paused, wondering if the garden had been neglected during the last year since Takarrub had passed away. Tentatively, she advanced, looked around her, and smiled with relief. Moonlight Mahal, bathed in warm sunlight, bloomed as wondrously as she remembered. Moving down the familiar walkway, she remembered every tree, flowering bush, and shrub.

Then she stopped and looked around her carefully. Here was a newly planted bed of flowers. The comely fountain in front of her hadn't been there earlier. What was the large shadow in the chenar

Ahnkus

tree near the lake's shore? She should be able to see the tent from this spot but did not find it.

Behind her, Khurram had halted, waiting for her reaction to the surprise he had prepared for her. He could see her begin to suspect a change and the hope that came with the thought. Slowly she raised her still-clenched hand and carefully opened her fingers. Inside was the key she'd used to open the gate. Not interested in the key itself, she looked at the attachment joined to the key that would confirm or deny her hope. The enameled strip hanging from the key ring no longer displayed the lotus crest of Takarrub's family but an outline of a crouching lion.

Moonlight Mahal now belonged to the Mughals! She and Khurram owned It! She turned to meet his eyes, and by the time she rushed toward him, his smile matched her own.

When Khurram had heard of Takarrub's death, he had made inquiries about the ownership of the garden that had come to mean so much to him and to Taj. When Takarrub had been alive, he would not have thought of asking his friend to sell this Garden that carried such personal meaning. After the older man's death, Khurram had discovered Takarrub's only daughter was married, lived far away, and seemed to have no further interest in what had meant so much to her parents. She gladly sold it to Shah Jahan.

Since his acquisition, he had had gardeners plant new flowerbeds, plasterers smooth the surrounding walls, engineers clear the fountains, and builders create a marble tree house for two.

He took Mumtaz' hand and strolled slowly to the spot near the water's edge where the white silk tent had been. Nearby its former place, built among the branches of the chenar tree, was an open room reached by dainty marble steps curving upward along the outside of the tree's trunk. Protected by branches all around and offering a nest-level view of the lake and the smaller garden below, their private space awaited.

Mumtaz stood at the railing of their tree house inhaling deeply, internalizing everything Moonlight Mahal meant to her. Then she noticed the same float had been recovered with new silver cloth.

Khurram's nearby, soft voice whispered to her that there would be a full moon. Their eighteen years of marriage had not diminished their physical need. It had taught Mumtaz, among other things, what it meant when Khurram ran his thumbnail softly down her back as he did now. She turned toward him, her desire matching his.

38

Moonlight Mahal ~ 1630

Mumtaz was no longer the untouched woman who had first embraced her husband on their wedding night. The first time they were together her fears of a loveless marriage had quickly been replaced by a passion totally new to her. Khurram, already experienced in the physical act of love, felt a depth of emotion he had never known before he and Mumtaz were married.

Through the years, Mumtaz had learned the most pleasurable positions and movements and had become her partner's equal in the art of lovemaking. To Khurram, Taj's beauty had developed and changed with their years and glowed irresistibly to him. With her he had reached his greatest levels of passion

In this most private spot of their exclusive garden, the two of them unabashedly pressed their bodies together with pleasure and anticipation. Slowly, enjoying the luxury of time, they removed the clothing which obstructed the intimacy of skin touching skin. Sensually, intimately, wearing only jewelry, they fully embraced.

Aroused by his wife's nakedness, Khurram responded to her aroma and warmth as he began gently touching the length of her arms. No matter how often he stroked her he was never satiated. When their skin connected, tingles of desire shot through his pores, mingling his hard angularity and her soft curves. The erection rising between them signaled his body's desire to move beyond the euphoria of foreplay.

Mumtaz wove her fingers behind Khurram's neck. With closed eyes she welcomed the slow and sensual uncurling of her internal response and the gradual, powerful, and encompassing knowledge that she was able to both give and receive pleasure. Khurram's touches slid further down to her hips and pulled her even more tightly toward him.

With a small sound of pleasure, Mumtaz, no longer able to hold still, began moving in an age-old rhythm. Pressing her hips tightly against him, she encouraged his hands to glide smoothly and tantalizing upward until he found, then held, her soft, heavy breasts. Larger than usual in preparation for their child within her, they were also connected to the core of her sexual energy. The couple moved with deliberate slowness, aware of the journey they had begun.

Moving his thumb over her responsive nipple, Khurram softly kissed Mumtaz' eyelids, nose, cheeks, and finally her lips. Bending further, careful not to scrape his bearded chin on her delicate skin, he included her neck, shoulders, and the tantalizing cleavage formed when his hands gently pushed her breasts together.

Mumtaz, increasing the circular, stimulating pressure of her hips, clasped her hands around her husband's neck, signaling him with her breathing that she was aroused. He stimulated her nipples with licks and flutters of his tongue.

A primitive need moved them onto the bed that had been scattered with fresh flower petals. Mumtaz' fingers and the palms of her hands tingled with desire when they caressed the soft black hair growing on Khurram's arms. Even when her pregnancies had prohibited lovemaking, touching one another had communicated messages of past memories and future fantasies.

Though he was quicker and hotter than Mumtaz, Khurram did not slip inside her until he was certain she was ready, allowing her slower pace to relax his own quicker response. He waited for her body's cue that she was ready to progress—a quickening breath overlaid with the aroma of musk.

Khurram sat with his legs straight in front so Mumtaz could rise onto her knees over him. She guided his hard member to the opening they both wanted him to enter. Locking eyes, she slowly lowered herself onto him. Without breaking eye contact she deftly moved her feet behind his back as she slid her hands to the outside of his shoulders.

They looked deeply into each others' eyes and lifted their tongues to the roofs of their mouths to complete the circle of sexual energy within each of them.

Moving into the role of the other, each shared sensations of entering and being entered. Intimate sounds, hums, breaths, and words filled their sensitive ears as they increased internal tension. Eventually, they relinquished the satisfaction of the moment for the potential ecstasy of the future. With sharp intensity, they were gripped by an internal wave that curled and crashed around them as their sexual energy erupted.

Mumtaz' peak traveled up her spine and out to her fingers and toes, then languorously back again. Khurram continued to stare into the open eyes of his wife even as he experienced a column of cool water moving from his center to the top of his head. Their mutual orgasms allowed them to gain access to the other's soul.

When their world was again quiet, they remained entwined. Mumtaz dropped her head on Khurram's chest and listened to his still-hammering heart. He brought his feet together behind her and they melted closer than before. Their arms, breath, and bodies mingled as their sexual energies retreated, ready to be accessed again.

When her breathing resumed normalcy, Mumtaz lifted her head from Khurram's shoulder, placing her hands on his forearms. He put his hands atop her arms. Gazing at one another, more softly than earlier, they meditated to receive revelations from Allah in their joined position.

Warm energy again radiated from their sexual centers, slowly moving upward and filling their bodies. They knew if they placed their hands on the other's head, they would draw this energy up from its base. Choosing the peace they had attained, rather than a second flood of heat, they remained still.

❈ ❈ ❈

THE SKY WAS NOW FILLED with moonlight. Moonbeams dappled their still-naked bodies with the same pattern of leaves that had shielded them from the sun's earlier heat and brightness and threw intricate shadows on the marble floors.

Unaware that they had slipped apart, Mumtaz awoke hours later and opened her eyes. Khurram was on his elbow, staring at her, pleased by her look of a woman who had been loved to fulfillment. "I'm envious of the jewels you still wear because of their nearness to your body."

Mumtaz smiled and Khurram continued. "I've found more in our relationship than I would have thought possible. When we are together, the most important part of my life is being your husband and lover. When I sense you are happy, it intensifies my own happiness in a way nothing else can."

Mumtaz reached for his hand and put it on a bare breast, her gesture and look warming him with reciprocated love. Then she glanced at the sky and the full, round moon. Her eyes darted back to Khurram's with her eyebrows raised in question. Words were not needed between them, and Khurram nodded agreement. With a last gentle movement before he rose and ran his hand from her breast to her knees, feeling the usual and delightful tingle. Mumtaz commanded the preparation of the float, and, dressed casually, the two of them descended to the lake.

Comfortable cushions, wine, and sweetmeats were in place by the time they slipped aboard. Pushed onto the water and illuminated by the white brilliant light of the moon, they rocked gently atop the water. Filled with the languorous satiation, they reclined lazily. Their fingers brushed as they raised their goblets to one another. They touched when crossing their legs. Wordlessly, they reached for the other's waiting hand and softly locked gazes. The pleasurable closeness and their memories of recent activities in their treehouse began awakening the energies and passions they had not long ago tucked away. The familiar flow was starting to rise and envelop them.

"Taj…"

The sensual feminine movement of her eyelashes told him she understood. "There's only one reason I'd want to leave the lake and the moonlight, Meerijan," she whispered suggestively.

Responding by signaling for the float to be pulled in by its chain, Khurram agreed. "We'll view the full moon from under the branches of a tree."

The movement of Mumtaz' hips under her skirt as she climbed the stairs that twisted up the trunk of the chenar entranced Khurram. As he followed her, he anticipated a repeat of the loving they had shared in what was now their moonlit room.

39

Burhanpur ~ 1631

"Mmmm." Shah Jahan's deep satisfaction was contained in a relaxing exhalation of breath. Godar, a Turkish Body Servant, was giving him an oil massage. He was enjoying the deep rhythmic motions of the strong-fingered woman. Jahanara was with her father this summer night in Burhanpur, a city in the Deccan, Mumtaz had taken her pregnant body to bed. As Godar continued, the emperor carried on a conversation with his attractive seventeen-year-old daughter, now almost as old as Mumtaz had been when he had first met her. Educated and cultured, Jahanara shared Mumtaz' same delicate features, heart-shaped face, and long black hair. Knowing she would never wed, Jahanara had formed strong bonds with her father and brothers—the only men she would know.

"Uhhg." Godar's pressure on his right lower back forced a grunt from the emperor. Ruefully Shah Jahan said, "That's the way I feel about the rebellion I'm here to quell."

"How long had you been friends with Khan Jahan Lodi?"

"I've known him much longer than I've been emperor. When I was a youngster he was already a handsome, daring man that my father liked. We should be enjoying each other's company right now rather than fighting, but his devious actions and nighttime escape from the fort have destroyed my trust in him."

The man under Godar's hefty hands had tensed while he spoke.

He jerked when another spot on his back was pushed.

"What does that feel like?" questioned Jahanara when she noticed his movement.

The emperor tried to answer her strange question with the thoughts that were on his mind. "That was the pain I feel for the farmers and their families in the Deccan for having to deal with monsoons that didn't come, crops that failed, and pestilence that is taking a heavy toll. The last time I rode through this country it was filled with life. This time the horror and destruction of famine and plague surrounded us".

Shah Jahan knew there were concerns, such as Khan Jahan Lodi and the plight of his peasants that he could talk about, yet there was another matter he was not able to mention. Not even to Jahanara. He was uneasy about Mumtaz though his wife had not complained. There was nothing definite he could point to, but she seemed more withdrawn, more easily tired than with her other pregnancies. She was a woman who had always been strengthened by gestation and able to withstand the additional weight she incurred with each one. She had usually glowed with the awareness that she was carrying a new soul.

When he had had these thoughts before, he had chided himself. *What did he expect?* he asked himself. *She is near the end of her thirteenth pregnancy. This is the time her thoughts and energies are on the child that will soon be born through her. She births babies rather easily, and I haven't worried before. Why would this time be any different? She'll have the best of everything for the birth and afterwards.*

As he contemplated Mumtaz, Shah Jahan knew he was not only concerned for his wife and her oncoming labor, but was petulantly wishing she were more available to him. He missed the physical closeness that was now awkward, but more than that, he missed her sage advice and counsel. Even when she was in the room with him lately, he felt part of her mind was somewhere else. It was almost as if she was concerned about something. Nonsense, he scolded himself. He was her husband and an emperor of a grand empire. He could protect her.

"What are you building now, Bapu?" Jahanara broke the silence that had fallen.

Shah Jahan's passion for architecture was well known to his daughter. He had already added a multitude of buildings in the empire to symbolize his reign as well as additional mosques to proclaim the strength of Islam. Her question effectively moved his thoughts toward the relaxing topic. His face brightened, Godar felt his muscles relax, and his muffled voice became happily conspiratorial as he decided to share a secret with his daughter.

"There's something I'm doing right now that's a surprise. I'll tell you if you keep the information from your mother."

Reluctantly, Jahanara promised, even though his request would be difficult. She agreed with her father that her mother was a treasure, an influential presence wherever she was.

"I'm building a brand new apartment for Taj in the Agra palace. It will be larger and finer than the one she now has. In the new one, she'll be able to take better advantage of the breezes off the river and will be more removed from sounds of the palace and the fort. I'm using white marble for the walls and the roof is beaten gold."

He talked on about the design, the balconies, and the fountains of the apartment that would be finished when they returned from Burhanpur. As Shah Jahan continued voicing his enthusiasm and the delight this elegant surprise would bring Taj, Godar's sensitive fingers on his back noticed continued relaxation of his muscles.

Jahanara sighed. The love so evident between her parents surpassed anything she had found in the poetry she read. She realized her father, now silent with thoughts of her mother filling his mind, was no longer aware of her presence. She stood, walked toward the prone man both she and her mother loved, and kissed him on the top of his head before she glided smoothly from the room. Uncharacteristically, she allowed herself to grieve that she would never inspire a man the way her mother inspired her father. *Since I can't marry and have children,* she consoled herself, *I have to enjoy other people's babies. There are many from mother alone.* Even that thought caused sadness to Jahanara this evening, for she remembered the brothers and sisters who were no longer alive.

Jahanara, particularly sensitive to Mumtaz, would have agreed with her father that this thirteenth pregnancy was somehow more troublesome than the others had been. No wonder, she thought. Not only did we witness famine and plague on the way south, but Mother's trusted daiya, the woman who had delivered her last seven babies, was too old to make the trip to attend her during this birth.

Jahanara recalled the differences in this pregnancy of her mother's. Her shape and her walk looked uncomfortable. Perhaps, she felt all right, however, for she didn't complain. *Soon, I will be playing with a new baby, maybe even a sister.* Jahanara smiled at the thought of tiny hands and feet and baby rattles and her mother returning to being the woman she usually was.

40

Burhanpur ~ 1631

Shah Jahan heard little of the battle around him and was only partially aware of charging soldiers, heavy cannons, and flashes of vividly colored fabric. He was, as he had been twelve times before, mentally with Taj as the baby she had been carrying was about to be separated from her to begin its own life. Swords met, rifles shot, arrows hit shields, and the men and animals around him shouted, whinnied, and trumpeted as he gazed through unseeing eyes and heard the sounds as if they came from afar.

Mumtaz' petite body didn't seem robust enough to have produced so many children. He praised Allah, knowing a child could be replaced but Mumtaz couldn't. I've a choice between not one but four sons to follow me onto the throne, he thought, and two daughters besides. He reflected again at how differently the boys had developed even though they were born of the same parents. *We have produced a mystic, a playboy, a puritan, and a bully,* he mused.

His reverie ended suddenly when he spied a lone maroon-turbaned messenger riding swiftly toward him. When he scanned the scrolled paper the messenger handed him, Shah Jahan smiled and gave the order for eighteen guns to salute the birth of a princess. Taj would be pleased to have another daughter, and he hoped she would grow to resemble her mother. There would be prayers, alms, feeding of the poor, and gifts to celebrate this royal birth.

But he must have missed information about Taj. He reread the message for word of her condition, but there was no mention. He commanded the rider to return with haste to the palace and then back to him with word of the empress' health. Waiting with impatience, he was relieved to finally read that Taj was fine, desired a nap, and wanted to see him later.

Knowing his nagging sense of unease would diminish only after he had seen his wife, he accepted he could do nothing for her yet. He would see her when he held his newest daughter, kissed her forehead, and gave his prayer of thanks for the birth. He would, as always, include a prayer for Taj as well.

When the battle halted for darkness, Shah Jahan eagerly rode to the palace only to be told his wife was still sleeping. Understanding her need to rest after childbirth, he turned toward his own sleeping quarters with disappointment but a certainty he shouldn't disturb her.

That night he dreamed of floating in a vast darkness, unable to tell if he was facing up or down, trapped by a total lack of light. He was adrift in a soundless, endless universe. Waiting for him in this void without light, just out of reach, was a nameless pain moving nightmarishly toward him. He didn't understand why such ugliness was present, only that he must avoid its nearness.

It was from this dark suspension in the sunless hours of early morning that a frantic servant unceremoniously shook Shah Jahan awake. The emperor opened his eyes to the light of a lantern that allowed him to recognize his own quarters.

"The queen! Hurry! She needs you right away!"

Shatum's panicked voice matched the emotion Shah Jahan had felt in his dream, and compelled the emperor to run to Mumtaz' room. Before him was Pakhini, the midwife. Her reddened eyes and her heaving chest pierced Shah Jahan's heart with alarm. Her blood-smeared clothing added to his fear, as did the tears she was no longer trying to conceal.

When she saw Mumtaz's husband, Pakhini sobbed. "She came to the birth already tired, Your Majesty." Her tears fell freely.

"Even so, the birth was not unusual. She even fell asleep after the baby was born. When I looked in at her hours later, she hadn't awakened but was lying in a pool of her own blood.

"I couldn't stop her bleeding, even though I tried everything I know." Her sobs were beginning to make her words unintelligible. "The blood just kept coming and coming."

Wringing her hands in despair, her large bosom heaving up and down as she talked through gulping sounds, Pakhini went on. "She wasn't rested today. Her heart was heavy with sorrow for the suffering of the people around us." Speaking the very words Shah Jahan had been thinking, she rambled on. "The many times her small body created life has taken its toll."

Noticing the stricken look on Shah Jahan's face, she hastened to add, "She loves you and wants your children, Your Majesty." Her anguish came to her again, and she wept unabashedly. Struggling to speak again, she frantically looked at Shah Jahan. With courage born of desperation, she ordered her emperor. "Go see her quickly. She doesn't have much more time with us."

He had never moved more quickly. Striding through the door and to his wife's bedside, Shah Jahan slashed with his hand to keep others out. He wanted to be alone with Taj. In the dim candlelight, he could see the prone figure of a woman lying on a bed with her silk sheet tucked under her arms and her royally crested blanket folded down. He approached quietly, knelt by her side and took her unnaturally frail hands between his own. He was so very close to the face he had loved for nineteen years. When she felt his touch, Mumtaz slowly and heavily opened her eyes.

He leaned forward to press his lips on the hands he held. Releasing one of them to lift a strand of hair from her face and softly stroke her cheek and forehead, he marveled how, even now, her skin remained welcoming to his touch.

"I'm so sorry, Meerijan."

She had spoken in a faint voice just as he had bowed his head to pray that she would live. Looking up quickly, hoping his request had been answered, he saw although life had returned to her midnight eyes, it wasn't the sparkle that usually lived there. The realization that she was moving to another world crumpled the hope he had felt when he had heard her voice.

She *couldn't* die. He loved her. He wanted her to smile at their children, turn her face to the moonlight and touch his cheek. For nineteen years, she had been close to him, traveled with him, and had given him children. She had loved him, had accepted his love, and had freely shared her mind and body. All that she had and was belonged to him. She had freed his heart to love beyond all expectations.

She tenderly repeated the words, "I'm so sorry, Meerijan."

"Taj." As he spoke his special name for her, his soft voice reflected what she was to him.

With a small smile, she continued in a barely audible voice. "I'd always thought you and I would have more time together."

Speaking as gently as she had, he interrupted her attempt to speak. "And we will. You need to rest now, Taj. Sleep and allow your body to restore you." Although he spoke lightly, a heaviness in his heart told him his words were powerless.

Powerless! Surely, as the Great Mughal, I could keep her alive. If I could exchange this one precious life for the dozens I have already sent to Azreal, I would. I would even forego my position of power...wealth, and, yes, Allah please understand, my children. Nothing, absolutely nothing, meant as much to me as this woman. As suddenly as it arrived, his vehemence departed, leaving in its place the initial tendrils of a numbing awareness of his inability to change the course of the next moments. She was journeying alone and leaving him behind. She was leaving him...

Mumtaz struggled to speak to this man who'd been her life. "Meerijan, don't sorrow." With shallow breathes she whispered, "I've lived the life many women have only dreamed. Allah has granted me your arms, your voice, your protection, your love. I'll wait for you in Paradise. We are meant to be together."

Though her breath was uneven, she was determined to finish. In a voice softer than a whisper, she managed to say, "Perhaps my greatest sin was loving you more than I loved even Allah. Perhaps that's why He's taking me from you so soon."

Still holding his eyes with hers as her life force slowly drained away, she spoke a single word.

"Please…?"

"Yes, Taj? Whatever you want." His world was beginning to darken. He leaned over so that his ear was close to her mouth and she could make her final request with less effort.

"A queen…"

"A queen? You are my queen, Taj. You are my queen."

"Please, Meerijan… Don't take another." The last touches of pale color drained from her face.

Before he could assure her that no other woman would ever have her place in his heart, she pressed his hands gently. "I love you, Meerijan."

Her eyes closed. The pressure was gone.

Taj was gone.

Shah Jahan held very still, paying no attention to the cooling of the hands he still held. He was, for the second time that night, adrift in darkness surrounded by pain. This time no one would awaken him.

41

Burhanpur ~ 1631

The sound of a soft voice coming from Mumtaz' room caused the midwife to wipe the tears from her eyes and listen. Could it possibly be that the empress had been revived by the nearness of her husband? Even though Pakhini could not hear the words clearly, the daiya was certain someone was talking.

Hesitantly, silently, she padded to the doorway. Hoping a miracle had somehow occurred, she peered into the room. Her heart sank.

Neither her distance from the royal bed nor the shadows in the room could mask the lifelessness of the woman on the bed. The words she heard had not been coming from the late empress, but were flowing from the lips of the only other person in the room.

Shah Jahan, holding his wife's hands in both of his was murmuring to her as if she could hear him. The daiya retreated, leaving him to deny his wife's death as long as he could.

※ ※ ※

"SLEEP NOW, DEAREST TAJ. Sleep and get your strength back. Birthing our daughter was strenuous, and you'll feel better after a rest. Perhaps women in the zenana can tell you how to prevent further pregnancies, so we can avoid this exhaustion in the future." He placed her hands together on her chest. Straightening the blanket that covered her body, he continued. "You know, I'm not your only admirer. Many others love you and wait for you to be fully and vibrantly part of their lives again. You lighten the zenana with your sunshine.

"Our children adore you. Though they have ayahs and servants, you're the woman they cherish the most. You've carried them, stroked them, crooned to them, and rocked them. You've filled them with memories. They know you'd grieve for each of them as you have already done for their unfortunate brothers and sisters who are no longer with us.

"Our lovely daughter Jahanara is a young woman now. I can see you in her walk, her laugh, and her song. She'll have everything she desires, other than a husband, of course.

"Taj, you were born for me to cherish. I've loved you since the night when you were so very unsure about being my wife. Our talk was my first interesting conversation with a woman. By the time we consummated our marriage, I already knew that you were meant for me in some important way...a way that I didn't understand then, and maybe I still don't today."

With great tenderness, he leaned over and gazed at her tranquil face. Putting his hands together at the top of her head and drawing them down along her cheeks until his fingertips met below her chin, he touched her face for the last time. The gesture, buried deeply in his subconscious mind, was identical to the one the fakir had used in farewell to the infant Khurram long ago in the royal garden.

"I like myself best when I'm with you. You help me to see my wisdom, compassion and sense of justice." He gazed at the woman who had filled him with so much happiness. Then he cocked his head as if listening. His voice changed, his eyes became wider, and his breath quickened. He stiffened.

"Something dark is lurking in the corners of the room, Taj." He'd leaned down to whisper to her urgently. "If I can hold your hand, it won't move any closer."

Saying so, he took her hands into his own. The threatening darkness did not move closer. Focusing again on the soothing and calming words as before, he continued in his normal voice.

"You're my wife, the mother of my children, and my lover. I can't imagine life without you."

Beyond the shadowy corners, the ominous presence moved again.

"Something is slithering nearer, Taj. Even though I can't see it, I know it's evil. It's using the air in the room, and it's becoming difficult for me to breathe." He let go of her hands and turned his body to face the unknown and protect her from the threat.

"It's creeping toward me, edging closer and closer. It's touching me and trying to tear me away from you." Thrusting his hands behind him, he expected Taj, who had always been there for him when he needed her, to take hold of him and in so doing disintegrate the grief that steadily advanced.

"Help me, Taj. Hold tight to me," he shouted desperately.

But she didn't respond in any way. In that terrible moment the veil of denial was lifted. Shah Jahan did not have to touch her skin, lift her wrist and allow it to fall limply back upon the blanket, or watch her chest for signs of movement. He knew again what he had known but denied immediately after she feebly squeezed his hand.

Mumtaz, his Taj, was dead.

Shah Jahan, no longer an emperor as much as a despairing husband, wailed his intense agony and loss. His cries echoed down the hallway, as the lurking grief could no longer be held off.

Hours later, Jahanara, one of the only people allowed to enter the room, joined him. Her tear-streaked face revealed her own loss. Aware of her father's indescribable pain, she stood near Shah Jahan, saying nothing. After looking for the last time at the face of her much loved mother, she gently touched her father's shoulder and led him away. June was hot in Burhanpur, and the women waiting to prepare the body needed to begin soon if Mumtaz were to receive the swift burial required by Islam.

The room became the center of activity as Body Preparers entered to begin their important and delicate tasks. From all directions, women appeared to share their deeply felt loss of Mumtaz Mahal. They lamented the death of their empress with their voices even as they had embraced her in life with their hearts. They ignored the Koran's prohibition against loud wailing and notified Allah with ululations of sorrow that Mumtaz had been taken from them.

The royal body was washed in cold camphor water, rather than in the warm baths Mumtaz had chosen in life. Fine garments and jewels belonged to the living; she was to be buried wearing a plain white shroud of five pieces of cotton with no other adornments.

Shortly before they had finished, the women received a single piece of jewelry delivered to them by a royal messenger. With it was a note written in Shah Jahan's hand. He had sent them a ruby and pearl earring and asked that it be buried on, not with but on, his queen. Just one? Curious. Unwilling to refuse the wish of their grieving emperor, they obediently slipped the earring into Mumtaz' ear for the last time, paused, then covered her face softly with a strip of cotton.

Mumtaz' prepared body was placed gently in a coffin, her head pointing north and her face turned toward the Kaaba. Shortly thereafter, four relatives carried her to a temporary home in a garden on the banks of the Tapti River. A stunned Shah Jahan silently watched the white bundle disappear and mourned deeply for the woman who had died so suddenly that not even a single verse of the Koran had been recited at her bedside. As the mullahs read the appropriate verse of burial, the emperor wailed for Taj and for the part of himself that was being buried with her. Before he turned away, Shah Jahan tore his hair as anguish freshly assailed him and he again experienced the wrenching pain of losing Taj twice in one day.

Mumtaz' life was finished, but her husband felt none of her peacefulness. He returned to her grave daily, always leaving with tears glistening on his cheeks. Rage, anguish, and desolation mingled with his devastation. Physical movement was difficult for him, and each step felt as if he was pushing his heavy body through deep water. He walked, leaning against another to prevent a fall, and he had difficulty holding up his own head.

He ordered that only white clothing could be worn and no alcoholic drinks could be served for two years. Music and perfume were banned and no one was allowed to wear Mumtaz' special scent. The strict mourning requirements stunned the lavish and pleasure-seeking court in Burhanpur and throughout the reaches of the empire.

For days after Mumtaz' death, Shah Jahan ignored affairs of state in any form. He canceled his morning durbar and stopped appearing at the jharoka window. Two weeks after Mumtaz was buried, Shah Jahan remained overwhelmed with his loss. He broke into convulsive weeping whenever he was reminded of the woman he would never see again. He ignored the zenana because the sight of a woman or any of their female activities sent him into convulsive depression. He appeared unable to recover or become involved with life.

Shah Jahan's world had lost its flavor. His goodness, light, and color were leaching from him and formed an inaccessible knot deep within his slowly diminishing life force. He had no energy. His despair had become an expanding mass within his body continuously denying him less space for breathing. He understood that he would certainly die unless he confronted the darkness that was consuming him. He had to do it immediately—and he had to do it alone.

Abruptly, consulting no one, he barred the brass-covered door of his room from the inside. Unable to go to the aid of the man they could hear within, those who waited outside eventually had to accept that their knocks, pounding, and cries would remain unanswered.

Four entire days passed before Shah Jahan slowly opened the thick wooden door and moved out of his room. Gasps escaped the lips of all who saw him. The Shah Jahan they had known when

Mumtaz was alive was tall, proud and wore fine, well-cut fabrics with rich adornments. The man before them appeared small, frail, and slightly stooped. Rather than his usual costly clothing, he was wrapped in common white cotton, loosely tied in the fashion of a penniless mendicant.

But the most shocking sight of all was his hair. Shah Jahan had always enjoyed dark hair under his turban. Even his facial hair had been a glossy black that needed no charcoal to keep its youthful hue. When he emerged from his rooms, every strand had turned white. Although he had not shaved his head and mustache as Akbar had when his mother died, the change from black to white hair revealed the depth of his sorrow.

Shah Jahan had won the fight for his life, but he'd lost the eagerness and thrill of ruling his massive empire. He was anguished that Mumtaz had left him when she had promised not to do so. He bewailed that he was nothing more than a living corpse without Taj at his side. He imagined her lying peacefully in her dark grave and wept because not even a thousand lamps could light the darkened world that surrounded him. The most precious flower in his garden was gone.

42

Burhanpur ~ 1631

"I almost lost my mind, Jahanara." Shah Jahan was walking along the Tapti River in Burhanpur with his daughter. In a few weeks, he would follow the slow-moving funeral cortege led by his second oldest son, fifteen-year-old Shuja. The procession that was to leave soon was transporting Mumtaz' body to Agra where it would remain.

Although only seventeen, Jahanara saw the distress, grief, and lack of direction that assailed her father. She was shocked by his appearance. Had he actually lost height? He had suddenly become older, white haired and shaky. His eyes were sunken, and his cheekbones protruded beneath his tight facial skin. But most of all she was disturbed by the flat look in his usually alert eyes.

"What happened when you stayed in your room, Father? We heard terrible sounds but were unable to make sense of them."

Shah Jahan bent his head and clasped his hands behind his back, walking several steps before he spoke. His mind had returned to the day, only two weeks ago, when he had closed the door to the world. For the first time, he began to speak of the days he had spent by himself.

"I don't ever want to go through a time like that again." He shuddered at the memory of what he had lived through. "It started calmly enough," he began slowly. "I looked at the Persian carpets on the floor…the expensive tapestries on the wall…the exquisite marble. I thought about my embroidered clothes...my containers of jewels...the enameled incense holder...golden goblets and chalice...silver trays...hundreds of slippers.

"I was surrounded by luxury and heavily protected from enemies without." Here he paused, absentmindedly smelling a nearby rose, and then nodded as he spoke his next words. "The most destructive enemy was within."

"I was smothered by grief when your mother left. I had thought I'd accepted never having her in my life again, but I came to learn this wasn't true. What I was still hoping for was that my longing for her would provide a bridge for Mumtaz to rejoin me. Eventually, I knew I had to accept that she was gone...forever." It again became difficult for him to speak. "Because I hadn't yet allowed myself to fully accept my loss, I was unprepared for the thunderous forces threatening to overpower me." He shivered in the hot sun.

"I went from blaming the riches around me for not being able to save Mumtaz to being assaulted by dark, agonizing waves of despair surpassing anything I'd imagined. Between the first and second waves, I realized a dreadful sound was coming from deep within my being. This struggle with waves of the darkest and most foul forces I could imagine was what I'd have to face if I wanted to remain on earth.

"I was being dragged farther and farther away from the shore of life. I thought about Taj and wondered if I would find myself with her again if I succumbed.

"The feeling was stronger, more frightening, and more persistent than what pulled at me when I ventured into deep saltwater as a boy. I was frightened and fought back and was bashed, battered, tossed, and tumbled until I understood I couldn't resist the great power of the ocean. My realization became lifesaving then for it was only in surrender that I relaxed enough to allow other swimmers to save me. My strength this time was also in surrendering.

"I don't know how long I lay in a crumpled heap on the carpet in my room. I only know the waves of torment covering me with despair were slowly, so very slowly, abating, and my shouts and groans were becoming more human as they escaped my lips. Even though each onslaught brought physical pain, it became increasingly endurable."

Jahanara clearly remembered her fear when she stood outside her father's door, unable to assist and hearing his howling cries.

"At last, I realized I could move," Shah Jahan was recounting the rest of his ordeal in a rush. "I opened my eyes and saw the familiar room and knew I was still alive.

"Life was what I fought for, Jahanara, precious life. For some reason I would not allow myself to lose it. Many times I wanted nothing to do with living without Taj, but the decision did not seem to be mine. Why that was true, I don't know."

He had to stop speaking to allow the ache in his throat to subside. "But I do know this: I will never again be blessed with a love like the one I shared with Taj." He walked away heavily.

43

Burhanpur ~ 1631

Though Jahanara believed her father had told her everything, she was mistaken. He had actually kept to himself part of his experience that occurred prior to his emergence from his room dressed as a mendicant.

Finding no solace in the wealth within his room or his jewels, Shah Jahan had stripped off his clothes and wrapped a piece of plain cloth around his body. He slowly went from his room to the connected garden.

He stopped, surprised. He was not alone. His room was the only way into the garden, yet there was a stranger sitting comfortably as though he belonged in the private area. Shah Jahan shook his head, wondering if his days of seclusion had contributed to hallucinations. No...the stranger had not disappeared. Looking toward the spent emperor was a man also dressed in plain, wrapped cloth. His lean body was topped with a head of flowing white hair and each eyebrow was slashed in the middle with a band of black hair.

Shah Jahan had no idea how or why this man had entered his private garden nor did he understand his lack of inclination to summon the guards to have him removed. He somehow understood that this particular person was the one he needed at this dark moment in his life.

The cross-legged stranger held out his fisted hand, fingers down. Stepping forward as though commanded to do so, Shah

Jahan extended his own hand, palm open, under the stranger's fist. Something pleasingly heavy fell. Lowering his eyes to identify the object, Shah Jahan experienced flashes of disjointed and puzzling memories: a garden, this man, a cradle. He had been looking up at the same bushy eyebrows, an effervesant feeling in his body.

The yellow stone in his hand with its miniscule red flecks, appeared to be identical to the one he had kept close during his childhood. His ayah had never understood why, with all the lavish playthings available to him, he had so frequently carried it in his small hands. As he grew, he had tucked the large pebble inside his cummerbunds.

He had come to think of the yellow stone, warm and smooth as amber but not as opaque, as a talisman. He remembered the graceful shape etched into one side, engraved deeply enough to feel with his thumb. With his free hand, he now turned the weight over in his palm. The dark lines of an inverted lotus blossom sprouting a tall kalash and topped with a crescent were there—just as he remembered from long ago.

Before Shah Jahan could speak, the stranger's rich voice said, "I'm so sorry." Shah Jahan knew he was speaking of the loss of Mumtaz and was comforted by the sympathy conveyed in the simple words.

As he closed his fingers around the stone, Shah Jahan knew questions were unnecessary. He was filled instead with a need to pour out the torment he had been living. Not asking how the stranger had come to the garden or where he had found the stone, Shah Jahan sat and began talking.

He spoke of Taj, how he had deeply loved her. He spoke of his wife's loving ways, kindness, and intelligence. The way she held their children, the bleakness of his life without her. How he could no longer abide colors, perfume, music, wine, or entertainment, for they reminded him of their days together. His now-vacant world was no longer the glittering vista of endless gaiety and possibilities it had been when she was with him. Time dragged without Mumtaz rather than danced as it had. He cried that his soul was surrounded with darkness and that Allah had stricken him where he was the least able to resist.

"I don't understand the reason she left me. Why did she choose to live in a spiritual paradise rather than the earthly one I've created here for her?" he agonized.

The thought of returning to Agra without Mumtaz was bleak and cheerless. He spoke of walking away from his now-joyless position as emperor. He would leave everything he had and wander as a humble fakir throughout the land he had ruled for over two years. His eldest son, Dara, could sit on the throne.

The stranger with the zebra eyebrows had not spoken, nor had his eyes left the face of the emperor during the tormented man's cathartic monologue. When Shah Jahan finally stopped speaking, he hung his head and allowed large tears to fall. Sobs began to convulse his body but he made no move to hide his crying. The fakir gave no physical comfort to the weeping man before him, simply allowed him the opportunity to complete his needed cleansing.

Darkness crept into the king's garden while the two white-haired men sat facing one another. The elder produced a short, fat candle from his garments and placed it between them, lighting it as he did so. Eventually, within the circle of the candle's golden light, Shah Jahan's sobbing ceased and a comfortable silence lengthened between them.

When the fakir finally spoke, it was with a question. "Can you forget her?"

"Never," came the immediate reply. Then Shah Jahan wondered about the answer he had given so quickly. If he changed his life and never again saw anything he had shared with Taj, there was a chance he could forget her. Yes, it was only slight but there was a chance. He knew he could not return to Agra where they had lived and where her new apartments, begun so happily, would mock him. If he lived as a humble wanderer, perhaps his memories would keep their distance and fade.

Another question from the stranger. "Shall everyone else forget her?"

"Never!" It was the same word but spoken commandingly this time in contrast to the wistfulness of the first reply. "She'll be remembered forever by all the people who knew of her. They'll tell their children about Mumtaz, and she'll be honored through the ages. Their hearts will sing when they think of her, where mine only hurts."

"How will this happen?"

There was a thoughtful pause while Shah Jahan considered.

"Stories," he finally decided. "I'll command the court, and storytellers to speak of her goodness to all. She'll be given extra honor because of her death in childbirth."

"And who will obey the command of a beggar?"

Nodding agreement to the logic the stranger spoke, Shah Jahan changed his mind. "Then instead of ordering spoken memories, I'll build a monument for her. One proclaiming by its size and beauty that Mumtaz Mahal was loved by a mighty king."

The fakir thought about this reply. "Will you build this mausoleum from the rupees in your begging bowl?"

More silence.

Shah Jahan stared at the man before him. Assuming he would learn how he could abdicate his royal position but still build a grand mausoleum for Mumtaz, he settled back to listen.

I have to remove myself from all reminders of Taj to forget her. A magnificent monument would proclaim her importance, but I'd have to be a king to build such a mausoleum. I'd give away the treasure in Agra to have her back, but since that isn't possible, I can use it to honor her in another way. Time passed while Shah Jahan wrestled internally. Did he, after all, need to remain ruler of his empire to build a monument to Taj?

"Yes." His own voice, reluctant though it was, startled him in the quiet of the candlelit garden. "I must," he finished sadly.

Immediately, he was overwhelmed with the immense scope of the task—the time, effort, and constant thoughts of Taj. *I can't do it. I can't even imagine anything more heartbreaking than concentrating on the woman who has left such a void in my life. In a few years, it might be possible. Now, even the thought is unbearable. I can't transform my feelings for Mumtaz into a building. It would reveal too much of my heart, my very soul, in public for others to see.*

In despair, he voiced his thoughts in two words contradicting his previous utterings: "I can't."

For the first time since the two had met, the stranger touched Shah Jahan. Leaning over and placing his hands on either side of his head, he firmly pressed above the emperor's ears.

Shah Jahan was surprised to feel hands against his skin, for few others had touched him since he was a baby. Without a doubt, Shah Jahan realized he was in the presence of a great power. *But, who could it be? I'm the most influential man on earth,* he thought. *Only Allah...* his mind jerked to a stop. It was beginning to make sense. He felt the omnipotence of The One True God through this pair of thin brown hands. All too soon, the fakir removed his hands from the royal face and resumed a relaxed lotus position across from the bereaved man. Shah Jahan's awareness of the power from the Ultimate Source evaporated as soon as the fakir released his touch.

Looking sadly at the man before him, Shah Jahan spoke sorrowfully. "I'd like to build something as beautiful as Mumtaz was to me." He shook his head slowly before the next words were spoken. "But I can't," he whispered. "It can't be done."

Although this was the moment he had been awaiting since he had first seen Khurram as an infant, the fakir was reluctant to proceed. The man before him was the one Allah had selected to create a building exquisite enough to be His own abode on earth. Shah Jahan had lost a wife he had loved deeply, he was passionate about grandiose construction, and he commanded the treasury of an astoundingly wealthy kingdom. All the ingredients for a masterpiece were present, yet the zebra-browed man felt the sorrow Shah Jahan was living and wondered if the price for the mausoleum was too high. Shah Jahan's riches and artistic genius could be utilized only if he was willing to commit them.

Fakir knew during this night's sleep, Shah Jahan would see the vision Allah had designed. The ruler believed becoming emperor was the high point of his life. He did not yet suspect that he would be remembered for something still to come if he would accept what he woulddream. Shah Jahan had the opportunity to construct the essence of beauty and loveliness on earth.

Dejectedly, Shah Jahan stood and returned to his chamber. There he sat alone, certain he could not transform the radiance that had been Mumtaz into a mere building.

44

Burhanpur ~ 1631

Never suspecting a dream would influence his decision to stay on the throne, affect the lives of thousands of men, or change the skyline of Agra, Shah Jahan closed his eyes. Almost immediately he saw such a strikingly beautiful building that he gasped and found it difficult to take a deep breath. His heart pounded, for he recognized that the building was a dream in line and proportions.

Four sided but not square, it stood proudly before him, an original use of familiar arches and domes faced in white marble. In the vision, a large arch commanded the center of each of the four sides, and the whole was capped by an enormous dome. Four kiosks crowned with compatible, smaller domes encircled the neck of the dominating dome, thus continuing the swollen upper shape toward the building's sides with an elegance that appeared to have simply floated to its resting spot. The two sandstone buildings on either side served as anchors to keep the marble poem from floating away. Four minarets provided visual protection.

A reflection in the wide waterway repeated the glory of the shimmering marble edifice. Shah Jahan knew without a doubt that this was a dream from the spiritual world, not from the reality of life.

As magnificent as it was, the breathtaking structure before him would be difficult to build. To attempt such an ambitious task demanded a passionate commitment of materials, manpower, and wealth that he did not have. All feeling had been ripped away from him by the loss he had suffered. The contrast of the brightness of the vision and the darkness of his waking hours was heartbreaking. Wrapped in grief, he was alone, lost, languishing in the nadir of his life. He could not even yet bear to decide on a mausoleum design for Taj.

With the vision looming before his closed eyes and his thoughts on Mumtaz, Shah Jahan was instantly awake, sitting straight up. The vision faded and disappeared.

Taj. *Somehow there was a connection between her and what he had just seen. As much a lyric as a building, it radiated an aura of…of…* Unable to find the word to explain the impact he had felt, he snorted forcefully in exasperation.

Then it came to him. The word that explained why he had thought of Taj. The word he had been looking for, the word that explained the romantic emanation from the white marvel was… femininity.

With mounting excitement, Shah Jahan examined the image closely to confirm his thought that a building could incorporate features of womanhood. Taj had possessed astounding beauty, as did the vision he had just seen. Both she and the structure were unique, both pleased the eyes, and both exuded quality.

The simple, curved lines of the dome added to the graceful, rounded look. He remembered Taj's smooth loveliness that had had this same allure to his fingers and lips. Neither building nor the woman presented sharp corners to snag the eye or hand. Each corner of what could have been a square building had been removed leaving a short flat wall where the sides met. Nothing stopped a visual embrace.

So caught up was he in the stimulating comparison, Shah Jahan was unaware of the tears that flowed as they did regularly when he remembered Taj's death.

The building was a complex accumulation of curved lines, arches, and cupolas that echoed Taj's own depth. She had been a woman, a wife, and a lover. But she also had been a mother, a daughter, and a friend. In the zenana, she was the highest-ranking woman and the organizer of the women's durbars. She carried, birthed and loved their children, she traveled with him. She had been publicly proper, devout, educated, and cultured while privately she had also been sensual. Oh yes, she had been a complex woman.

Intricate features of the construction were increased and multiplied when the sky behind it changed. The sun-touched dome would be pink in the morning, white in the afternoon, and orange at sunset. At times, the backdrop of the sky would paint the dome with cloudy hues. Moonlight would create its own shades. Yes, both Taj and this dream structure were many-faceted.

Another comparison pleased him: a blend of cultural patterns. Persian and Indian styles increased the shapeliness of the design. Mumtaz, with her Persian background yet born and raised in Agra, was a feminine blend of the same influences.

Suddenly he understood. A man with zebra eyebrows and thin, brown hands softly cupping his face were part of this. The intense love and completeness he had felt with Mumtaz. His destiny to rule. They had all led to this vision. Beyond wearing the royal turban, he had to construct this most enchanting of buildings. It would be a marble palace fit for Mumtaz Mahal, his own Chosen of the Palace. He would give her the most dazzling mausoleum in the world by erecting on earth what now existed only in Allah's Paradise.

The more he put the pieces together, the more committed he became to turning his intense sorrow into a monument of powerful beauty. It would embody the emotions and soul of Mumtaz.

Before he slept again, Shah Jahan realized the stranger in his garden somehow had precipitated his acceptance of the huge task. How, he was not certain, but the last words the fakir had spoken lingered in his head.

"I cannot remove from your heart the powerful sorrow that is there," the old man had said. "What I can do is enable you to transform the depth of your private love to an external monument which will wordlessly say what you feel."

Shah Jahan rushed to where he had been the previous evening, wondering if the stranger had really been there, seen him sob, and touched his head. He had to know if it had been reality or part of his dream.

His private garden was empty. Not even malis were there to water, cut or trim the flowers. Walking to the exact area where he had sat, Shah Jahan noticed two objects on the ground. Slowly, he knelt to see them more closely. The first was a thick candle with a dark, used wick. The second was a smooth, yellow stone etched with the same graceful shape he had seen atop the dome in his dream. Holding the candle in one hand and the yellow stone in the other, Shah Jahan knew he would never see the fakir again. It was up to him alone to direct the next phase of his destiny.

45

Indian village - 1632

Chundar's village was a flurry of excitement. Farmers came from their fields, and women put aside their chores. Children scampered as they tried to help, pulling their mothers' skirts while excitedly attempting to move them toward the road. Villagers, resigned to repetitive days of cooking, cleaning, and farming, enthusiastically greeted the diversion. The excitement that lured them away from their usual routine was not to be missed: the Mughals would be passing soon.

Chundar had heard the news in his field and his thoughts returned to the memory of his experience in Agra. Even though he had received his lands back, Chundar wondered if the price of Malador's continued silence was worth the cost. A simple man, Chundar had come to place blame for the loss of Malador's voice on Shah Jahan. Turning back to his soil, he chose to not watch the procession.

The lure of glimpsing royalty, even as it passed their village only briefly, was strong, and few could resist. Even old Narayan had insisted he should be piled into a cart and rolled to watch. Villagers craned their necks as the cloud of airborne dust, at first a speck on the horizon, moved closer. Excited children ran ahead, then back to their parents, chirping their descriptions of what was coming.

The unknown reason for the procession was not as important as the fact that it was coming near their village. This display promised a brief glimpse of another world, a life they could live only vicariously. They were certain to see colorful clothing on the men and ornate coverings for the women's conveyances. If they were lucky, rupees would be thrown to them.

The children brought back more information about the procession. They returned with the somber news that the purpose of the stream of people and animals coming toward them was to take the body of Mumtaz Mahal to Agra where Shah Jahan would build a monument for her.

The villagers were stunned. The empress was dead. How did that happen? When did it happen? When Mumtaz' casket rolled by, they bowed their heads in silence. She had never been in their homes. She had never talked to them or to their children. She had not given them money. But they loved her. Loved her from the stories of her kindness, her beauty, and the love she shared with their emperor. Mumtaz' generosity with women and children and her affectionate nature had been well known throughout the land. Although distant, her glory had brightened their lives and now they were no longer able to live through it. No more stories about Mumtaz. No more wistful daydreams about their empress.

Women who died giving birth were particularly revered, and her frequent pregnancies elevated Mumtaz in the eyes of mothers from all walks of life. Women who had been blessed by their chosen gods and goddesses to produce a baby, shivered to learn that the most exalted woman in the land had not emerged alive after sharing this experience. She had, in this exclusively feminine way, given all she had to her husband.

Sorrow was woven into the fabric of the lives of the onlookers. Thousands of hearts knew and mourned a beloved woman, wife, or mother who had been taken from them in the same way Mumtaz had died. Their hearts went out to Prince Shuja who rode bravely with his back straight and his eyes forward attempting to hold in check his feelings of sorrow. He led the procession conveying his mother's casket to her second burial in Agra.

❋ ❋ ❋

BEFORE THE FUNERAL PROCESSION left Burhanpur, Shah Jahan had asked Shuja to come to him. He explained that Mumtaz, buried temporarily here, was to be taken home where he would begin to build a mausoleum for her remains.

"Before you even stop at the palace, take Mumtaz directly to the site of clear land a mile west of the fort. See to it that your mother is interred there on the bank of the Jumna, a river that fascinated her. I've traded four of my palaces to Raja Jai Singh for the plot of land that is to be used for the mausoleum."

The emperor seemed to drift away memories while Shuja waited for him to recall he was in the room. The power and force Shah Jahan usually exuded was noticeably subdued, causing Shuja to hope his father was still vibrant enough to build a proper monument.

As if reading his son's thoughts, Shah Jahan said, "The tomb I'll build for your mother will represent what she was for me." The design continued to be privately his, giving purpose to his life. He held onto it for stability as the rest of his meaningless world threatened to consume him.

Shuja, proud to be assigned the important task, did not appreciate the strength it took for his father to order Taj taken to Agra where he would be further from her in death than ever in life. He had agreed to follow in a grand entourage, for he couldn't bear the thought of spending days seeing Taj's casket. Weeks after Shuja left Burhanpur, Shah Jahan's military duties in the Deccan were finished, Khan Jahan Lodi had been taken care of, and it was time to return to Agra.

❋ ❋ ❋

IN HIS VILLAGE, Chundar was faced with a decision. His wife and sons would certainly watch the Mughals when they again came nearby. Indeed, they had talked about the first occasion incessantly.

Certain this day's event would be repeatedly discussed as much as the first had been, Chundar knew it was only if he was there that he would be included. The storyteller in him wanted to be heard.

Should he leave his field and join them? When he heard Shah Jahan was expected, he remembered his last view of the emperor and the changes that fateful experience had put into motion. He missed his relationship with Malador and still was not used to the subservient attitude his mute friend had taken toward him. He knew it was Malador's way of showing appreciation for his life, yet Chundar would immediately return to their equal relationship if it was in his power.

He wondered how Shah Jahan looked now. Did the loss of his wife show on his face? Was he still as imposing as he had been, or would he be different off his throne and away from his balcony? At that point, Chundar dropped his planting stick and called to his family to wait. He wanted to ride with them to the road and again see the man who had so altered his life.

Arrival of camels, elephants, carts, and coaches indicated the traveling emperor was close. The simple village carts belonging to the farmers were primitive compared to the intricately designed vehicles now passing in front of them. They waited through the spans of nothingness created when so many people and animals move a long distance. Faraway palanquins could be seen with women inside comfortably protected from stares.

Several hundred rocking, swaying camels bedecked in red passed before the wondering eyes of the villagers. Although there had been camels in the advance guard, the ones before them now carried slave women, servants, and attendants. Pack elephants transported the luggage, tents, chests, and bedding that had been securely tied onto their backs with thick ropes.

Finer elephants followed, their status proclaimed by jewels, paint, cloth, and elegant howdahs on their backs. Flags fluttered, some with the personal designs of nobles, some identifying each marching division, and many with the familiar Mughal crest.

Children climbed trees and hung from branches to get better

looks. They gazed at the animals and were awed by the voluminous fabrics draped over them. Cloth of a quality most villagers would never own hung on howdahs, palanquins, and was made into uniforms.

More than twenty coaches, copies of an English gift to Jahangir, bumped along the rutted roads. Uncountable uniformed men on dressed horses rode rigidly facing forward. Enthralled, the onlookers did not notice the gritty dust they were inhaling.

Another gap stretched before riders advanced with silver staves high in the air and loud voices ringing, "Make way! Make way!" Following them, fifty men sprinkled the ground to settle the dust. The emperor was near.

Chundar, in spite of having already seen the emperor, was as excited as those who were waiting for their first glimpse. Remembering the opulence, the presence, and the self-assurance he had seen on the throne in Agra, Chundar was unprepared for the appearance of the man sitting atop a dark gray horse.

Shah Jahan was wearing neither his famous jewels nor rich clothing but was swathed only in white. "Village clothes" thought many people who watched him. Cleaner perhaps, but much the same. With his white hair, the entire effect was of a ghostly, shrunken man.

"Is this the emperor you've spoken of?" whispered Chunder's wife quizzically. She had heard her husband's colorful descriptions of Shah Jahan and could not match them to the man passing before them.

Looking intently at the approaching rider, Chunder was uncertain. Surely, he thought, these changes could not have been brought about only by the death of Shah Jahan's wife. But, yes, this was Shah Jahan weighted down with a heavy load of grief. The emperor was much more subdued then he had been in Agra, Chundar thought. He is now a man I can relate to, a man feeling a great loss.

After Shah Jahan, thousands of mounted cavalry clopped by in perfect formation as the rear guard. Nobles, riding back to avoid the dust, were mounted on garlanded elephants and followed by their own horsemen.

Bringing up the rear of the procession were the war elephants. These beasts of burden, not gaily decorated as the earlier ones had been, carried small field pieces strapped to their backs. These reminders of the war this army had been fighting signaled to the onlookers that the procession was over.

Children climbed down from the trees and found their families. Chundar brushed his sleeves, pleased to have observed the hot, dusty and lengthy spectacle. Even as the villagers returned to their carts, they began talking with descriptions that would be repeated for years. The quality of that velvet! Those horses...beautiful! Thousands of them. Maybe more than that. Did you see the jewels on the first palanquin? Imagine, seeing the emperor in the same clothing as my husband.

That night as they rolled out their balls of dough for chapattis, cut vegetables for curry, and pulled down the charpoys for sleeping, the villagers' heads were full of the splendors they had witnessed.

What had not been visible were Shah Jahan's thoughts. Without Mumtaz he no longer noticed smoke gracefully rising from thatched huts, a bright pink bloom within its thorny bush, or silhouettes against the sunset. With her, he had found delight where now there was flatness. He had lingered on the brink of insanity, had spoken with a messenger from Allah, and had a dream that gave him a reason to continue. As he rode, barely conscious of the people around him, Shah Jahan was thinking of Taj and his monument for her. He continued to create a space around himself that his companions were reluctant to enter. He was consumed with thoughts of the most complex and daring venture he had ever attempted. His silence hid his inner determination to honor Taj with the vision he had seen.

Slowly Shah Jahan was beginning to heal.

46

Agra - 1632

Consumed with his building plans, Shah Jahan was unaware of how his mind's numbness was being gradually replaced by the return of life. During this time he concluded he would erect the four minarets slightly out of plumb so if they ever fell, they would fall away from his masterpiece. The soaring top would be a double dome to accommodate the enormous size. It would have a false bottom to form the interior ceiling so Taj's mausoleum would not feel like an open cave. The closer he came to Agra, the more he grappled with his ambivalence about the end of his journey. He was eager to begin the construction, but he would have to live with daily reminders of Taj's loss.

What was he going to do about decoration? Were the graceful shapes and the smooth marble of the shape enough? Statuary was forbidden on Muslim buildings, but he could use intricate mosaics and inlay of geometrical designs. Maybe there could be black and white chevrons climbing the towers. Human or animal forms were not allowed but calligraphy was a possibility. He liked the idea of black, flowing Arabic letters on a white background incorporating words from the Koran that flowed up, over, and down the four large openings. Why not both: chevrons *and* calligraphy. Yes, this was coming along very well.

But it was not enough. The details of building the arches, walls, and cupolas were easier than deciding on ornamentation. Something more was needed, a detail that would transfer his masterpiece into something as subtle, delicate, and exquisite as Mumtaz herself had been. *What I have,* he thought, *represents her dignity and grace. But she was also charming, colorful...*

Colorful. Mmmm.... Perhaps I can find a way to incorporate pigment onto the building. He straightened in his jeweled saddle. *I could hang cloth from the sides even as Taj draped beautiful garments over herself. No...too cluttered and would spoil the lines. No cloth.*

The word "colorful" kept returning to his mind. Cosmetics are colorful. *Taj used cosmetics to outline her eyes and paint her hands. Maybe I could paint the building with her favorite colors.*

He thought of painting the luminescent marble but concluded the white luster was an important part of the vision and should not be covered.

Flowers? Taj loved them in life and they surround her in Paradise. Flowers could be profusely displayed around the building. He shook his head sadly. The reality of fresh flowers during the many hot months of Agra posed a serious problem. *I'd have to arrange to have them changed several times a day to avoid wilted and bedraggled displays.* No, flowers were not the answer.

Hardly noticing the walking servant whisking a pesky fly away before it reached his leg, he rode on, wondering if he should drop the idea of color. He almost let it go, but not quite.

Unable to stop himself, he brought to his mind a clear likeness of Mumtaz. Tenderly, he remembered her as she had been: her eyes, her cheeks, her lips, neck, ears, earrings...her earrings. He again sat up straight. *Her earrings.* The excitement he felt within alerted him to the presence of an answer to his search. *Taj wore earrings. She also wore necklaces, rings, jeweled belts, anklets, nose rings, hair ornaments, rings on her toes, and of course her thumb ring. Mirrors, combs, and vases adorned with jewel surrounded her. There were jewels everywhere.*

That's it! I'll imbue the memorial for Taj with colorful jewels! Excitedly, he recalled his brimming treasury—perfect for enhancing the black and white he had already designed.

Riding and nodding, he decided to definitely incorporate jewels. They were, he thought as he scratched the back of his neck, just what had been missing. Before long, his horse and his thoughts slowed.

How do I use them? If I adhere them to the outside of the building, they would add lumps to the smooth lines I find so appealing. Maybe, I could use them inside where their protrusion from the marble would be more acceptable. I could cover the entire panels around her cenotaph. But then they would remain away from the sparkle of the sun.

I could have the stones set in the minarets leaving the building itself free of bulges and protrusions. Or, perhaps the gems should go inside only on the cenotaph itself?

Not satisfied but knowing he was on the right track, Shah Jahan decided to present his thought to Salih Kambir, his talented and creative jeweler. Certainly Salih would grasp what he wanted. With the decision made, he thought no more about the issue.

Months later, Shah Jahan watched the work begun on the mausoleum that had already taken an enormous expenditure of manpower. The ground had been cleared and the reinforcement of the site was underway. Engineers calculated how much the shoreline needed to be strengthened to accommodate both the constant current from the Jumna River and the massive weight of the structure to come. Simultaneously, the land was being reconfigured allowing the building to be positioned most advantageously for viewing from his palace a mile up the river. When the ground work was finished, the first portion of the building would begin. This would be an enormous sandstone platform, or plinth, which would be topped by a smaller marble plinth, upon which the marble building would be erected.

While the activity downriver continued, Shah Jahan awaited the arrival of Salih Kambir in the Design Room. "The grave-mosque must be decorated and I want to do it with jewels," he announced bluntly to the man walking into his chamber. "I've already thought of cloth, paint, and flowers to add color but dismissed them. I've settled on gems. Mumtaz wore them, they'll add color, and I want to use what I already have in my treasury. How do I do this?"

Salih had experienced working with Shah Jahan on projects before. He walked through the doorway toward his emperor and made his teslim even as Shah Jahan was speaking. He had gained prominence not only because of his rare artistry with gems, but also because he understood human nature. Hearing Shah Jahan's comments, Salih's mind raced. This idea was beyond anything he had ever considered doing with precious stones. Yet, tantalized and excited about this idea of jewelry for an entire building, he realized it was possible. Outrageous, yes, but possible.

Wisely, he listened without interruption. When the emperor had finished Salih deliberated. He spoke cautiously.

"We can make the gems into any shape you want, Your Majesty. What would you like?"

"I don't know yet." The impatient emperor was irritated that his glorious idea required explanation. "Surely, you can give me answers rather than more questions. I've been asking myself all the questions I can think of, and now I'm ready to decide!"

"Let me think about this for a moment, Your Majesty. I know you will want only the best, the finest. Therefore, I request that you grant me the moments I require."

Perspiration formed on Salih's forehead, neck, and trickled down his chest. He had done superb work for Shah Jahan in the past, including the famous earrings he had created from Prince Khurram's design. But this day he questioned his own limitations. Perhaps he was not up to the task of adding gems to an entire building. Yet, to preserve his life and his livelihood, he needed to maintain the emperor's good graces.

Shah Jahan became quickly impatient. "If you must think, do so aloud. I want to hear your words and not just watch your face." Salih knew an excited or passionate Shah Jahan sounded angry, as he did now. He began to speak.

"Gems. We could put shaped gems into the marble so that there would be no intrusion upon the smooth surface. I know a man who has skill in that. There is a wide expanse of marble. There could be gems on the minarets as well. How many gems will we need?"

Gradually, Salih became less aware of his surroundings and the intensity of the man who watched him as he sorted through his random thoughts. They led him toward the familiar point of his creativity where he had found the most satisfying solutions to the challenges that had faced him in the past. He hoped the usual multitude of ideas waited for him there this day. If so, he would select a possibility, carefully wrap it in words, and hand it to Shah Jahan who continued to emanate anxious impatience.

"No matter the amount of gems needed, the emperor will have them," he realized aloud. "If he doesn't, he'll find them. He's already mentioned cloth, paint, and flowers. Cloth by itself isn't particularly interesting although designs on it could be. Perhaps the gems could represent designs of Mumtaz' favorite garments. Or rugs.

He continued mumbling through his thoughts. "Or we could use a background of paint studded with gems. No, too contrived, and I don't see it touching the level of sophistication the emperor seeks. Paint would mask the marble design, which is simultaneously intricate and simple.

"Flowers. Mmm. We could use the gems in the shapes of flowers. They would also represent the bounty promised to the faithful in Paradise. If we use the stones for the flowers, then the blooms would never die..."

Shah Jahan, listening intently to the ramblings of his Gem Master, leapt from his divan and strode to the wooden model of the project that he kept in his room.

"Flowers! That's it," he exulted. "The gems will be in the form of flowers that never die. This is the right idea, Salih. This is the very thought I was close to."

Turning away from Salih, Shah Jahan's hands stroked the wooden model of the building that would stand on the bank of the Jumna River. His voice took on a gentle tone. "Flowers and gems for you, Taj. You'll be surrounded in beauty as you wait for me to join you. I couldn't keep you from dying," he whispered to the model, "but I can surround you with flowers that will live forever."

Salih was inspired by the combination of everlasting flowers and his emperor's commitment to the memory of his beloved empress. Putting pen to paper, he began excitedly sketching his thoughts in much the same haphazard and exploring way he had fumbled through the words to get to the idea both men recognized as brilliant. Soon, his paper was full of beautiful blossoms, graceful vines, and realistic leaves. With ideas flowing now, Salih created flower-filled vases, flowers growing from the earth, and a wall of free flowers, leaves, and vines. He sketched frantically, sliding the finished papers to Shah Jahan only to fill another blank sheet with more ideas.

Servants entered and exited the room, keeping the lanterns burning while the fire of creativity sparked between the men. They conferred, argued, and eventually agreed. Only when the first light of the sky announced the new day, did the two of them stop, both satisfied with the masterpiece they had accomplished together.

Returning the sketches produced during the night to Salih, Shah Jahan clasped the Gem Master in a surprising embrace of gratitude. "We have done wonderful things here tonight. Return to me when you have completed the everlasting flower designs." Shah Jahan left to attend his first prayers of the day and give thanks to Allah for the idea of using gems to enliven the mausoleum.

Salih, in a mosque outside the fort, sent a different prayer to Allah. He asked for the strength to finish what had been started. Unlike Shah Jahan, the jeweler's feelings about the night were less of joy and more of enormous responsibility.

When the jeweler returned to Agra Fort later in the day, he headed to the treasury to tabulate the gems there. Although the wealth overloaded his ability to comprehend what it represented, he counted it with the calculating eye of a man measuring materials. When he had enumerated what was available and what would be needed, he sat dejectedly with his head in his hands. There were not enough stones to fill the need. No man owned treasure as vast and fabulous as Shah Jahan, not the kings of Europe, not the emperors of China. But even Shah Jahan's wealth fell short of what was needed. He would have to reduce the grandeur of the design, or he would have to obtain more gems. Lifting his head, putting his hands on his knees, and pushing to rise, Salih knew he must tell the emperor. This was, after all, the Great Mughal's decision, not his. His first task was to present a plan to Shah Jahan.

❉ ❉ ❉

HE WAS FINALLY READY to present what he had created during the nearly sleepless days since the memorable night with Shah Jahan. Dildil, Salih's apprentice, was aghast when he looked at the parchments prepared for the Great Mughal. "These drawings are not complete, Master. Surely you are not going to take them to the emperor in this condition. There are spaces to be filled, color that needs to be added."

Even his untrained eye could see the blanks that usually were not seen by anyone outside the jeweler's design room. Refusing his offer to add even a single brushstroke, Salih moved the papers out of the young man's reach. Seeing the boy's obvious confusion when his sincere offer of assistance was refused, Salih explained.

"Whenever you are dealing with a client, always keep in mind that he is affected by much more in his life than jewelry. In this case, Shah Jahan's interest goes beyond that of an architect. He's building a memorial to his beloved wife. More than that," the jeweler corrected himself, "it is becoming almost an image of her and brings a touch of her back into his life. It will be richly decorated, lovely beyond anything we've seen, and in all ways a tribute to what he feels for her." Acknowledging the incompleteness of the papers of his hand, Salih lowered his voice, rolled the papers together, and turned to leave.

His parting words to Dildil were spoken as he walked away. "The eyes and hands that caressed Mumtaz Mahal when she was living must also caress and touch these drawings. The emperor will complete them."

Entering the emperor's chambers, Salih began carefully to unroll his designs. When Shah Jahan showed his delight with the results, the jewelry-maker mentioned the insufficient number of stones in the treasury. Shah Jahan did not hesitate before he authorized caravans to collect what was needed.

❉ ❉ ❉

THE CARAVANS LEFT AGRA traveling to Baghdad, to Yemen, to Tibet. Some would be crossing waters to Ceylon, and still others would traverse the River Nile. Diamonds from Golconda, garnets from the River Ganges, conch shells from the seas, and granite, crystal, and bloodstone would be purchased in India. Agates, jasper, and rubies would be brought to Agra from within the empire. Other caravans would travel to Afghanistan and China. Forty-three different kinds of precious and semiprecious stones were necessary for the inlay.

As Salih watched the first lengthy camel caravan leave Agra and listened until the tinkling bells were only a faint sound in the distance, he reflected upon the dangers the men would face before they returned. Beyond finding or bargaining for gems and the dangers of unknown lands, they could learn firsthand of the greed of the men riding with them to the reaches of the known world. Salih philosophically put his worries in Allah's hands and relaxed, accepting that what would be, would be. If jewels were meant to adorn the edifice, Allah would smile on the caravans. If not, nothing a simple jeweler could do would help.

47

Agra ~ 1632-1654

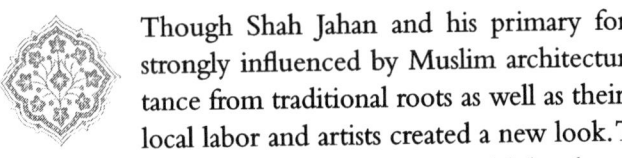Though Shah Jahan and his primary foremen were strongly influenced by Muslim architecture, their distance from traditional roots as well as their reliance on local labor and artists created a new look. The Taj Mahal was a blending of Islamic architecture with borders and parapets created by Hindu artisans from indigenous marble and sandstone.

Thin square bricks were made by slapping straw-thickened mud into forms which were then sun baked. Used for scaffolding, these blocks also formed the shape of the structure that would eventually be hidden by a covering of marble. Earthen ramps were continuously extended, enabling the bullock carts to deliver the cut marble facings where they could be used on the growing structure. By the time the soaring dome was ready to be faced in marble, the earthen roadway was a mile long.

The dome, larger than any previously built, was topped by a finial pointing heavenward. The pinnacle began as a massive iron rod. Several hollow pieces of brass were then shaped and forged to fit around the center pole. This finial shape was then surfaced with more than a thousand pounds of gold. Finished, it appeared molten in the sunlight as it held the Islamic moon and star at its tip

Funereal quotations from the Koran were calligraphied dramatically around the arches in black letters on a white background. The chosen words were written full size with attention to gradual enlargement that ensured readability as they traveled upward. If the mason erred, he filled the incorrect black letter with white marble pieces, carved another shape, and inserted the new black slate.

Across the Jumna River, a smaller parcel of land of equal width of the Taj Mahal became the Moonlight Garden. From there the mausoleum could be directly viewed as it seemed to stand above the spray of twenty-five fountains within the smaller garden's octagonal pool, or indirectly as it was reflected on the river.

The walled Moonlight Garden, though by far the smaller of the two locations, required tons of rock, earth, brick, and stone. With these materials, workers fashioned terraces, walls, and a landing platform in a continuation of the design across the river. This Moonlight Garden existed at the outside of the Jumna's curve, so its shore received the troublesome brunt of the forceful, flowing water and required a sturdy bulkhead.

Constructed for pleasure, the Moonlight Garden lacked the somber formality of the imposing gate, the long approach, and the breathtaking tomb that existed a river's width away. Mahtab Bagh, the Moonlight Garden, celebrated life even as the nearby mausoleum revered death.

As the building, the gardens, the waterways, and the Moonlight Garden grew, so did a small city nearby. It was in Mumtazabad where the architects, builders, designers, and workmen lived. The many rooms of the serais were filled with those needing temporary living space, and bustling shops lined the streets.

Salih had been busy long before the caravans returned from their travels. He gathered men familiar with the inlay he had in mind who would assemble their own groups of artists. The inlay would be more costly and time consuming than mosaic would have been, but the result would last longer and actually strengthen the surface of the marble. Although mosaics were used in most Islamic buildings, the technique of adhering comparatively fragile pieces of tile to the building's surface was not appropriate for the slender, flowing designs that would embellish Shah Jahan's vision.

When the caravans began to trickle back, Salih was ready and

Flowers of the Taj

soon had the artists beginning the intricate work of creating flowers by slipping slender pieces of colored stone into incisions in the marble. Using combinations of varying shades of stones, delicate blossoms began taking shape in the firm, unvarying bed of Rajasthani marble.

The work was exacting, time-consuming, and persistently destructive to the fingers and eyes of the men who turned their grindstones for many hours each day. Artists transformed a seemingly unending supply of marble panels into opaline wonders that became iridescent in the sunshine. The finished panels were carefully stored until they were placed around the building, even as jewelry would encircle a woman's neck. Their skillful creations were additionally incorporated around the tall archways and were used to turn Mumtaz' sarcophagus into a dense garden of undying flowers.

Before the inlay could begin, the white stone was cut into panels that fit together along the bottom of the mausoleum. Blades lubricated with sandy water from the river were the only tools sharp enough to cut the exact shapes which were then delivered to the artists' workrooms.

Salih, wanting the panels more quickly, grew restless with the slow progress of the work. Suspecting it was possible to increase output, he arranged to visit the workshops himself. When he arrived in Mumtazabad, he asked the overseer how he could hasten production. Was more money needed? Another incentive? Threats? He had arrived expecting to stay an hour or so. Maybe, he would stay until noon. At dusk, he decided to spend the night at a nearby caravanserai and return the following day.

Though he had created jewelry his entire life, Salih was impressed by the constant attention and precision each man contributed to the huge panels. The hours spent shaping a colored stone to fit the exact shape cut into the marble were brutal. Holding small gems firmly against stone wheels spinning in water caused many men to lose feeling in their hands and sometimes even portions of the fingers were inadvertently sacrificed. Creating without patterns, they used long sticks to turn the wheel while regulating its speed with the pressure of the stone. The miniscule pieces produced in the dusty workshops fit together so snugly that even Salih's jeweler-sensitive hands could not feel space where the individual stones in a twenty-piece blossom had been fit into the marble.

Painters who paused at these workshops noticed a similarity to the art they themselves created with Mughal miniatures. Their paintings, produced in the fort's ateliers, exhibited exquisite detail and richness from pigments, ground stones, and burnished gold. The inlayers achieved a similar effect with colored stones.

The chiselers who prepared the openings in the marble had developed an equally essential artistic skill. As young boys with malleable bones, each had been taught the complex and unnatural grip necessary to hold the slim metal chisels effectively. Delayed training meant increasingly inflexible bones and additional months of practice to achieve success. Before they began their exacting work, the chiselers first sprinkled a soft reddish powder on the marble. This colored the stone and allowed the marks they would then incise to be easily seen.

Men with hunched shoulders and bent backs created cornelian flowers, buds of jasper, and chrysolite vines. They twirled, cut, shaped, incised, filled, and ever so slowly created colorful gardens from marble and stone.

Fatigued by simply watching the exacting process, Salih stepped outside to discover the marble was not finished when the stones had been set. The henna-stained marble had to be rubbed clean with pieces of broken grinding stone that removed the color yet left the stones intact and unscratched. The panels were rubbed again, this time with beeswax to bring the sparkle back to the crystals, then set in the sun, and finally rubbed once more before they were inspected and put into place.

A thoughtful Salih returned to his home with an increased appreciation for the charming stone flowers and a determination never again to suggest faster production.

❊ ❊ ❊

THE WIDESPREAD ACTIVITY around the Taj Mahal, although it looked unorganized and undirected, was highly structured. Draftsmen, stonecutters, and sculptors completed their jobs as carpenters, dome-makers, gardeners, and engineers contributed their specialized skills. The monument that resulted from the contributions of twenty thousand men for over twenty-two years was a testimony to organization, technical skill, and artistic talent. The towering mausoleum was a masterpiece.

48

Agra ~ 1654

Shah Jahan's twenty-two year old ache for the woman he loved was brought to his attention this day. The decades-old loss continued to dilute the pleasure he took in his many accomplishments as emperor. During those years, projects had diverted his feelings and masked his grief, but today he was without distraction; tomorrow the Taj Mahal, as it had become know, would be formally dedicated.

As he prepared to enter through the main gate on the southern end, he realized it would be the first time he had see the completely finished complex. Although he had made many visits during construction, he had entered from the royal barge on the opposite side. This was his last opportunity to be here before the morning's formal dedication.

Several of the men accompanying him had already viewed the completed Taj Mahal from the Moonlight Garden across the Jumna. Shah Jahan could not bring himself to walk in that pleasure garden, for fear that thoughts and feelings of Mumtaz' loss would assail him there.

Even though he was no longer grieved outwardly, he still couldn't visit the downstairs crypt that actually held the remains of Mumtaz in a coffin as intensely covered with inlaid flowers as the one in the "public" area of the mausoleum. He'd been wrong two years ago, he remembered, when he'd ventured down the steps. As he now approached the courtyard, he relived the moment when his knees began to weaken at the bottom of the stairs, and he'd leaned against the doorway to remain standing. He could touch the coffin of the woman he'd loved for so long. Although she'd been dead for over twenty-two years, his heart pounded loudly and a fresh wave of grief washed over him. The memories were still too great, the feelings too vivid for him to be this near to the woman who had filled his life with joy. Wordlessly, he'd rushed back up the stairs, breathed deeply, and accepted once again that he still wasn't free of the ache of Taj's loss. He'd take no chances this evening and would avoid a repeat of the painful experience.

Forcing his attention to the present, he observed the nobles in the space between Mumtazabad and the entry, waiting for their late afternoon visit. The sun was becoming low, and the emperor felt a need to show the building and his now-famous design in the light that would illuminate the design and workmanship.

Proud to be included with the emperor at this important pre-dedication visit, the men were lively with anticipation. They would be the first official visitors to see this monument inspired by marital love. It was one thing to see the construction of the Taj Mahal; it was far more prestigious to see the masterpiece in the company of the man who had made it possible.

Because he'd been closely involved with the details of the mausoleum, as well as the additional buildings, the wall, and the garden, Shah Jahan was expecting no surprises this visit. His personal and emotional involvement assured this mausoleum surpassed all religious and architectural requirements. For the imams, there was a mosque; for his friends, a garden to enjoy; for him, a poem in white marble representing Mumtaz' femininity, beauty, and grace.

He was barely aware of the murmuring and words of praise for the flowing ebony calligraphy on the outer face of the gate. It was here, at the entrance to the walled garden, that the cares of the world were left behind: visitors stepped from the secular world into the spiritual arena of peace and contemplation.

The next morning, ladies of the zenana would sit on the marble platform behind red velvet screens, unseen. Revered mullahs inside the mausoleum would intone prayers of praise for Mumtaz, read from the Koran, and burn heavy incense. There'd be great feasting in costly tents. Thousands of rupees would be distributed to the poor who would receive their food on the far side of the gate. Even during the dedication, the garden wouldn't be open to the masses.

As he strode slowly along with the others who were seeing the interior marvels for the first time, Shah Jahan knew the arrangements had been made and the final details of the morning's ceremony were complete. He was here simply to relax, enjoy, and absorb the compliments he knew were coming. He strolled, listening to several conversations behind him, thinking of nothing in particular. When he looked up he stopped as abruptly as if he'd hit a wall. Framed by the arch of the entrance gate, the sight before him was breathtaking. Although he knew the building at the end of the waterway was larger than his entire living quarters in the palace, from this distance, it appeared small enough to hold in his hand.

Those behind him quickly became aware of his complete halt. Their low voices turned even softer to whispers, and then even those faded. Slowly and respectfully, the men who'd eagerly anticipated a preview of the building came to understand that that their pre-dedication visit was already finished. Seeing their emperor deeply moved, they wordlessly gave him privacy and returned to the entrance and their bearers. They re-entered the still warm chariots and palanquins and returned home.

Shah Jahan, standing alone, was bewitched into speechlessness by the magnificence he beheld. The glimmering sight went beyond the architectural drawings he'd handled. Before him was nothing less than magic, feminine magic. Soft, curved, full.

Overwhelmed, hardly believing what he saw, Shah Jahan felt, more than he understood, what was before him. The harmonious design of garden and canals presented the proud form of the Taj Mahal with tender grace. The sight spoke to his heart of the loveliest moments he'd known—those with Taj.

His reaction surprised him because he'd assumed he knew everything there was to know about this Taj Mahal. True, this was the first time he'd seen it with the evidence of construction removed and the white marble tinged with a sunset orange. Nonetheless, the coordination of the mausoleum, the gardens, and the flowing and spraying water had become more than mere finishing touches and combined to create nothing less than enchantment. Perhaps, it was the monument's elevated place of honor that set it apart without seeming to separate it from the masterful integration of the whole.

He'd been involved in the project; he knew thousands of facts and measurements concerning the size, the cost, the types of stones used, and the measurements of height, width, and length of each face, wall, and arch. Yet, at this moment, the concrete realities and numbers fled. The overall finished result had become so real he could feel the essence of Mumtaz in front of him.

The rainbow of spray from the flower-shaped fountainheads gave the impression that the building he knew to be massive was weightless enough to float upon droplets of water. The pair of sandstone buildings on either side set off the dazzling marble of the delicate mausoleum, and their smaller domes softly echoed the shape of the prominent double dome. As he reverently walked nearer, the Taj increased in size. The sky deepened in color as oranges and reds darkened the hue of the curving top as dusk approached.

Shah Jahan was unaware of how he came to be seated on a rug. As he sat in front of the Taj Mahal, the sky became emerald green before fading into darkness. The moon began its nightly journey from east to west, pearling the elegant dome with its reflected light even as it outshone the smaller heavenly bodies.

The night was silent except for the faint sound of the river flowing between the two gardens. Even the birds, particularly noisy at dusk as though trying to delay the loss of sunlight, had quieted. Shah Jahan's tender pain receded in the peace that entered his body as he rested.

Surely, I'm imagining things. Even to him, his words seemed dreamlike as he noticed the radiance coming from the building similar to the radiance on the face of the woman coming toward him. The woman looked like Taj. He felt reality slipping even further away as he waited for her smiling approach. As he watched, his longing to be with Mumtaz again overcame his certainty of her death. It couldn't be her, but no one else had her particular silhouette, her lissome movement and dignity.

She took a seat beside him. For several moments it was quiet as they filled their eyes with the sight of the other. Shah Jahan broke the silence. "This building is for you, Taj. I'm overcome that you are here to share this moment." As he spoke the words, he knew their truth. He was unaware that Allah had altered reality, so young Mumtaz could return to him for a short time.

Shah Jahan reached for Taj but his hand touched nothingness. His disappointment flared, then disappeared quickly. That she was here, even if it was without substance, was an unexpected gift.

She moved behind him, knelt, and put her hands on his shoulders exactly as she'd done so often. He could feel the gentle pressure of her fingers. Automatically, in response to the natural movement he remembered from uncountable instances where he had enjoyed the same touch, he placed his own hands atop hers. Again, he was unable to touch her flesh and felt only the cloth on his shoulders. Even though he couldn't feel her hands with his own, her fingers gripped him in the familiar, never-to-be-forgotten blend of massage and caress. It was Taj. No one else had touched him like that. An aroma circled him, one as enticing as the garden's bouquet. The fragrance, like the monument shimmering in the moonlight, was unique. He smelled the blend of oils that had been created solely for Taj.

She'd come to him in the shadow of the monument he'd built to proclaim the love he, a mighty emperor, had for her. He could see her, and enjoy her touches and the sweet smells of the woman he still loved.

"I've been watching everything you've done since I've been

gone, Meerijan, and I'm proud of you." He heard the familiar voice behind his back. Exulted, he was unwilling to speak and risk her departure.

"This mausoleum is your finest creation." She continued in the voice he recognized, "and our love will be remembered because of it."

"You and I need nothing to remind us, Taj. The building is for others to see." His heart seemed to speak softly to the presence behind him.

"You've taken no other queen. Our children will never battle the children of another woman to earn the right to sit upon your throne. I've never doubted your love for me or your generosity as you continue to surround me with extravagance and beauty even after my death. You've given much to me, Meerijan; now I have two gifts for you."

Although he heard the words, they were lost as he rejoiced in the wonder of being with Taj. That they were together transported him to a high level of bliss, and there was no curiosity about the gifts she had mentioned. Taj was with him, and that was all he wanted.

She sat beside him, and he perceived her touch as she slipped her hand onto his and rested her head on his shoulder. The magic of the night surrounded the emperor and Mumtaz Mahal.

For many hours while the moon traveled westward and returned to the opposite horizon, they sat gazing at the silent stone that publicly expressed the tenderness of their private love. They spoke of the moments they'd shared throughout the nineteen years they'd had together. Private and happy memories, to be sure, yet still painful for Shah Jahan even as he visited them with Taj. The portion of his life they'd shared was untouched pain deep in his heart.

He spoke of the magnificent Peacock Throne. They discussed the burns Jahanara had suffered when her diaphanous scarf had touched an open flame and burst into fire. There was great promise in their oldest son, Dara Shikoh who would follow Shah Jahan on the throne. The emperor was proud of him and kept him close by his side. And of course there was Shahjahanabad, the beautiful city and fort Shah Jahan had designed to the next to near the old city of Delhi.

They relived their lives, polishing remembrances until they gleamed anew. Their laughs perplexed the guards walking discreetly in the shadows. These men on their protective rounds heard their emperor's one-sided conversation, and his laugh that danced toward them in the night. Unable to understand the sounds, they nonetheless smiled that their much-loved ruler, whose reign had provided nearly thirty years of peace and prosperity, was enjoying himself.

49

Agra - 1654

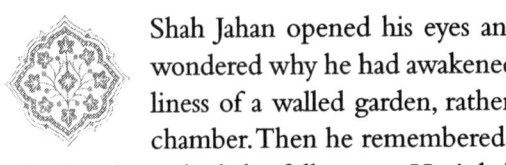Shah Jahan opened his eyes and, for a brief moment, wondered why he had awakened in the pre-dawn loveliness of a walled garden, rather than in his own bedchamber. Then he remembered sitting with Taj as they talked and watched the full moon. He inhaled sharply and looked around him. Where was she?

Hundreds of birds filled the air with their sweet trills, greeting the light that was returning to the sky. The faintly illuminated horizon added subtle shadowlines to the relief carvings of the Taj Mahal. The dark silhouettes of the round, open balconies nestled against the dominant dome emerged as the sun awakened the sky. Greens in the garden became individual leaves in the first ray of light. The dome absorbed a soft luster of pinks from the rosy dawn and sparkles flashed as spears of sunlight struck the necklace inlay that ringed its slender neck. As he listened and watched he knew he was receiving a message from within the mausoleum.

He strode across the marble platform that was already being prepared with the velvet screen for the zenana and cushions for the guests of the formal dedication. Soon, the level marble would be adorned with superb tents for the princes, grandees, religious scholars, and visiting dignitaries in a ceremony combining pomp and restraint.

Monkeys scampered playfully along the top of the wall and

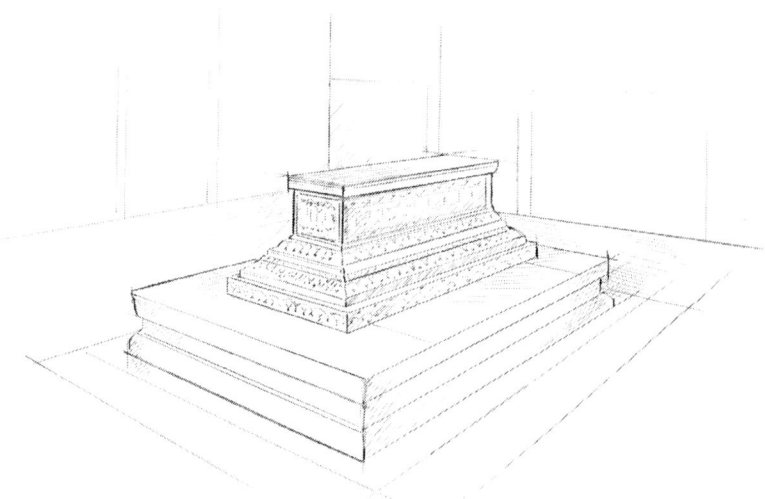

Mumtaz' Tomb

birds swooped and chirped as Shah Jahan climbed the marble steps. Carpets muffled his footfalls as he hurriedly moved into the shadowy interior. The large open room under the dome had been built to display a highly decorated casket surrounded by a fence of gold. He inhaled the air tinged with the aroma of incense. Lilies, narcissi, iris, and tulips were abundantly carved in relief upon the walls. Some of these everlasting flowers grew from mounds of marble earth, others were arranged in vases that would never break.

The huffaz standing near the casket continuously recited passages from the Koran, intoning the sacred words with his mellow voice. Shah Jahan looked for Mumtaz even as Allah's ninety-nine names were chanted, resonated in the spacious dome, and descended in heavenly reverberations.

He moved across the marble floor to the elaborately carved fence surrounding the decorated but empty cenotaph. Stepping through the railings' opening, he searched for Mumtaz. Though the early morning sun was already glittering on the outside marble, the mood within was softer. The lacey grillwork of the doors and windows diffused the sun's rays and highlighted the colorful cenotaph that was centered directly under the highest point of the marble sky.

His fingers softly caressed the smooth marble with Persian script: The illustrious sepulcher of Arjumand Banu Begam, called Mumtaz Mahal. God is everlasting, God is sufficient. He knoweth what is concealed and what is manifest. He is merciful and compassionate. Nearer unto Him are those who say: Our Lord is God.

He had seen all of these marvels before. This morning, he was searching for Taj. He steeled himself, knowing the only other place she could be: the downstairs crypt. Remembering his previous experience, he shuddered. Before contemplating further, he turned to descend the stairs.

Though much smaller, the crypt mirrored the richness of the floor above and held an equally beautiful inlaid casket. Walls and ceiling were lined with sheets of gold and studded with precious stones. Turkish and Persian carpets covered the floor. Gold cloth, a lamp with golden chains, and silver candlesticks filled the room. A canopy of pearls hung over the coffin. Solid jasper doors sealed the entryway. This was where Muslims, and *only* those of the One True Faith, would be able to enter and pay respects to their former empress once a year.

Relieved that he had experienced none of his previous anxieties, Shah Jahan found the woman he sought sitting on her own cenotaph atop the brilliantly inlaid arabesques. With a lurch in his heart, he realized again how much he had missed her.

"You left me alone, Taj."

His statement was meant only to reflect his relief in finding her again, but it chilled him with the memory of the moment in Burhanpur when she had left him alone the first time. Mumtaz saw his eyes glaze and knew this direct reminder of her death had led her husband to a place of anguish. She quickly began to talk.

"I spoke of two gifts I have for you." Her soft voice filled the small room. "We didn't discuss them last night. I know you don't believe there is anything you want that you couldn't arrange for yourself. You may have even asked what a woman living in Paradise for twenty-two years could think you'd possibly need. If you have had these thoughts," her eyes sparked in the way they always had when she was about to rebuke him, "you are wrong...Meerijan."

That did it. Her use of the name only she called him. Not only did it caress his ears, but it deflated his fear that he could be mistaken. This woman who called him Meerijan was still one of the few people who could dare tell him he was wrong.

"My first gift to you is the promise that today is the last time I'll leave you."

The word that jumped at him from her sentence, although she had spoken it with no additional volume, was 'leave.' A spasm of panic clutched Shah Jahan at the thought of losing her again. After the previous night, he could not accept being apart from Taj.

"No! Don't leave me again," he cried brokenly. "I won't be able to stand it."

"But you *will* be able to stand it. It is not time for you to live in Paradise, but when you do, I'll be waiting for you. We'll be together for eternity."

He was silent while Mumtaz allowed him to absorb the meaning of what she had said. Then she continued.

"The second gift is my gratitude." A husky whisper was her only indication of the anguish caused by another separation from Shah Jahan. "You've honored me with your love, with this magnificent monument, and with the assurance that one of my sons will inherit your royal turban. For all of these things, I return full memories of our love to you—with one important change." She touched his face, and he felt her soft fingers along his temple and down to his chin. A touch she had used so many times.

"From now on, there'll be no more hurt, anguish, or pain when you think of me...when you think of us." Her voice was an even softer whisper. "From this moment, your memories will comfort you and provide only happiness."

Even as she spoke, Shah Jahan felt in his chest that her words were true. Mumtaz would forever live in his heart, but she had transformed his pain into pleasure. The deep happiness he had shared with her for so long was now alive for him to enjoy. He could remember what they had been to each other without the agony that had previously come with the memories. He could luxuriate in wrapping the reminiscences around him.

Taj had understood why he had dismissed the idea of her gifts. She had bequeathed to him treasures beyond price. Now, if his life couldn't include her, he had everything he could ever want. He had warm memories of love for Taj in his heart, the Taj Mahal to publicly commemorate the feelings they had shared, and the knowledge that at the end of his life on earth, he will be with Taj once more.

Accepting humbly what only she could have bequeathed, he looked at her. A lump came to his throat as she caressed his hands. He knew there was soon to be another farewell.

"I love you, Taj."

"I know, Meerijan. And I love you."

Then she was gone.

Epilogue

Agra - 1666

The 76-year-old man lying on his couch in the apartment above the Jumna River bore little resemblance to the angry and disbelieving emperor imprisoned eight years earlier. Only in imagination or memory did he command great armies, wealth, and politics.

For more than sixty years before his imprisonment, he had enjoyed life's pleasures and lived with the greatest advantages. The war, murder, usurpation, and imprisonment of his last eight years no longer caused the anguish they once had. Death, an anticipated release from his human and his marble prisons, was finally approaching. He would soon be in Paradise with Allah and Taj.

The thought of beginning an everlasting life with Taj had distracted him in ways he did not realize. Earlier in the day when a mullah had come to pray with him, he had turned his prayer beads in his hands and spoke the ninety-nine names of Allah. Forgetting the last one, his eyes closed, his fingers moved automatically, he spoke the name, "Taj."

The mullah had dropped his prayer beads at the sacrilege of Shah Jahan speaking the name of a mortal while reciting the names of Allah. When he realized the former emperor had not been aware of his error, the religious man peered closely and saw that Shah Jahan was clearly at the end of his life. That he was speaking at all indicated he had been forgiven his earthly sins. The

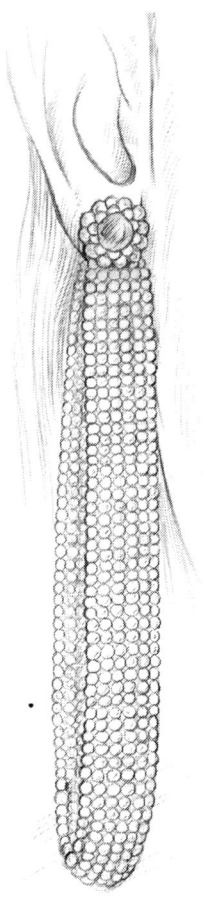

Wedding earring

indiscretion could be overlooked.

Jahanara hovered over her father feeding him ice chips to help him resist temptations as he traveled to Paradise. She knew the newly dead were known to be thirsty, and she wanted her father prepared for the journey.

Political unrest and intrigue within the Mughal Empire did not start with Shah Jahan—nor would it end with him. Because of his own experiences as he waited to be acknowledged as his father's heir, he was determined that the son he chose to succeed him, his eldest, Dara Shikoh, would know his intentions far in advance. From an early age, Dara was aware of the strategy and kept near his father. Gifted, tolerant, handsome, and intelligent, Dara was compared by many to Akbar because of these characteristics as well as his respect for a variety of religions.

Dara's three brothers, Shuja, Aurangzeb, and Maurad, however, were not among his many admirers. To keep peace in Agra, it was necessary for Shah Jahan to give teach of his sons a high-ranking position far away from the capital city. Shuja became Provincial Governor in Bengal, the eastern part of the empire where his ambition to become the Mughal Emperor rusted in the tropical climate.

Aurangzeb was the most militarily talented of the four sons. His hatred for Dara partly stemmed from his older brother's acceptance of religious differences which contrasted sharply to his own narrowly orthodox view of Islam. Aurangzeb was given a high position far to the south of Agra in the Deccan. From the son he referred to as The Snake, an unsuspecting Shah Jahan would one day receive yet another disastrous blow from an area that had already provided many.

Maurad grew from being a spoiled bully of a boy into a spoiled bully of a man. His father frequently had to smooth over the results of Maurad's temper and self centeredness. Once, after a successful campaign, when a military leader was expected to remain in the area of the conflict to oversee the finishing details, Maurad had returned to Agra just because he wanted to.

While Shah Jahan spent the years building the Taj Mahal and the new city of Shahjahanabad in Delhi, adding distinctive architecture to his empire, and creating a throne of jewels, his sons were usually far from his presence. Their jealousies of Dara grew and they were increasingly susceptible to rumor and gullible to flattery.

In 1657, five years after the dedication of the Taj Mahal, a celebration recognizing thirty years of Shah Jahan's rule turned his city into an extended fairyland of lights, color, fireworks, feasts, and entertainment. Within months, however, Shah Jahan became seriously ill and implored Dara to assume a position of leadership. By sending notices of this choice throughout the land, Shah Jahan unwittingly ignited the hatred and resentment within Aurangzeb.

Through trickery and lies, Aurangzeb separately assured both Shuja and Maurad that his army would fight to make each one of them emperor rather than allow their oldest brother to become their ruler. He, of course, had no interest in the kingdoms of the world. When he had their trust, he disposed of his brothers then moved against his father and removed him from power. Part of his justification was that Shah Jahan had set the precedent when he violated the Timurid code and killed royalty to become emperor.

Aurangzeb ruled as the Great Mughal, sitting in splendor upon the prized Peacock Throne while the man who had fashioned it remained a prisoner.

The princess' eyes fell upon the crude, plain leather slippers at the side of her father's bed. When Shah Jahan was emperor, he had owned embroidered velvet slippers designed to match his every outfit. More than having his correspondence read, his jewels taken, his treasure carted away, and an attempt made on his life, his being forced to wear these common slippers eloquently summed up the indignities he had faced while imprisoned.

If Shah Jahan had looked at his daughter's face at that moment, he would have seen her love for him there. Knowing her presence gave her father one of his few remaining comforts, she had chosen to remain imprisoned with him, declining the opportunity to live freely as Aurangzeb's sister.

However, Shah Jahan's last gaze was not toward his faithful and attentive daughter. It was down the Jumna River to the Taj Mahal, indistinct to his aging eyes. It hardly mattered that he did not see it clearly, for he had long ago memorized each and every detail of the mausoleum, its surrounding garden, the Moonlight Garden across the Jumna, and the waterways with their gentle fountains. A Paradise on earth.

Jahanara was watching her father when he closed his eyes and simply quit breathing. Saddened, she bent to kiss his forehead for the last time and saw that in death her father was smiling.

As her lips touched his brow, she became aware of a velvet pouch tied with a silken cord around his neck. Curiously, Jahanara touched it and could tell that whatever was inside had the approximate shape of a walnut. Widening the neck of the small sack and turning it upside down, she wondered which exquisite jewel her father had hung near his heart.

She was puzzled when a rather common, smooth yellow stone with faint markings on one side fell into her hand. What value could it have had to Shah Jahan? Still holding the stone, she noticed the fingers of one hand were tightly curled. Was there another mysterious stone within? Before she could open his hand, she was filled with a sudden wave of uncharacteristic self-pity for losing her last parent, the man who had been the center of her life for the last nine years. Still holding the stone, she bowed her head to be nearer to her father. Her gesture of grief signaled the waiting women who immediately filled the air with their ululating, keening wails.

As the light of the world was extinguished for Shah Jahan, he felt soft lips touch his forehead. He saw before him a young man with an energetic spring to his step, jet-black hair, and a smile illuminating his entire face. This man wore fine garments as though born to be so dressed. With surprise, Shah Jahan recognized himself as he had been long ago.

Slipper

No longer encased in the aging body that remained at the Agra Fort, he was now as he was the day he had married Taj. He stopped and stood still, slightly puzzled by the familiarity of his surroundings.

Of course. The plants were larger than the last time he had seen them, but he recognized the garden he had often visited, the garden he'd built for Mumtaz. He was at the Taj Mahal.

Aware of another presence, he turned and as he did so, his heart leapt. There was Arjumand Banu Begum, Mumtaz Mahal, his own Taj.

"You're here, Taj."

"Yes, Meerijan. As I promised. Forever."

He noticed she wore a single earring of many graceful strands of pearls long enough to loop beneath her earlobe and back up to her ear. On the front of her earlobe, small pearls encircled a stunning ruby. It was one of her wedding earrings.

Daring to hope there was still something in his left hand after his passage to Paradise, he raised his fist and slowly opened his fingers. Lying on his palm was the matching earring he had kept since the day of her burial.

Pleased, Mumtaz placed it in her other ear and reached out to him. Hand-in-hand they walked together in Paradise.

Glossary

AIGRETTE ~ Turban ornament
AYAH ~ Nursemaid
AZREAL ~ Muslim Angel of Death

BABA ~ Son
BAPU ~ Father

CARAVANSARIES ~ Inns
CENOTAPH ~ Empty tomb
CUMMERBUND ~ Wide sash worn
    at the waist

DAIYA ~ Midwife
DIWAN-I-AM ~ Public audience—open to all
DIWAN-I-KHAS ~ Private audience—
    restricted attendance
DOWRY ~ Money and goods a wife brings
    to her marriage
DURBUR ~ Gathering, audience

EUNUCH ~ Castrated male

FAKIR ~ Religious ascetic
FIRMAN ~ Order from a high authority

HOWDAH ~ Traveling compartment on
    the back of an elephant

IMAM ~ Muslim leader or chief

JALI ~ Carved screen
JHAROKA ~ Balcony that protrudes from palace wall

KOFTA ~ Ground meat balls

LASSI ~ Drink of yogurt and cucumber

MAHAL ~ Palace
MAHOUT ~ Elephant handler who rides on animal's neck
MALI ~ Gardener
MEERIJAN ~ My life
MULLAH ~ Muslim teacher

PLINTH ~ Platform
PURDAH ~ Seclusion of women

RANA ~ Male ruler, Maharana

SHAH BURJ ~ The most exclusive of Mughal meeting rooms
SHARBAT ~ Sherbet
SHIKARA ~ Small open boat used in Kashmir

TESLIM ~ Bow of obedience
TIMIRUD ~ Of the Mughals (House of Timur)

ULAMA ~ Body of scholars who are authorities of Muslim law and religion

ZENANA ~ City of women; harem

Author's Biography

Sandra Wilson first visited the Taj Mahal while teaching in India and has returned many times to visit this Wonder of the Modern World.

She has four grown children and lives with her husband on one of the San Juan Islands in Washington.